THE DEBUTANTE

'Is this really necessary?' Lucinda demanded, as she preceded Norris into her bedroom.

'In what way would that be, miss?' the manservant enquired coolly.

She stood facing him, little fists tightly clenched. The man's insolence was all the more galling for being subtle.

'I mean, is it necessary for me to be . . . caned by a servant?'

Norris maintained his usual sober expression but Lady Lucinda was damned sure she could see an infuriating twinkle in his eyes.

'It is part of the training programme at Hurtwood House, miss; I do assure you that all the girls who come here are subject to it. Now, if you would be so good as to take your frock off, we should be getting started.'

THE DEBUTANTE

Jacqueline Masterson

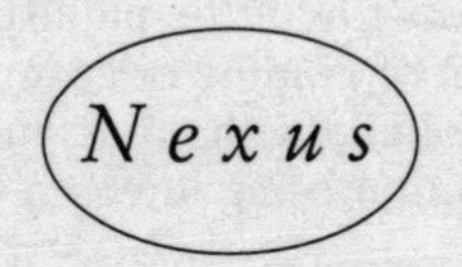

This book is a work of fiction.
In real life, make sure you practise safe, sane and consensual sex.

First published in 2003 by
Nexus
Thames Wharf Studios
Rainville Road
London W6 9HA

www.nexus-books.co.uk

Typeset by TW Typesetting, Plymouth, Devon

Printed and bound by
Clays Ltd, St Ives PLC

ISBN 0 352 33802 4

All characters in this publication are fictitious and any resemblance to real persons, living or dead, is purely coincidental.

Prologue

'*Very* nice,' Lord Randolph Southdean drawled as he let his eyes linger on the photograph. The girl was dark and delicately pretty with enormous brown eyes and beautiful long lashes. 'I say,' he continued. 'Woof! Woof! Woof!'

'Sweet little piece, isn't it?' Valencia Dacourt said, watching him with evident amusement. 'According to Anais and George, she is the daughter of those poor souls who got eaten by lions in Happy Valley, back in forty-one. Tragedy, because they were definitely *our* sort.'

'So has she been in Kenya all this time? With all that hullabaloo in Suez it will be a bloody long voyage back.'

'No, she was packed off to boarding school, and since then she has been staying with some fusty relatives in a godforsaken suburb of Birmingham.'

'Birmingham? Christ! Poor lamb! So what's Anais got in mind?' He rolled his eyes. 'Planning to rescue the little poppet from a hell of privet hedges and powdered egg?'

Valencia laughed. 'Actually, I don't think they still eat that stuff, even in Birmingham, Randolph! Apparently, she is a distant relative of George's. Anais was happy to have her out of the way until she was grown up enough –'

'To be introduced into society!' Randolph finished for her archly. 'Excellent. She looks so innocent and naïve with those doe eyes. What's her name?'

'Her name is Angela Carstairs and she has just turned twenty-one. Spit of Audrey Hepburn, don't you think? Only with more curves, apparently, not that you can tell under that bag she is wearing. Sweet, innocent, and headed our way in time for the season. What more could one ask?'

Randolph looked up from the photo and caught his friend's eye.

'Well . . .' he said, never one to be easily satisfied, 'any chance of Lucy Beaufort-Grey coming out as well?'

'You want Grace Kelly as well as Audrey Hepburn!' Valencia said, throwing up her hands in mock outrage. 'Well, actually, I'm working on our little Lucinda. She wants to join the fun and games very badly. That girl has a cruel streak and she is desperate to unleash it.'

'But if she wants to play . . .' Randolph said with relish.

'She is going to have to pay!' Valencia finished for him.

They both chuckled. He looked back down at the photo, and then at Camilla who was serving as his footstool. The voluptuously blonde young woman had been laced tight into a black satin corset. This, sheer nylons and matching black lace gloves were all the clothing she had been allowed, other than restraints. The girl's ankles were locked into steel manacles and her hands were handcuffed behind her. She knelt prone on the floor before Randolph, her chin in front of her knees and bottom just above her implausibly high heels. Above Camilla's shackled wrists, on the corset lacing in the small of her back, Randolph let his riding boots rest comfortably.

'I thought last season was the best,' he said, smiling fondly at the shackled girl.

There was a whimper from Belinda. Red-haired and more slender than Camilla, she had been costumed and bound in exactly the same way, and was serving as a footstool for Valencia. She was still Randolph's property, however, and he looked at her with a frown.

'Be quiet, Belinda!' he ordered.

There was no reason for her to make a fuss, he thought, the girls had only had to maintain their cramped positions for half and hour or so, and it could hardly be so very vexing for them. After all, Camilla was still enduring her discomfort in respectful silence. Then Lord Randolph realised that he could only see one of Valencia's viciously narrow heels resting on the small of the red-head's back. His friend's other nylon-sheathed knee was slightly raised, and he guessed that the other stiletto heel was being dug into soft thigh or buttock flesh. He chuckled. Valencia could be such a bitch sometimes.

'Yes, last season's debutantes really were a toothsome crop,' he said in a slow drawl, looking at Camilla and Belinda thoughtfully before returning his attention to the photograph. 'But, something tells me this season is could be even better!'

One

'Angela, baby! My, look at you, my dear!'

Lady Anais Fakenham threw her arms open in a dramatic gesture of welcome and Angela found herself engulfed in fur and expensive French fragrance. To her chagrin, Angela could not help blushing in response to her exotic relative's continental manners.

'How do you do, Lady Fakenham,' she said politely once finally released.

'Oh, don't be so formal, child. Call me Aunt Anais, I insist. Come along, let us go to Eaton Square and get you settled in.'

Lady Fakenham was not really Angela's aunt. In fact since the letter inviting her to London had arrived, Angela had been puzzling about the exact relationship. Lord George had been some sort of second cousin to her poor father, it seemed. Really it was too distant a relationship to explain this sudden summons, and her 'aunt' and 'uncle' had shown little interest in her before her 21st birthday. Still, London had to be better than the stifling boredom of Edgbaston and Mrs Muncaster's endless rules and mean-spirited propriety. Whatever this new life meant, Angela was only too eager to explore.

Lady Anais signalled for a porter and Angela's trunk was swiftly found. The elegant little woman had a quick conversation with the porter and a white banknote changed hands. Angela was astonished as five pounds seemed to her an extraordinary amount to pay.

'La! It is all settled.'

'Thank you, Lady . . . Aunt Anais, will they send it on tonight?' Angela asked, anxious to be reunited with her few possessions.

'I said it was settled!' her aunt said, a little tartly.

Angela coloured a little and held her tongue. Anais linked arms with her, as if to reassure her, and steered her out of the station to a waiting silver-grey Rolls-Royce. The uniformed chauffeur jumped out at their appearance and opened a door for them. Angela smelt the leather and the tang of expensive cigars as she sank into the plush seat. She felt intoxicated by the heady scent of privilege and wealth, so different to Mrs Muncaster's house and its pervasive smell of TCP.

London was every bit as grimy as Angela dimly remembered it when she's arrived back from Kenya. Eaton Square was rather elegant, however, and the house impressively grand. She followed Lady Fakenham up a marble stairway. As if by magic the door was opened for them. A maid, plumply pretty with blonde curls and a neat uniform, stood holding it, her eyes a little downcast. Aunt Anais paused.

'Don't forget I have promised you a skipping, Mary. I shall see you in the billiard room at four.'

The little maid gave a bob, two pink spots appearing on her dimpled cheeks.

'Yes, ma'am,' she said in a husky voice.

'Mary, Mary, quite contrary,' Aunt Anais said and broke into a peal of laughter as they walked on into the house. 'The trouble I have with staff. Too soft with them, I suppose. Mary broke a glass so I have promised her a whipping. The cane, I suppose, though I might try the tawse.'

Angela listened with astonishment. Could her aunt be serious? she wondered. The little maid had certainly seemed uncomfortable and anxious. But this was 1956, not 1756. Surely the days of thrashing servants were long gone, even amongst the aristocracy?

Aunt Anais looked at her elegant little watch and made a tutting sound.

'Look at that now. It is quarter to four already. No wonder Mary looked so glum.' The dark little woman laughed again. 'I will show you your room after tea if you don't mind.'

'No,' Angela managed, somehow, 'not at all.'

'Good, good! Well, let us take it in the billiard room. Mary has the sweetest little bottom; you will enjoy to see it smacked, I am quite sure, chérie!'

Perhaps it was the effects of the journey, but Angela found herself feeling a little faint. So she was glad to follow Lady Fakenham into the billiard room. This was a large, dark-panelled chamber, dominated by a big billiard table. There were some comfortable seats set around this, and Angela sank into one of them with some relief.

'Ah, Simmonds, there you are. This is Miss Carstairs!'

Angela looked up to see that a tall, grey-haired butler had arrived. He greeted her with the briefest of bows.

'At your service, ma'am,' he said in a way that made her think that somehow he was not in her service at all. His eyes were grey too, though darker than his haïr, and there was something in their gunmetal glint, Angela found, that she did not like at all.

‘We will take tea in here. Arrange it,’ Aunt Anais said crisply. ‘And send in Mary with a good Lochgelly.’

The butler nodded, as if her instructions were quite normal, and silently withdrew. A few moments later two maids appeared, well laden. Both were dressed like Mary had been, soberly and neatly uniformed, and both were quite as pretty. One had a shock of nut-brown curls, barely held in check by her white lace cap. The other was an exotic beauty, olive complexioned with jet-black hair in a bun and exquisite almond-shaped eyes.

‘Put it there, Yvette!’ Aunt Anais ordered the brown-haired girl.

Yvette put down a small table between Angela and Lady Fakenham. The other girl carried a tray laden with tea things. It was not easy for her to place the cups, tea pot, milk, sugar, and plate of cakes on the table in an elegant manner, and Angela noticed that her aunt watched the maid like a hungry hawk, almost as if willing her to make a mistake. There was a palpable air of tension in the room until the last teaspoons had been set in their proper places.

‘Very well,’ Aunt Anais said at last. ‘Tie back the curtains, Leila, and then you both may go.’

Angela had not noticed the gloom in the room until the maids tied the heavy velvet curtains right back and let in the evening sun. Now it was much brighter and lighter, and she could see how high the ceilings were and how opulent the décor. However, she did not have long to peruse her surroundings before there was a little knock on the door.

‘Come!’ Aunt Anais said imperiously.

The little blonde maid who had opened the door for them entered with every appearance of reluctance.

‘There you are, Mary. Ready for a belting?’

'Yes, ma'am,' the maid said in a hoarse little whisper, that suggested that she was not ready at all. She carried a split-tailed strap, holding it gingerly in front of her, almost as if the brown leather belt was too hot for her hands.

'Well, we are not ready for you, miss!' Aunt Anais said sharply. 'Go to the middle of the billiard table and place the tawse upon the baize.'

Angela watched with astonishment as the blonde maid did as she was bid.

'Now,' Aunt Anais continued, 'face the table and lift your skirts and petticoats up and drop your knickers!'

Fascinated, despite herself, Angela watched as the girl pulled up her skirt to reveal surprisingly fancy, frilly white panties. These she eased down with obvious reluctance to reveal a plump, pale peach of bottom, with dimpled cheeks that matched those on her face. Angela swallowed hard.

'Tuck your skirts into your suspender belt and bend over the table. No, feet further back and legs apart. That's better. Now you can wait there!'

Mary had on a substantial white suspender belt and she managed to tuck her skirt and petticoat into the back of this. The garter belt supported black seamed stockings. These were sheer and to Angela's eyes looked expensive. Like the frilly knickers, they seemed to be finer and more frivolous than Angela would have expected under the neat maid's uniform. She wondered if the girls who had served the tea also boasted such fancy lingerie beneath their sober skirts and aprons. The idea seemed strangely exciting, though Angela could not have said quite why.

'Do take some bread and butter,' said Aunt Anais, interrupting her thoughts. 'It will be a good while until dinner is served.'

Angela found the situation quite surreal. True, she was tired from her journey, but surely not so exhausted that she was hallucinating? Her aunt poured more tea and discussed the deficiencies of English cuisine and inconvenient mealtimes. Mary's peachy bare bottom trembled slightly in anticipation. Angela could hardly take her eyes off the maid's presented buttocks, but found herself forced to make conversation with her new-found relation.

'Well, enough of tea!' Aunt Anais said at last, putting down her cup.

She stood and looked at Mary steadily. 'Such a pretty bum, it is always a real pleasure to punish it!'

As Lady Anais walked over to the waiting maid, Angela watched in a state of some agitation. Her palms had become distinctly moist and there was a pounding in her temples.

Aunt Anais reached Mary's side and gave the girl's behind an affectionate pat. The maid squeaked anxiously in response and her bottom cheeks flinched visibly. Picking up the tawse, Angela's aunt hefted the thick leather thing thoughtfully, before swinging it through the air a couple of times, the action producing a most ominous-sounding whistle.

'In my country they favour the martinet, in yours the cane, but I sometimes think that the Scots have the best idea of all,' she said with a chuckle. 'This is a genuine school extra-heavy tawse, made by Mr John J Dick; look, how thick the leather!'

Angela did look. Indeed, she could barely keep her eyes from the wicked-looking thing. The dark brown, well-oiled leather strap was about three feet long and an inch across, split down half its length into two tails. But it was the thickness of the leather that was most astonishing. From where she sat it looked thicker than Angela's forefinger.

There was a loud crack as Aunt Anais brought the tawse down hard on the green baize of the billiard table, the impact producing a little cloud of chalk dust. Mary let out a startled squeal and her bare bottom started twitching once more.

'Now, Mary,' Anais said in a husky, excited-sounding voice, 'I told you last time that clumsiness would not be tolerated. I'm going to have to give you eight.'

Mary let out a little strangulated sound but Angela could not tell whether it was a sob, a gasp or a whimper. Despite the tea, she found that her mouth had gone quite dry. She watched her aunt slowly raise the tawse and hold it high above her.

It was as if time had stopped. Angela was transfixed by the tableau: the little blonde maid with her flinching bottom waiting for the stroke; elegant Aunt Anais, the embodiment of chic in her black Dior dress; the thick tawse, poised to strike, incongruously brutal in her delicate hand.

It should be a slender riding crop, Angela thought absurdly, the moment before her aunt brought the belt down. It almost seemed to travel in slow motion to begin with. Then the thick leather tails became a brown blur as they picked up speed and thwacked across Mary's bottom cheeks. The impact was sufficient to flatten the chubby rounds momentarily, before the flesh bounced back resiliently.

'Ooh!' Mary gasped, slowly writhing on the billiard table.

'Are you counting, girl?' Aunt Anais demanded.

'Ooh,' the maid said again, 'one . . . thank you, ma'am.'

As Angela watched, two lines appeared deep pink against the pale peach of the maid's chubby bottom. There was a strange and urgent tingling between

Angela's legs. She bit her lip and did her best to ignore it.

Aunt Anais lifted the tawse again, waiting until Mary had stopped writhing, before cracking the belt hard across the blonde maid's buttocks. This time Mary made a sort of hissing noise and jiggled her bare bottom furiously. It was some time before she could thank her mistress for the stroke. Indeed, by then the furious pink stripes had bloomed across the paleness of her bottom.

The third stroke seemed even harder. Certainly its effect was dramatic.

'Ooh, ah, no! Please!' Mary gasped and babbled, putting back her hands to clutch her punished bottom. 'Ooh! Ouch! Please, ma'am . . .'

'Get back into position, you silly girl!' Aunt Anais ordered in a gruff and slightly strained voice.

Mary did not do so at once, jiggling her bottom and writhing on her belly, kicking her legs back almost convulsively.

'Angela, you will have to help or we will be here all day.'

'Me, but Aunt . . . I . . .'

'Go around the table,' Aunt Anais said, just as if Angela had enthusiastically agreed to help, 'and take hold of her hands.'

Heart pounding in her breast, Angela did as she was bid. She rounded the big billiard table and found herself facing the little maid across it. Mary's face was red now, her crimson cheeks emphasised by the contrast with her corn-gold curls. These had largely escaped her maid's cap, which was in danger of falling off altogether.

Angela found herself looking into wide, pleading blue eyes. Tears had formed in the corners of these orbs and started to trickle down Mary's cheeks. The sight sent a stab of pity through Angela's heart, but also made the tingling sensation lower down feel even more desperately urgent.

Reluctantly, Mary stretched out her hands across the billiard table. Only slightly more willingly, Angela bent over the cushion on her side and stretched out to meet her.

'Fireman's grip, girls, you know how that is?' Aunt Anais demanded.

They did. Angela took hold of Mary's wrists. The little blonde maid gripped Angela's wrists in turn, grasping them almost tightly enough to hurt in her desperation.

'Getting warmer, are we?' Aunt Anais said with a chuckle as she reached down to squeeze Mary's bottom.

The blue eyes widened and the maid's sweet little mouth formed a pained 'O'. Angela could hardly tear her gaze away from the other girl's face. The blue eyes had a lost, almost glazed look. Then there was a whooshing sound, followed by a crack, and Mary's face was contorted with pain. Angela felt her wrists gripped even tighter as the blonde maid let out a shrill squeal.

'Be quiet, you silly girl.'

'Really Aunt Anais, I don't think that you should be whipping her like this . . .' The words came out unbidden. Mary's eyes opened again and regarded her with astonishment.

'Do you not?' Aunt Anais said calmly. 'Well, perhaps you would like to take the rest of her strokes in her place then.'

'What?' Angela said, astonished. 'No, please, wait . . .'

But it was too late. Aunt Anais was striding around the billiard table. Angela let go of Mary's wrists and tried to stand.

'Hold her hard, Mary,' Anais ordered. 'If you want her to take the rest of your punishment I would not let her go!'

Mary, it turned out, was a lot stronger than she looked. All that scrubbing floors and polishing, Angela thought wildly, must have given the blonde girl a formidable grip. In vain Angela struggled.

'Now, there are four strokes left. Keep pulling away like that and I will double it.'

Something in her aunt's tone told Angela that she meant it. She made herself stop fighting Mary's grip. Then she felt her aunt push up her skirt.

'Dear me,' Anais said dryly. 'Whatever is this? Ugh, one of those appalling girdles! We do not wear such things here. They cover half the bottom! Well, you will have to take your strokes lower down, chérie.'

Angela felt the blush suffuse her cheeks as her baggy and substantial bloomers were pulled down. She knew only too well how shabby her shapeless drawers must look; even her stockings were coarse lisle. The worse thing was that Mary, the little minx, was staring at her with those wide blue eyes, and the expression that had been so pitiful now looked distinctly amused. The sympathy that Angela had felt for the little maid was dissolved in a surge of impotent fury. She silently swore that she would never try to help the little tart again.

Unfortunately, Angela was not given time to dwell on the perfidy of servants. Before she knew it the tawse was whistling through the air again, impacting on Angela's buttocks with a meaty crack. This time, however, the sound was the least of her worries.

'Ow!' she yelped as a hot stinging sensation suffused her hindquarters.

'Keep still, girl. Stop that kicking back and squirming. Mary, hold her tight!'

The pain had barely begun to subside when the second stroke lashed across her underbum. Angela gave an agonised gasp as she was stung again. Helpless in Mary's unrelenting grip, she moved what she could and furiously wiggled her bottom, as if this might, somehow, disperse the stinging. Only after some time, however, did the scorching sensation simmer down to more a bearable level. Of course, as soon as that happened, Aunt Anais unleashed another scorcher.

Angela had never been tawsed before, let alone with a real Lochgelly. By the time her aunt delivered the fourth stroke, her whole bottom felt as though it were ablaze. Despite Anais's orders, she kicked and yelped and squirmed on the billiard table. Nothing did any good, she simply had to wait until the scorching became stinging and then a sort of not unpleasant glow.

'Well, my dear, I did enjoy that,' Aunt Anais said in an amused tone.

The belt landed with a thud on the green baize beside Angela. Then she felt her aunt's hands grasp her still hot bottom and could not prevent a hiss of pain escaping.

'You really do have a lovely arse, my dear. It's every bit as pretty as Mary's. A little chubbier, perhaps, but just as firm and positively bouncy. Oh, but wait a minute, what on earth is happening here?'

Angela ground her teeth in vain as she felt her aunt's cunning fingers probing.

'It's all wet and sticky, Angela, have you peed yourself?'

Angela felt her already red cheeks go a deeper shade of beetroot. To her utter horror, Mary was grinning at her knowingly and even had the impertinence to wink!

'No, ah, ooh, please, Aunt . . .' she babbled, writhing despite herself in helpless response to Anais's manipulations.

'Not peed?' Aunt Anais said with a chuckle. 'But surely, ma petite, you are not telling me that you have become aroused? That would be too shocking!'

Lady Fakenham's right hand had reached between Angela's legs and kept probing until three of her slender fingers were buried deep inside the gasping girl. The other hand had gone around Angela's hip, and was now gently teasing the girl's clitoris. To Angela's bewilderment, the shame of being fingered in front of Mary and the soreness of her still throbbing bottom just seemed to make her more excited. Even the sheer humiliation of her situation could not stop the older woman's fingers from driving her to complete distraction. She had never experienced anything like this in Edgbaston; what on earth was happening to her?

'Oh, please, ah, ah, ooh . . .!' She babbled as arousal quickly bubbled over into unstoppable crisis.

'Hold her tight, Mary, she seems to be having some sort of seizure,' Anais said with amusement.

Angela was engulfed in a great wave of pleasure. It was like nothing she had ever known, or even imagined. For a few moments she howled and shrieked and writhed on the billiard table, oblivious to everything but her own thunderous orgasm.

'What an extraordinary performance!'

The little aftershocks of ecstasy had begun to ebb away, and Angela slowly became aware of her situation. She was bent, bare bottomed, over the billiard table, moaning and crooning, as her aunt mocked and the maid regarded her with amused contempt.

'Let her go, Mary. Angela, I want you to get down on your knees to thank me.'

'Thank you?' Angela mumbled, confused and astonished.

'Mais oui, of course, you must thank me for chastising you. Get on your knees and make it sincere if you do not wish for another dose.'

Aunt Anais picked up the tawse from the billiard table and flexed it between her hands thoughtfully.

Fear, outrage, humiliation and half a dozen other emotions warred in Angela's breast. She did not doubt that her aunt would belt her again if she did not obey. But then a warning voice in her head told her that if she got down on her knees she would, somehow be completely in this strange woman's power. Part of her rebelled, urged her to walk right out and away from this strange compelling house. Angela raised her eyes and found herself impaled on her aunt's glittering green gaze.

'On your knees, now!' Anais said, gently but firmly.

Angela was not aware of making a decision. The fact was she was in a sort of daze. It was as if her legs made the decision for her. She got down and felt the thick carpet beneath her stockinged knees.

'That's better. Now say, "thank you for chastising me, ma'am."'

Refusal bubbled up within her, but Anais dropped the tawse and Angela found herself compelled to watch its pendulous swing as if it were the swaying watch of a hypnotist.

'Thank you for chastising me, Aunt . . . ma'am,' she mumbled somehow.

'You are quite welcome, my pretty,' Anais said with a sly smile. She stepped closer and lifted Angela's chin with her free hand until the girl had to look into those cold green eyes again.

'Now,' Anais said quietly but firmly, 'get right down on the floor and kiss my feet.'

* * *

'Cheer up old son, it might never happen!' the barman said with a grin.
'That's just the trouble, mate,' Jem Wingrove muttered. 'It never bloody does! Working for those old fossils is like living in a very boring museum.'
Albert stopped drying glasses for a moment and regarded him quizzically.
'Oh, so you fancy more excitement in your life, do you, old son?' he said.
'I fancy any excitement, Albert!' Jem said mournfully.
'Ah, but can you handle it?'
Jem looked up from his pint, wondering what on earth the barman was going on about.
'What do you mean?'
'How much excitement can you handle?'
The challenge was clear in the barman's eyes. The Rose and Crown was one of the few pubs in Mayfair where servants felt at home, and Albert was well known to run it as a sort of unofficial employment agency. So, Jem did not simply dismiss the barman's remarks as the meaningless pub banter that he might otherwise have done.
He had had five pints, however, and he had had more than enough of the doddering old fossils that employed him. Hell, there was not even a maid under fifty for him to indulge in a little bit of slap and tickle with now and then. How much excitement could he handle? Jem shook his head slowly and grinned.
'How much have you got?' he demanded.

'Come along, Mary! Stop daydreaming, girl!'
Mary Bunting tried to pull herself together and concentrate on polishing the silver, for Mr Simmonds was not a man she dared provoke. Fortunately he carried on walking through the dining room and disappeared through the doors on the other side.

It was not fair! It simply was not fair! Mary had been quite happy for that stuck-up Carstairs girl to get a share of her belting. It was what had happened afterwards that made her fingers tremble with frustration and fury. Punishment always seemed to have the same effect on Mary. Watching Lady Anais bring off Angela while she had to wait and watch impotently had been close to unbearable, but she had consoled herself with the thought that she might sneak off to her room afterwards and give herself a spot of quick relief. Unfortunately she had been caught by Simmonds as she left the billiard room, still wincing from the pressure of her panties on her sore bottom. The butler had ordered her here and Mary had been obliged to begin polishing the silver.

There was so much of it, she thought with a sigh. There was no hope of finishing the job before dinner and then she would have to serve at table. She was so diabolically aroused that she could hardly concentrate, however. The memory of her mistress's hands on her bottom, and the expression of Angela's pretty face contorting as the tawse bit, simply would not leave Mary's thoughts.

The candlestick that she was polishing was solid and mostly rounded. It had somehow got between her legs and pushed her skirts right up. Mary began to rub the shaft against the silk frills at the front of her knickers. She put her free hand in her mouth and bit it to stop herself from crying out. This was madness, she realised, and stopped for a moment. She took a deep breath and listened for approaching footsteps but could not hear a thing.

Bugger it! she thought, and began rubbing harder, polishing the rounded shaft on the tight knicker material stretched over her clitoris. Within a few short minutes, she had to bite her left hand harder, as the rubbing of the candlestick had its inevitable effect. First a shudder, then a judder, then a great convulsive rictus of pleasure gripped her body. Somehow, almost completely doubled up and panting hard, Mary managed to stay on her chair as the climax shook her.

'Well, well,' an amused male voice said behind her.

Mary stiffened and sat up, a sudden stab of panic cutting through the post-orgasmic glow of well-being.

Lord George Fakenham walked around her and regarded the maid with an amused expression. He was a big, slightly portly man with old-fashioned mutton chop whiskers and a jovial expression. To Mary's appalled gaze he looked even more amused than usual.

'That's an interesting way of polishing the silver-ware, Mary.'

He reached out his hand for the candlestick. Reluctantly the maid handed it to him. Lord Faken-ham took out his reading glasses and put them on, then regarded the gleaming object carefully.

'My word,' he said at last, 'your method certainly seems to work well, my girl!' He chuckled. 'I think you should demonstrate it to the rest of the household.'

'Oh, no, please . . .' Mary said with panic churning in her vitals.

'Oh, yes, Mary,' he said, a hint of menace entering his amiable tone of voice. 'Let's have a little exhibi-tion after dinner, shall we, my dear?'

'But, Aunt . . . I can't go down like this,' Angela said in an appalled whisper, blood rushing to her cheeks.

'Tsk, tsk, of course you can, child. Far better than those dreadful things you came in,' Lady Fakenham said briskly.

Angela had been taken to a bright, pleasant, feminine-feeling room with pale yellow wallpaper.

There, Lady Fakenham had told her to undress. Sheer shyness would probably have provoked a refusal an hour earlier. Angela had eyed the tawse that Anais still carried, however, and reluctantly complied. Only when she was standing completely naked, covering her breasts and sex and blushing furiously, did Lady Fakenham ring for a servant to attend.

Terror had seized Angela at that point. For some reason the idea that the butler, Simmonds, would appear in answer to that summons came into her mind. So it seemed a huge relief when Yvette bustled in.

'Take those awful things away and burn them,' Anais said, wrinkling her nose in disgust and pointing to Angela's girdle, bloomers and other clothes. 'Then fetch me those garments Barbara wore before she "came out".'

Angela had watched her clothes disappear with something close to panic. Of her trunk there was no sign and something told her that she would not see it again. She had the leisure, standing naked in the little bedroom, to wonder who Barbara was, and what had happened to her. Still, she had told herself as she tried to shield her naked body from her aunt's amused gaze, at least there would be clothes.

Then Yvette had come back and Angela had almost fainted. The 'garments' which Barbara had apparently worn were utterly ridiculous and shameful. White knickers, even more frilly and flouncy than Mary's, came with opaque white stockings that finished just above the knee. These were gartered with white satin ribbons that had big bows at the back. The real problem was the dress, however. A tiny pink silk thing, it had puffy little quarter sleeves and frills above her breasts. Below this smocking, however, the gossamer material failed to veil her nipples completely, before falling in translucent folds to cover only the top two thirds of her absurd panties. It was a sort of parody of a little girls outfit, completed with black, patent leather, shoes. It would have looked silly on a young Shirley Temple. On a 21-year-old woman it was not only absurd, it was close to obscene.

'Of course you will come down to dinner with me,' Lady Fakenham said with a smile, not bothering to hide her amusement and fingering the tawse. 'You look quite lovely, though I must say that your face has gone a deeper pink than your little frock.'

She stepped forward and, raising the doubled tawse in her right hand, she tapped Angela's hot cheek. Then she gave the blushing girl a gentle kiss right on the lips.

'You will come down with me, chérie, and all will be explained. But first, I think we must send Yvette to get some ribbons for your hair!"

'I won't do it! Why should I? I'm not some silly little tart like Belinda Congreave or Camilla Fosset-Knowles!'

'Well, of course, dear,' Valencia said demurely. 'If you do not choose to come out, then no one can make you. Many girls would love to be a debutante . . .'

'*Debutante*! Debutante indeed. What you people call a debutante is more like a white slave if you ask me,' Lady Lucinda Beaufort-Grey retorted. She tossed her exquisite blonde head crossly, her delicate nostrils flaring in outrage.

'Would you prefer to be the official sort of deb then, Lucy? With your family and title, I'm sure that it could be arranged.'

Lucinda regarded Valencia as if she were a beetle that had just crawled out from under the sideboard. 'Well, of course not,' she spat. 'If I wanted to die of boredom I could have stayed at home. All those witless Roedean girls and the *mothers*.' She shuddered dramatically. 'And chinless men called Jeremy who think that telling me about the drainage plans for their estates will get them into my knickers. No, thank you, Valencia, my dear.'

'Well then,' Valencia said firmly. 'You have a choice, don't you? If you want to enjoy the advantages of belonging to our set, then I'm afraid that you will have to pay the entrance fee.'

'One doesn't see many boys being put through this humiliation,' Lucinda muttered mutinously.

'No,' Valencia said patiently, 'but they have to endure their public schools, which amounts to much the same.'

It was a simply dreadful dilemma. While she did not know everything about the 'secret season', Lucinda knew enough to make her belly flutter with anxiety; months of training, followed by corporal punishment and humiliations for the amusement of Valencia and her debauched friends. It was a bitter pill for a girl as proud as Lucinda to swallow. However, it seemed to be the only way that they would let her in to play. She chewed her knuckle, riven by indecision. If she could endure the season, then it would be her turn. After all, she thought, she was tough enough to endure a spot of caning, even a whipping. They could only really humiliate her if she let them, couldn't they? She took a deep breath.

'Oh very well,' she said with the best grace she could muster. 'I'll bloody do it. Valencia, will you sponsor me?'

Valencia laughed. 'Well, Lucy sweet, not if you ask like that!' Her eyes locked onto the blonde girl's and glittered with amusement. 'First of all you need to get down on your knees.'

* * *

'So this is the Carstairs girl! I say, my dear, do you always go around showing people your frillies?' Lord George asked before letting out a delighted chortle.

Angela went a deeper shade of crimson and continued to stare miserably at her feet.

'Curtsey to his Lordship, Angela darling,' Lady Anais said gaily.

Feeling tears of sheer impotent humiliation welling, Angela took hold of the hem of her little frock on either side and lifted it up and out, horribly aware that she was displaying even more of the absurdly frilly knickers as she dipped her knees.

'I say!' Lord George declared, openly rubbing the front of his trousers. 'Damn me m'dear if that morsel doesn't look good enough to eat!'

'All right, Angela,' Lady Fakenham said firmly. 'You can stop that silly blushing. What you are wearing is what girls wear here who have not come out yet. If you do not like it you will need to have a season.'

'A . . . a season?' Angela managed somehow.

'To be brought out into society, to be a debutante. Of course –' Aunt Anais paused, '– as you might have guessed we have a slightly different sort of season to the one you read about in *Tatler*. The principle is the same. After a spot of training, when required, debutantes are brought out in a series of balls.'

At the word 'balls', Lord George, who had begun drinking from a glass of burgundy, suddenly chortled again for some reason, and very nearly choked.

'Well, we call them balls, though there is not always very much actual dancing,' Lady Anais said with a sly grin. 'Now, if you would like to be a debutante, you will need a sponsor. I am prepared to sponsor you for your dear departed parents' sake. The training can be . . . challenging, and the season is not easy. Afterwards you will, however, have a real place in society. The advantages are considerable if you are game.'

Angela was barely conscious of what her so-called aunt was saying. She could feel Lord George's eyes fixed on her nipples, which were impudently pushing out the gossamer material of her little frock. Most inconveniently, these had responded to the feel of the silk by standing out more stiffly than sentries on Horse Guards Parade. The truth was Angela could only really think about one thing at that moment.

'These debutantes . . .' she mumbled, still looking downwards. 'I mean, if I . . . do this, I will get proper clothes?'

'What's this?' Lucinda demanded, her voice high with outrage. 'Where it says, "The debutante shall not be permanently sold to any foreign sheikh or other potentate as a harem slave . . ." '

'Well.' Valencia shrugged and took a drink from her Martini. 'What on earth is the problem now? You don't want to be sold into slavery, do you, for heaven's sake?'

Lucinda looked down at the contract, and back up at Valencia. The older woman was wearing a full-skirted gown with a tight-fitting, sleeveless bodice that managed to display a tiny waist while simultaneously emphasising her impressive physique. Valencia was a buxom woman and her bare arms were sleekly muscled from fencing, tennis and other energetic sports. Lucinda did not know if she would like such powerful-looking arms herself, but she had to admit that they looked good on Valencia; almost as good as that canyon of a cleavage.

' "The debutante will not be tattooed or branded with any owner's mark or be given flesh piercings that will leave significant permanent scarring . . ." ' she continued in a disbelieving voice.

'There you are again,' Valencia said. 'I do not see your problem. It is the standard contract and we all had to sign it. After all, you don't want some brute like Lancelot Shaw to brand your bottom with his initials, do you?'

'You are deliberately missing the point, Valencia,' Lucinda said through set teeth. 'Of course I don't want to be sold to a sheikh or tattooed by some home-grown sadist! What bothers me is that word – *permanently*!'

'This him, then?' the blonde girl said, looking at Jem with a dubious expression. 'Looks a bit young!'

'That's him, Chloe,' Albert the barman confirmed. 'Leave you to it, shall I?'

'What do you mean?' Jem demanded, colouring. His auburn curls and pellucid complexion often had people thinking he was younger and it was more than a little annoying. 'I'm nineteen! Old as you, I bet!'

'I'm twenty-two, for your information, sonny!' the girl said with a grin.

It was not her features that made her look younger, exactly; it was something about her manner. She was perky and mischievous in a girlish sort of way. She was also very pretty. Jem found her manner both annoying and strangely attractive. Still, he thought, it had been months since he had spoken to a pretty girl. He would probably have found her attractive whatever her manner was.

'Stand up!' she ordered.

'What?'

'Stand up! Look, sunshine, do you want me to recommend you for a job with my mistress or not?'

His pride was piqued by her manner, but not as severely as his curiosity. So he stood up with ill grace.

'Turn around!' she said, twisting her index finger to illustrate her request.

Jem shrugged and performed a slow, ungainly pirouette.

'Old Albert says you want some excitement in your life,' Chloe said with a grin.

'That's right. I'm footman to the Coombe-Marlowes. Do you know them? Both in their eighties and as dull as bloody dust!'

'Well, Miss Dacourt is not exactly what you would call boring!' Chloe said with a sly smile. 'But I warn you, little Jem, if you come and work with us, you might find that you get more excitement than you bargained for!'

'Still a bit glum, sweetheart?' Lord George said, smiling fondly. 'Never mind, come into the drawing room. We are going to have a treat.'

Angela had hardly eaten a morsel. It was not just Lord George's eyes on her breasts throughout the meal. There were the maids, who moved about serving the courses, occasionally glancing at her knowingly. Then there had been Simmonds, who glided about supervising the maids, but always seemed to be standing on the opposite side of the table, so that his gaze constantly fell on Angela.

So Angela had simply sat and squirmed. Lady Anais and Lord George had barely bothered to hide their amusement at her discomfort. The servants had disguised their derision a little better, but it had still been plain to see. She simply had to get some proper clothes as soon as she could. But how? Dressed like this she could hardly run out into the street.

Lord George took her firmly by the arm and, with a glass of brandy in his other hand, steered Angela into the drawing room. Lady Anais sat down on an elegant chaise longue while he settled into a comfortable leather-upholstered armchair, pulling Angela onto his lap and causing her to let out a startled squeak.

'That's it, m'dear, sit here, nice and comfy for the show,' he said with chuckle.

A meaty hand gripped the side of Angela's waist through the silk frock. He put down his brandy next to some papers on an occasional table. Then his freed hand gripped the bare leg above her stockinged knee. Angela bit her lip and tried to ignore the stiffness in his trousers that pressed against her upper thigh.

'All right, Simmonds,' he said at last, 'I think it is time for Mary to demonstrate her new polishing method. Send in the other maids as well, they might find it instructive.'

Angela was only too glad of the distraction. Mary came in clutching a silver candlestick and looking distinctly apprehensive. Yvette and Leila followed, both with more candlesticks, glancing nervously about them. Simmonds brought up the rear, closing the double doors behind him. As he turned, Angela realised with a start that he was carrying a cane.

'Now, Mary,' Lord Fakenham said, 'I want you to sit on that ottoman and show us all the way you polish silver.'

Red spots spread out from the dimpled centres of the little blonde maid's cheeks until her whole face was suffused with a blush.

'Please, sir . . .' she mumbled uncomfortably.

'I would have thought you would have had enough discipline for one day,' Lord George said with a sigh. 'But I asked Simmonds to bring a cane in case we had to polish your bottom instead of that candlestick.'

Mary looked around wide eyed and saw the cane in the butler's hand. Angela watched her swallow and turn back. Licking her full lips nervously, the maid sat down on the ottoman and reluctantly pushed her skirts up. As the frills of her knickers were revealed, she opened her legs and placed the candlestick between them.

Angela watched entranced, so astonished by the sight of the silver stick pistoning up and down between the blushing blonde girl's legs that she almost forgot Lord George's hand stroking her own thigh.

'You see, it is a most singular method!' he declared.

'I do see, George, and it's effective, you say?' his wife asked blandly.

'Terrifically. Shall we ask the others to try it?'

'Yes, why not, but I think their skirts are rather in the way.'

'I take your point, m'dear. Simmonds, have them all take off their dresses, would you?'

To Angela's astonishment, all three maids took off their uniforms, and confirmed her earlier speculation. Each of them wore sheer black nylons and frilly white silk knickers. The secret of their narrow waists was also now revealed, for the three girls each wore tight-laced white satin waspies. These did not come up to the maid's breasts and Angela was startled to see that these were now bare. All three girls proved to have shapely bosoms; Yvette's were full and round, Mary's a little smaller, and Leila's apple sized and delicately pretty. The stiffness pressing against Angela's leg gave a noticeable twitch, and her loins were now tingling so furiously that she was forced to try, without success, to ease the itch by shifting surreptitiously.

There was a small stool on one side of the ottoman which Yvette sat down on. On the other side a wooden chest had been set and this Leila took. Thus the three maids sat, facing their mistress and master, at roughly the same height. At a word from Mr Simmonds, each girl opened her stockinged legs wide and placed her candlestick against the frills of her knickers. Mary was still blushing furiously, Yvette had a glazed look and Angela thought that even the calm Leila looked a little pinker than her usual olive tone.

'Now, I want you all to polish those sticks thoroughly,' said Sir George, when all was ready. 'There is one thing, however. This is work, not frivolity. Thus, I have asked Simmonds to give the first girl who brings herself off a thorough caning.'

Angela was aghast, but less so than the maids, to judge from their various expressions. Simmonds stepped into their line of sight and cut the cane through the air by way of demonstration. It made an ominous whooshing sound and three pairs of eyes watched it with appalled fascination. At a word from Lord Fakenham, the maids began rubbing their candlesticks. Gingerly at first, but orders from the butler soon made each do her job with energy and vigour.

It was almost instantly obvious what effect the task was having. Mary bit her lip and glanced at the cane from time to time. Yvette let out a series of stifled moans of pleasure. Leila kept her eyes closed and her exquisite lips parted. The only question seemed to be which one would climax first.

'So,' Lord George said languidly as Mary also began moaning, 'Anais tells me that you wish to be a debutante this season.'

'Um, ah, yes, if . . .' Angela managed.

The pistonlike pumping of the silver candlesticks seemed almost hypnotic. Angela looked from face to flushed, excited face, fascinated by this diabolical competition.

'Well then, you had better sign this.' Lord George took the sheaf of papers from the table and put them on her naked lap, then he took a pen from his lapel pocket.

Leila, who had stayed silent the longest, let out a lost-sounding groan.

'What . . .?' Angela glanced down at the papers as he put the pen into her hand.

'It's your contract dear, for Anais to be your sponsor. Just a formality.'

'Oh, God!' Mary said suddenly.

Yvette gave a gasp of pleasure.

'Just sign there!' Lord George said firmly.

'Ooh . . .!' Leila moaned and started pumping even harder.

It was a close-run thing in the end, but Mary must have suffered from her head start, because she began shrieking first. Closing her legs around the candle-stick the blonde maid fell off the ottoman and onto the floor, squealing with delight and shuddering with pleasure.

Leila's climax began only a few seconds later. She too closed her legs around the stick, but she retained her seat and let out a high, clear scream of sheer ecstasy.

Yvette arched her back back and began to shout in French, before falling off her stool and curling up in a foetal position.

'Well, Mary,' Lady Anais said mildly, 'you do get yourself into some scrapes! Simmonds, take her away and give her a thorough caning.'

'Very well, ma'am.'

The butler bowed and walked over to the still prone blonde maid. Bending stiffly from the waist, he took hold of her left ear and hauled her, squealing with pain, to her feet. The cane still clutched in his other hand, he marched her out to meet her fate. This time, however, the only remorse that Angela could muster was a pang of regret that she was not going to get to witness Mary's punishment.

'Well, that is all settled,' Lord George said jovially. 'Yvette, put these papers in my study!'

The contract! Angela looked at the sheaf in his hand. There was her name. She had been so distracted by the spectacle of the masturbating maids that she hardly been aware of inscribing her signature. With a sudden pang of panic, she realised that she had signed the contract without having the least idea of what the document contained!

Two

Angela awoke, tried to move her hands and panicked. For a few futile moments she fought the chains that bound her hands tight to the collar round her neck until she remembered where she was and what had happened. The memory caused another jolt of panic to course through her body, but this time she managed not to fight against her bonds.

Lady Anais had buckled the leather straps onto her wrists and secured the collar around Angela's neck with a padlock.

'After my maids' shameful exhibition, we must guard against self-abuse, my dear,' she had said with a sly smile.

The wrist cuffs had been secured with a padlock to the collar and then ankle straps had been buckled on and chained to the foot of the brass bedstead.

'There now, that will put a stop to any masturbatory pranks!' Aunt Anais had said with a chuckle. She had pulled the bedclothes up to Angela's chin and planted a kiss on the pinioned girl's forehead.

'Tomorrow, you will go to Mrs Frobisher's to start your training. The season will be on us in a trice so we had better get you started.'

With this puzzling titbit of information she had gone, saying that, 'Yvette will be going cold,' before pulling the door to.

It had been a long night. Tired as she was, Angela found that she had been strangely aroused by the maids' silver-polishing performance. The tickling, tingling, itchy little urge had come back with a vengeance. The bedclothes were light, however, and provided just enough pressure on her sensitised clitoris to torment her further. However she moved in her bonds, she simply could not get enough pressure to give herself relief.

Exhausted by the long, strange day, Angela had drifted off into strange dreams of being spanked and inspected by elegant people in evening dress. Every so often she would wake up with a start and jingle of chains, to find herself still secured in bed and bathed in perspiration. She tried not to think about Mary being caned by Simmonds, about what Lady Anais was doing to Yvette or Lord George might be up to with Leila. It was no good. Strange fantasies haunted her feverish imagination and invaded her dreams.

If she had not been so tired, she might have spent all night perspiring and fighting the unyielding restraints that held her. She had been exhausted though, and so eventually she had slipped into a deeper sleep.

Now she was awake, she was almost sure. It took some minutes of going over the events of the previous day to convince herself that she was not still dreaming. Everything had been so utterly strange.

Proof, other than the fact that she was still in bondage, soon came with the appearance of Leila, once again the uniformed picture of respectability. The dark beauty regarded Angela with almond-shaped eyes for a moment.

'Good morning, ma'am,' she said in heavily accented but euphonic tones, 'I have been instructed to get you ready.

Angela had little time to reflect on the absurdity of being called ma'am while she lay naked in chains, as Leila began to unlock the chain that secured Angela's collar to the bedstead.

'Lady Fakenham is taking you to be fitted at nine,' Leila said solemnly. 'I am instructed to bathe you in preparation.'

Somewhat to Angela's chagrin, Leila did not release her hands, instead unlocking the ankle straps and taking the collar chain as if it were a leash, pulling gently so that Angela got out of the bed.

'Wait,' Angela said as soon as she was standing. 'What if I don't want to go?'

The truth was that she felt horribly vulnerable, chained like this and naked, and had no idea where the maid was planning to lead her.

Leila turned and regarded her with beautiful dark doe eyes. 'Lady Fakenham says if you do not do as you are told, I am to ask Mr Simmonds to give you a whipping.' The dark girl licked her full lips as if anxiously, her lustrous eyes quite solemn. 'Mr Simmonds,' she said in a low confiding voice, 'I think likes very much to whip you.'

A shiver of sheer terror passed up Angela's spine. She swallowed hard and made no further objection. Leila led her into a luxurious bathroom and, taking an elbow, helped her to step into a bathtub filled with scented water. Angela was so frustrated from her night in chains that she thought that she was going to explode when Leila made her kneel up in the bath and passed a sponge between her legs.

'Please . . .' she heard herself moan as the sponge passed on, 'I need . . .'

Leila regarded her again and for the first time there was the suggestion of amusement in those solemn eyes. 'I know what you need, ma'am,' she said in a low and husky voice. 'But this is not permitted, I'm afraid.'

Thoroughly washed and then towelled dry, Angela was led out and towards the stairway. There was a pounding in her temples. Surely she was not being taken downstairs, naked like this. The Shirley Temple outfit had been bad enough; this was simply too much for her sense of shame to cope with.

'Please, no . . .' she babbled, pulling on the chain.

'Mr Simmonds!' Leila said simply and shrugged.

With a despairing groan Angela let herself be led down the wide sweeping staircase.

Lord George was in the breakfast room, helping himself to sausages and grilled kidneys. Worse, Simmonds himself was replenishing the coffee.

'Ah, there you are, my dear! Looking lovelier than ever,' Lord George said with a grin. 'Did she give you any trouble, Leila?'

'No, sir,' Leila said simply.

Angela thought she detected disappointment flickering in Simmonds's eyes. Certainly Lord Fakenham gave a chuckle.

'Never mind, Simmonds,' he said brightly, 'maybe when she comes back from Mrs Frobisher's she will need it!'

At a gesture from Lord George, Leila led Angela over to him and handed him the end of the chain leash. Then to her enormous relief, the maid went out with Simmonds.

'All right, my dear, kneel down by me. All this is a bit strange, I know.' He patted her on the head and let the chain drop, to dangle cold between her breasts and on her belly. 'Are you hungry? Have a bite, Anais never rises before nine.'

Angela was starving, she realised suddenly, having eaten very little at dinner.

Lord George fed her titbits as she knelt naked beside him; a piece of sausage, a bit of toast, some kidney or a mushroom. It was bizarre but oddly comforting. Naked, she could not so much as cover herself with her pinioned hands. Yet, as she could do nothing, she felt herself relax into a sort of strange acceptance.

'For God's sake, George, what are you doing? I'm taking her to Madame Gelabert's!' Lady Anais announced her presence in a loud voice.

'The girl has to eat, Anais,' Lord George replied calmly, quite unruffled.

'Well, I suppose that it is only the first fitting,' Lady Anais grumbled, pouring herself some coffee. 'But it would have been a disaster if you had stuffed her face before we laced her tight. Thank God she will be at Mrs Frobisher's by the time her corsets are ready!'

'Why do I have to go to this Mrs Frobisher's, anyway?' Lucinda grumbled as Valencia's Daimler sped through the Surrey countryside.

'Because, my sweet,' Valencia replied, taking a bend too fast as usual and narrowly avoiding going off the road, 'you need to be trained before the season.'

'I don't need to be trained,' Lucinda retorted. 'I know how to behave. I'm not some little oik like Jemima Truscott!'

Valencia chuckled. 'You need training a damn sight worse than little Jemma did, Lucy, my lamb. You are spoilt, wilful and petulant and your manners are appalling. Anyway, there is no use complaining now. You have signed on the dotted line and your delicious arse is ours until we choose to release you.'

'You mean until this stupid season is over,' Lucinda retorted, a sliver of doubt making her suddenly feel chilly.

'No,' said Valencia calmly. 'After *this* season you will belong to whoever wins you, until the start of next year's season. And there, I thought that you had read the contract properly!'

They drove on in silence for a while. Lucinda tried to look bored and disdainful, but the truth was that there was a tight knot of anxiety in her belly. She had seen some puzzling references in the contract, but the bloody thing had been so long and strange that in the end she had just signed it.

Although she would not have admitted it for anything, Lucinda was feeling rather strange. A potent cocktail of fear, dread and even a strange excitement was making her quite dizzy, suddenly.

The roads were very narrow now, cut deep into the Surrey greensand, and even Valencia had to slow her maniacal driving a little.

'Nearly there,' she said, grinning at Lucinda as they sped through a pretty village and into deep woodland. 'This is called the Hurt Wood, you know; Maude Frobisher thinks that's awfully funny.'

The entrance to the house was so well concealed in the woods that Lucinda would have missed it. Valencia obviously knew it well, however, because she slowed the Daimler just in time to screech around the corner. There was a short drive to a handsome, Georgian-looking house, set in pleasant lawns and gardens, with wooded hills behind it.

A stocky woman wearing a tweed suit came out of the front door as they were getting out of the car.

'Ha!' she said, 'Thought it must be you, Valencia, when I heard that infernal squealing.'

So this was the famous Maude Frobisher. Lucinda thought, looking at the woman with some incredulity. She was a hefty, pleasant-faced woman in her late forties or early fifties; tweedily respectable and amiable looking. She would be bound to have Labradors, Lucinda sneered to herself, and be very keen on horses. Certainly it was hard to see why the very mention of her name made grown women of Lucinda's acquaintance blanch and tremble.

She does not look so very fearsome, Lucinda thought, feeling rather better about her situation suddenly.

'This must be Lady Lucinda,' Mrs Frobisher said, looking at her with frank grey-blue eyes. 'Delighted to make your acquaintance, your Ladyship.'

Good god, Lucy thought, she is going to curtsey in a minute. The fear that had gripped her moments earlier had gone. Lucinda Beaufort-Grey could deal with this fat sycophant, any day of the week!

'Quite still, child!' Madame Gelabert said sharply.

Angela gasped as the cold metal tip of the tape measure brushed her naked belly again. It seemed to be taking for ever. She had been made to strip down to her stockings in the corsetiere's plushly furnished fitting room. A chic girl had brought tea for Aunt Anais who sat and watched proceedings, chatting in French to Madame Gelabert. This lady was an elegant creature of about thirty, who had the tiniest waist that Angela had ever seen. This, and a tendency to creak slightly when she bent, suggested that the corsetiere was a woman who practised what she preached.

'You must lace her very tight, Lady Anais!' she expostulated as she prodded Angela in the soft flesh of her belly. 'These young girls with their flesh so . . . malleable and . . . opulent, they must be constrained . . . disciplined . . .' at which point she lapsed into French again.

She passed the tape between Angela's legs, though why such a measurement should be of use, the naked girl could not imagine. Then the little Frenchwoman tugged it tighter and Angela let out a startled cry as the tape disappeared between her labia and she was even more puzzled about the purpose of the measurements that the little woman called out to her assistant.

'Hello, dear, lovely to meet you. My name is Mrs Frobisher. I'm very glad that you are coming to stay for a while.'

The anxiety that had gripped Angela eased considerably as Maude Frobisher chatted away and beamed at her the most amiable way.

'Ah, here is Norris, my man. Norris, would you show Miss Carstairs to her room?'

'Certainly, ma'am,' the manservant said and invited Angela to follow him up the sweeping staircase with the subtlest of gestures.

'Bye for now, Angela, I'll come down and see you in a week or so,' Aunt Anais called up after her.

The anxiety returned as Angela followed Norris up the stairs. She could not quite have said why, but there was something about the butler she did not entirely like. He was not a tall man, and was inclined to be a little stout. If pressed Angela would have guessed that he was in his fifties, for what little hair he still had left was grey. In all he was the most unremarkable of men, and yet something about him frightened Angela.

They reached the top of the stairway and Norris led her down a thickly carpeted corridor.

'That is the girls' bathroom, miss,' he said, nodding towards a door. 'I expect that you would like to freshen up.'

They continued on.

'Here we are, miss.'

Norris produced a large bunch of keys from his pocket and sorted through them carefully until finding the one he wanted. Then he unlocked the door. He led the way into a large, bright room with lavender walls. It was simply but well furnished, and dominated by a comfortable-looking bed. A bay window looked out onto a wooded hillside. Once again, Angela felt, this place might not be so bad.

'I expect that you would like to shower after your journey, miss.' Norris said, taking a fluffy-looking bath towel from a chest of drawers.

The journey from London had taken less than two hours and Angela was hardly fatigued or dirty, but the way he said it seemed so certain that she found herself nodding her head. She followed the . . . well, she supposed he was a butler really, back down the thickly carpeted corridor. Just before they reached the door a young woman reached the top of the stairs and came along the corridor towards them. When she saw Angela and Norris standing there she paused.

'Ah, there you are, Lady Lucinda. I will be ready for you in just a tick. Would you be so good as to wait for me outside your bedroom door?'

The girl was elegantly dressed, blonde and delicately beautiful. The feature that struck Angela most forcibly, however, was the expression on Lady Lucinda's exquisite face. The blonde girl was plainly gripped by an internal struggle of conflicting emotions. Fear, anger and embarrassment seem to be fighting for supremacy, the emotions plainly too powerful to be quite hidden, despite the girl's obvious poise.

'Oh, very well!' she said a little petulantly after a moment.

Lady Lucinda stalked off down the corridor, completely ignoring Angela, who for her part noticed that the blonde girl's fists were clenched so tight that her knuckles had gone quite white.

'I'm afraid that Lady Lucinda is finding adjustment to our ways a little difficult,' Norris said as they watched the elegant figure disappear around the corner of the corridor. 'In particular, I believe that she finds it particularly hard to submit to being caned by a servant.'

Angela had little time to digest this information. That the proud Lady Lucinda was to be caned by Norris! The thought sent a little shock of panic through her vitals. For if Lady Lucinda had to submit to such painful indignity, what about . . . But she had no chance to dwell on the awful implications. For, to her surprise and further alarm, Norris looked through his bunch of keys again before unlocking the door to the bathroom. The fact that her bedroom door had been locked, and that she had not been offered any key, had given her a moment of anxiety, but Angela had told herself that this may have been for some reason of security. She could think of no reason for the bathroom being kept locked. Norris stood aside to let her enter, and Angela stepped inside.

The strange scent hit her first; the distinct and pungent odour of latex. The room was almost oppressively bright, with glossy white tiles from the floor to the ceiling. It was also much bigger than she had expected, with four shower stalls and the same number of baths, bidets and toilets. Clearly the girls staying at Hurtwood House got little privacy, Angela thought.

In scale it reminded her of her old school's facilities but there was an important difference. Here, every piece of porcelain gleamed; every stainless steel fixture glittered brilliantly.

It was not hard to find the reason for this. A strange figure bent, diligently polishing one of the bidets.

'Suzette, stop that and come here!' Norris ordered.

The bending girl had frozen at the sound of their entry and now she turned quickly to face them. Once again, Angela had to blink hard a few times to convince herself that she was not dreaming. Suzette wore a sort of parody of a French maid's costume, very low cut and with a flouncy little skirt of absurd brevity. What made the uniform so extraordinary, however, was that it was made of gleaming, skin-tight black rubber. Black latex stockings, held up by quite visible rubber suspenders and matching arm-length gloves, a little white latex cap and extraordinarily high-heeled, glossy black patent leather shoes completed the bizarre outfit. Except for the strangest part of all – the maid wore a gleaming steel collar about her slender neck and steel cuffs about her wrists and ankles. This collar was attached to a long steel chain, which was attached to a bolt set in the very centre of the ceiling.

'Suzette will undress and wash you,' Norris said, as if the chained, latex-sheathed maid was quite unremarkable.

'I, I can bathe myself, thank you . . .' Angela managed to mumble.

'That would be unfortunate, miss,' Norris said with a tone of regret. 'You see, it is Suzette's job, and if she does not do it, whether from her own fault or someone else's, I am required to punish her severely.'

The maid said nothing but her expression was eloquence itself. She looked up at Angela with wide brown, appealing eyes. For the first time Angela noticed how pretty the girl was. She had black hair pulled tight into a bun behind her cap, contrasting pale, pellucid skin and full lips that had been rendered startlingly crimson by her lipstick. The bottom lip trembled very slightly.

'I should, perhaps, also point out that Mrs Frobisher will require you to watch if I have to whip this girl or any staff member as a consequence of your behaviour. Now, miss, if you will excuse me.'

Norris went out and Angela heard the lock click a second or two after he closed the door. She turned back to the maid who was waiting with her head bowed very slightly.

'Will he really, I mean, what he said about . . . he would not really whip you because I didn't let you undress me?'

'Oh yes, miss,' Suzette said in a soft voice, keeping her eyes downcast. 'Yesterday we had another new girl and she –' the rubber-encased maid stopped as if trying not to sob '– she would not permit me to perform my duties.'

The girl turned and bent over to the sound of tinkling chain. She did not need to flip back the little skirt because it was so short that the act of bending lifted it clear of most of her bottom. This was nicely plump and encased in translucent white latex panties, so tight that they almost made the constricting uniform look loose. This was not what transfixed Angela, however. Thin, deep pink lines, much darker than the pale flesh that they criss-crossed, were clearly visible on the bare flesh between the panties and the latex stocking tops. Angela could even see welts through the semi-transparent latex of the knickers.

'Who . . . who?' was all she could manage, feeling her knees go weak as she stared at the maid's clearly well-whipped bottom.

Suzette stood up and faced her, once again taking up a submissive, head-bowed, posture. 'I believe her name was Lady Lucinda, miss. Please may I help you to undress now?'

'Is this really necessary?' Lucinda demanded, as she preceded Norris into her bedroom.

'In what way would that be, miss?' the manservant enquired coolly.

She stood facing him, little fists tightly clenched. The man's insolence was all the more galling for being subtle.

'I mean, is it necessary for me to be . . . caned by a servant?'

Norris maintained his usual sober expression but Lady Lucinda was damned sure she could see an infuriating twinkle in his eyes.

'It is part of the training programme at Hurtwood House, miss; I do assure you that all the girls who come here are subject to it. Now, if you would be so good as to take your frock off, we should be getting started.'

Lucinda hesitated for a moment longer. Part of her was considering refusing altogether, the rest just wanted to debate the point as a delaying tactic. Gallingly, Norris simply walked over to the wardrobe, as if quite sure that she would obey his last instruction.

When he opened the wardrobe door, Lucinda's mouth went dry. Hanging on the inside of the door were two canes, a riding crop, a tawse and a couple of heavy leather belts. As if by magic this startling array turned Lucinda's nettled pride to sudden fear. By the time Norris turned around with a cane in his hand, she was hurriedly taking her dress off.

'Do you spend . . . a lot of time in here?' Angela asked hesitantly, as she watched the maid pour perfumed bath oils into the rapidly filling tub.

'I am not permitted to make conversation, miss,' the girl said simply.

Angela was quite naked now. The maid had taken her clothes and put them into a sort of hatch set in one wall.

'What are you –?' she had protested too late as she realised it might be the top of some sort of chute, rather than the lid of a hidden basket.

Angela had run across the room, and hauled open the thing. Her stomach had done a little flip. It was a chute. There were no clothes, no shoes, not even any underthings. Feeling the blood flooding to her cheeks, she glared at the strange rubber-clad maid, who carried on imperturbably about her business.

The only sound was the occasional squeaking of tight latex as Suzette bent; the tinkling of the strange maid's chains and the pounding in Angela's ears.

It was not just Suzette's presence that made her feel horribly embarrassed about her nakedness, however. It was the knowledge that Norris might return at any moment. For all Angela knew the sinister butler might be about to turn the key.

'Now then, miss,' Norris said briskly. 'If you would care to stand here and bend over, placing your palms on the bed.'

Lady Lucinda's cheeks felt like they were burning as she stalked over to the point he indicated. She was wearing her best, expensive French silk lingerie; lace and silk bra in pale peach, with matching suspender belt and French knickers, and sheer tan nylons. To her absolute mortification, the butler did not bother to hide his admiration for her underwear or for the figure that it decorated and revealed. He looked at her quite openly with a half-smile on his lips. Lucinda bit back an acerbic comment, for he was also idly flexing the cane in between his hands. Putting Norris in his place would just have to wait.

Trying not to think about the sight she was presenting, she bent with ill grace and put her hands on the satin coverlet.

'Please try to keep your legs straight now, Lady Lucinda. I regret that if you do not hold still I shall be obliged to add to your six of the best,' he said gravely.

Lucinda gripped the coverlet so tight that her knuckles whitened. How was this to be borne? she wondered. His use of her title seemed designed simply to mock her further. The blush on her cheeks burned even brighter than before, if that were possible. To be made to bend in her underthings, to submit to being caned like a naughty child by this common servant. It was the most degrading and humiliating thing imaginable.

'Right, your ladyship. Time to have these expensive French frillies down, I think.'

To Lucinda's utter horror, she felt the butler insert his thumbs into the waistband of her French knickers and then slowly peel them right down to her knees.

'You have a very pretty bottom, Lady Lucinda. If you don't mind me saying,' Norris said with facetious deference.

'Of course, I mind you . . . filthy oik!' Lucinda said, unable to contain her fury one moment longer.

'Oh dear,' the butler said, regretfully. 'I am afraid that I am going to have to increase the tariff on account of that little outburst. If it was but up to me . . . however, Mrs Frobisher is most particular about the way her guests are expected to address her staff. That remark is going to cost you four more strokes, my lady.'

His hand, his ill-bred, middle-aged, servant's hand, actually had the temerity to pat Lady Lucinda's bottom. She bit back another insult with difficulty, clutching the counterpane even more tightly and screwing her eyes tight closed. He continued to feel her buttock flesh, pinching and stroking until tears of pure humiliation threatened to run down her flaming cheeks. Something told her that he was trying to provoke her, however. Something told her that he was trying to get her to insult him again so that he could give her more strokes. Well, she would just refuse to be provoked!

'What, what are you doing?' she demanded in a shrill voice as his fingers drifted to the bottom of the crack between her buttocks.

'Simply checking something, miss,' the butler said calmly. 'Good heavens, Lady Lucinda, you would appear to be all wet between your legs!'

She dropped her head and let a humiliated sob escape her as his fingers slid inside. The thing that mortified her most was not the fact that she was naked being fingered by the butler, however, nor that she was bent over like a naughty child awaiting the cane. The thing that caused the tears of shame to course down her lovely elegant face was that while Lady Lucinda Beaufort Grey was being fondled in her most intimate places by a servant, she was silently praying that he would not stop too soon.

'Ooh!' Angela said, unable to keep silent under Suzette's caressing fingers any longer.

The maid had helped Angela into the warm, fragrant bath water, and begun to soap her body with a luxurious lather. Even from the start this had felt very strange. The feel of the latex gloves against her naked skin was quite as unsettling as the pungent smell. The chain, though Suzette moved gracefully and was clearly quite used to this tether, fascinated and appalled Angela in equal measure. She found that she could barely take her eyes off the solid-looking padlock that affixed the chain to Suzette's gleaming steel collar, or stop herself from imagining how it must feel.

Once Angela's arms and lower legs had been soaped, things became even more disquieting, for Suzette worked up more lather from the soap bar and then began to stroke her breasts. Annette closed her eyes and bit her bottom lip. The urge to moan was almost irresistible as she felt her nipples stiffen in response to Suzette's soap-lubricated, latex-sheathed caress.

It was strangely pleasant, but hard to bear in silence. As Suzette's hands worked their way down her belly, she kept her eyes tight shut and gripped the sides of the bath as tightly as she could. The rubber-gloved hands gently worked her wet skin until Angela simply could not prevent a sight of pleasure from escaping.

'Oh, ah, no . . . not there . . .' she said between gasps as the maid's cunning fingers reached her sex and continued their almost unbearably titillating contact. She did not open her eyes, however, nor release her grip on the sides of the bath in order to ward off those caresses. Instead, her pelvis bucked in response to Suzette's exquisitely tantalising fingers as they brushed her clitoris and explored her pussy opening beneath the scented water.

How long this went on for she could not have said. It was as if the rubber-sheathed maid's fingering stroked Angela away into a rose-and-latex-scented dreamland; a warm and wet world, intoxicating, soporific, yet arousing.

'Your clothes, miss.'

If Angela had been slapped hard across the face the butler's voice could not have had more impact. She opened her eyes in shock, feeling the blood rush to her face, letting go of the sides of the bath in order to cover her breasts.

It was clearly a bit late for that, however. Norris was standing in front of her. How he had moved so silently she did not know, and she wondered how long he had apparently been admiring her naked body at his leisure. He continued looking for a moment. His face was a polite blank but Angela was sure that she could discern amusement if not desire in his eyes.

'I'll put them here. You are expected downstairs, miss. Suzette, you are here to help the guests with their ablutions, not to finger them for your pleasure. I shall whip you later, unless you wish to appeal to Mrs Frobisher?'

'Oh, no, Mr Norris,' Suzette said hurriedly.

Her pretty face looked paler than ever, Angela thought, and those wide appealing eyes turned on her again. Should she protest on Suzette's behalf? No, Angela thought, remembering Mary. Anyway the little tart *had* been fingering her! In truth, despite the adrenalin surge that Norris's presence had provoked, she still felt strange and tingly down there. This realisation only made her cheeks burn brighter.

Angela clutched her breasts until the butler closed the door behind him, and only then did she dare to get out of the water and let Suzette towel her dry.

'Oof . . . I can't breathe,' Lady Lucinda protested as the corset laces constricted her dainty waist ever more tightly.

'Sorry, miss,' the trim little maid said brightly, and hauled on the laces again.

Lucinda held tight onto the foot of her brass bedstead as the laces were inexorably tightened. The corset was an innocent-looking thing in pale pink satin, dotted with tiny flowers in fuchsia and trimmed with delicate lace. It did not come up as high as her breasts nor go down so low as to cover any of her bottom, and when the maid had taken it out of its tissue paper-lined box, it had looked so frivolous and feminine that Lady Lucinda had been shocked by the garment's brutal grip. Now it nipped her waist in like a garrotte tightening inexorably about her middle.

'No tighter, Lysette,' she said between gasps, 'I can't breathe!'

'Nearly done, miss,' the red-haired maid said, giving the laces one last hefty tug. 'There, I think that will do for your first time.'

'It surely . . . oof . . . can't be any tighter!' Lucinda said, alarmed by this remark.

The maid had finished tying off the laces and so Lady Lucinda turned to face the red-haired girl. Lysette stood with a critical expression, clearly admiring her recent handiwork.

'Oh, don't worry, miss,' she said with twinkling eyes and a mischievous expression. 'Once you have been tight laced for a few days we'll get you down at least another inch or three!'

'Can I have your attention please, ladies?' Maude Frobisher said, standing.

The stilted conversation in the drawing room paused abruptly. Five pairs of eyes fixed upon their hostess, attentively and not a little apprehensively.

'We have a new addition to our little party. This is Angela, everyone.'

The eyes all turned to Angela, who sat perched uncomfortably on the edge of her seat.

'Angela, let me introduce Lady Lucinda, whom we shall call Lucy for short.'

The delicately beautiful blonde whom Angela had passed in the corridor on her arrival nodded curtly at her. For all her poise and elegance the girl seemed to be having difficulty sitting still, Angela noticed. She could not help but wonder if this were an after-effect of having a freshly caned bottom. The appalling vision sent thrills of anxiety, and yet a strange excitement, coursing through Angela's body.

'Jane ...' Mrs Frobisher said, moving around to stand behind the chair of a tall, strikingly beautiful girl whose dark hair was carefully coiffed. Jane regarded Angela with wide, solemn dark eyes and nodded briefly.

Mrs Frobisher moved on to stand beside the other blonde girl in the room. In contrast to Lucinda, she was distinctly plump, although her smart, flower-patterned frock displayed a relatively tiny waist. This apparent contradiction was no mystery to Angela however as, after her bath, she had been tightly corseted by Suzette.

'Daphne ...' Mrs Frobisher said simply before moving on. 'And, last but not least, Anastasia – though, as we are not formal here, we call her Annie!'

This last girl was petite, brown haired and pretty. She nodded towards Angela and managed a strained smile.

'Now ladies, you all know why you are here, I think. Before your "seasons" start you will need to be prepared. Think of this as a sort of finishing school. If ever you think my discipline too strict, remember that your lives will become yet more exacting once you leave here.

'What I shall endeavour to instil, during your stay, is ladylike comportment in all situations. Submission and obedience will not be sufficient during the coming months. What I shall require from you young ladies is for you to submit and obey, elegantly.'

She paused, beaming around the room at each of the girls in turn. The tweedy woman's gaze ended up fixed on Angela.

'Angela, my dear. I understand that you have not been caned yet?'

Angela could not stop herself from colouring. There was a pounding in her temples, dryness in her throat. Mrs Frobisher's gaze seemed to pin her to her seat.

'Um, no . . .' she managed.

'Well, I shan't insist that you submit in public for your first time. Norris will cane you in your room, at, shall we say five o'clock? You may find that you need a little while to settle down before dinner. Would that suit, my dear?'

The expression on Mrs Frobisher's plump face seemed to suggest that she was expecting an answer. But what sort of answer could Angela give to such a question?

'I . . . er . . . suppose . . .' she mumbled, confused and flustered. She could feel the other girls' eyes resting on her, watching her reaction.

'Jolly good, that's the ticket!' Mrs Frobisher declared with a broad beam. 'Five o'clock it is! First things first, though. Jane, ring for Norris, would you? I do believe it's time we all had a drop of sherry!'

How long had she stood outside her room, like a naughty girl waiting outside the headmistress's study? It seemed to have been ages. Norris was making her wait deliberately, she realised; or was it Mrs Frobisher's instructions?

It did not really matter either way. Angela was obliged to wait outside her own locked bedroom door until it pleased the butler to come and cane her. It was intolerable, humiliating, and scary, and yet strangely exciting, all at once.

From time to time she glanced down the corridor towards the bathroom door. Was Suzette still in there, still leashed by that chain in her strange world of porcelain and latex? She could hear nothing, but supposed the maid was still diligently polishing and cleaning. The thought of Suzette on her chain, encased in rubber, and the memory of the maid's caress only increased Angela's strange arousal. This would not do; she must think of something else! The corset gripped her so tightly that she had to breathe shallowly even when she was quite calm. The thought of Norris with his cane was even worse.

There was moistness on the palms of her hands and Angela wished she had a handkerchief. It did not seem right to wipe them on the flared skirt of her new, pale blue frock.

So she tried not to think about Norris and what was coming, nor about Suzette and what had passed before. She banned all thoughts of Mary being strapped on the billiard table, and refused to let herself imagine proud Lucy bending for the cane.

'Sorry to keep you waiting, miss,' Norris said as he approached, silent as ever on the thick corridor carpet.

Angela did not believe he was sorry for a moment, but his expression remained the usual polite mask. He unlocked the door and stood aside to allow her to precede him into the room. Once in he went to the wardrobe and opened the door. Angela had not yet had time to look into this piece of furniture. There, to her confusion and astonishment, hanging from the back of the door were two canes, a tawse and several leather belts. Her heart was hammering so hard that she felt almost dizzy.

Norris selected one of the canes and turned to face her, flexing it between his hands as if testing its resilience and spring.

'Now, miss,' he said as smooth as a head waiter, 'if you would be so good as to remove your dress.'

'I'm going to miss this,' Lord Randolph Southdean said as he adjusted the spotlight to make sure it was trained on the two young women.

'I know what you mean,' Valencia Dacourt replied.

The buxom blonde Camilla and red-haired Belinda were naked except for sheer black stockings gartered above their knees and long black lace gloves. Randolph had shackled both girls' wrists to a chain which hauled them up until they had to stand on tiptoe. A narrow leather belt pulled tight around the pair's waists forced their bellies together and also caused their naked breasts to be squashed against each other – to Randolph's mind, most amusingly.

'Shall I fix their ankles?' he asked, once the spotlight was arranged on the naked girls to his satisfaction.

'No,' Valencia said slowly, 'let's let them dance, Randolph.'

She already held a whip; a five-foot signal whip in braided black leather, and she cracked this suddenly. In the confined dungeon it sounded like a gunshot. Both Belinda and Camilla jumped in response to the sound, and Camilla let out a startled little wail.

'We could keep them, I suppose.' Valencia said, archly.

'Tempting, very tempting. But Belinda is supposed to be marrying her fiancé!'

'Oh yes, Sir Jeremy Dickless-Twerp, wasn't it?'

'Something like that,' Randolph conceded with a chuckle. 'Digby-Tremaine, I think, actually.'

'Seems a dreadful waste of prime girl-flesh!' Valencia continued.

'Quite. Coming back from Kenya in a couple of weeks, eager to wed his virgin bride and all that, I believe. I suppose if he found out what his little fiancée had been up to for the last year, it could put the mockers on the match . . .'

'Oh, please, no, sir . . .' Belinda began, as he had known she would.

He had only to cock an eyebrow at Valencia. The black snake coiled back and cracked across Belinda's lovely bottom. The red-haired girl's pleas were abruptly interrupted by her shriek of pain.

'Actually, Belinda, old thing,' Valencia said in an amused voice as they watched the naked girls writhe helplessly in their bonds, 'no one is all that interested in what you might think!'

Randolph smiled to himself. She had a point: it would be a wrench to free Belinda. He suspected that the voluptuous Camilla would be around to abuse for a while yet, as the blonde had developed a real taste for submission during her season. So had his sweet Belinda, of course. But the red-head wanted money and Sir Jeremy had lots of it. He would just have to hope that she could wangle a way to stay when the rich Baronet went back to his coffee plantations.

The whip cracked again, this time lashing across Camilla's pale back. Bigger and fuller figured than Belinda, the blonde lurched forward as if by doing so she might somehow get away from the source of pain. This caused both girls to swing and spin a little on their chains. Both were squealing with pain and terror as Valencia whipped them expertly. Randolph felt his cock stiffen as he watched the naked girls dance desperately around in a doomed attempt to escape the lashes.

Yes, he would have to let Belinda go, there was no help for it. But as least the season would be starting again soon. Who knew what succulent delights might soon replace these dancing beauties? Sir Randolph smiled to himself as he took a sip of Armagnac. The whip hissed through the still dungeon air and wrapped itself around Belinda's chubby bottom. The red-head let out another agonised shriek.

'Thank you, miss,' Norris said, his eyes fixed on Angela's tightly corseted figure. 'Now, would you please bend over the rail at the foot of your bed for me?'

Angela's cheeks were glowing as if they had been sunburnt. She held her hands cupped over her naked breasts, wishing that the pale blue satin corset were not so short. However, the cane in his hand focused her mind, and she turned to do as he had bidden her. The brass rail at the foot of her bedstead came to a little below her constricted waist. As she tried to bend she encountered a problem. The stiff boning of the corset resisted her attempts to bend, creaking lustily in protest as she attempted to obey.

'Ah, I can't, it's too stiff . . .' she gasped as she fought with limited success to bend over the bedstead.

'I'm afraid I must ask you to put your hands on the counterpane at least, miss,' Norris said smoothly.

She felt the butler place his hand on her bare back, above the corset, and push. The whalebone creaked louder in protest but with this help she managed to bend just enough to grasp the satin bedspread.

'That's it, miss,' Norris said, removing his hand.

Only for a moment though for, to Angela's mortification, he rested it on her bottom next.

'These will have to come down, of course, miss,' he said evenly.

Angela swallowed hard as she felt him pull her new silk knickers down until they were around her knees. The hand came back and rested on her now naked bottom, gently.

'Lovely,' the butler said in a soft and reverent tone, 'simply lovely.'

Part of Angela was outraged, though she did not know why this might be worse than his usual crisp politeness. Bending over ready to be caned, however, she did not really feel ready to protest at this liberty. Indeed, another part of her was quite happy for him to stand and caress her bottom all day, so long as it put off the moment that was coming.

The hand was removed. Angela tried to swallow but found her mouth too dry. She sensed, rather than heard him step back and get ready. It was silent except for the slight creaking of her corset. Her knees began trembling uncontrollably.

'You are required to count, and thank me for each stroke, miss. The form is to enunciate the correct number and then say, "Thank you, Norris." I hope that that is clear?'

'Yes, ah . . . thank you . . . Norris,' Angela mumbled, gripping the satin cover as hard as she could.

There was an ominous low whistle and a meaty crack of impact. A line of fire was scored across the very middle of her bottom, intense enough to make Angela gasp in pain.

'One . . . thank you, Norris,' she said quickly, screwing up her eyes tightly.

Another whistle and another impact crack. He struck lower this time, scoring her tender under-bum. He struck harder too. For a few moments Angela was unable to say a word, rendered quite breathless by the pain.

'Two . . . ooh . . . thank you, Norris,' she gasped out at last.

Norris caned her with vigour and skill. Several times, Angela thought that she must let go of the bedspread and jump up to clutch her burning bottom. Somehow she stayed down. Somehow she managed to thank Norris for each stroke, though sometimes it was a minute or so after the event before she could compose herself sufficiently for speech. There was something curiously humiliating about having to thank the butler for each blistering cane stroke, as if thanking him, as she had done only minutes earlier, for serving her with a glass of sherry.

Tears came on the fifth stroke, though whether principally tears of humiliation or of pain, Angela could not have said. The last stroke was the hardest of all. She hissed and stamped her feet for a full minute before she could manage to speak.

'Six . . . Ow! Thank you . . . Norris,' she managed at last between sobs.

There was a long moment of silence. Angela could sense him looking at her freshly welted bottom. As the pain subsided she began to wonder what he was going to do next.

'There now,' Norris said in a softer voice than he had used before.

Angela winced as she felt his hand on her well-caned buttocks. Although he stroked her gently, the fresh weals stung anew under even that light touch. Yet there was something else stirring inside her. The urges that Suzette had awoken seemed to have seized Angela anew. She found herself desperate for the butler to touch her between her legs. The desire was so strong that she felt her thighs quivering.

'Would there be anything else, miss?' the butler said in a slightly thicker, more strained-sounding voice.

Angela bit her bottom lip to stop herself from moaning, and clutched the counterpane. She knew that if she gave in to the urge all dignity would be lost for good.

'Ah, no . . .' she said finally with enormous effort, '. . . no, no thank you, Norris.'

'Very well, miss,' Norris said calmly, withdrawing his hand. 'If you would care to dress for dinner, it will be served at six.'

Three

'Well, ladies.' Maude Frobisher beamed around the drawing room at the five girls in turn. 'After dinner, as those of you who have been here a few days know by now, I like to give my guests a little talk, about what will be expected of them over the coming year.'

At dinner, once again, Angela had eaten little. She had been too aware of her still sore behind on the dining chair, even through the layers of net petticoats that buoyed up her skirts. Her throbbing bottom, the unfamiliar restriction of the corset, the still insistent tingling sensation between her legs and the awful shame-inducing conviction that the other girls must know what had happened between her and the butler had left her with no appetite at all.

'Tonight,' Mrs Frobisher continued, 'I wish to talk about the subject of masturbation.'

Angela could not prevent the colour from rising to her cheeks at the word. A glance around told her that she was not the only one. Both Daphne and Annie were visibly blushing and Jane was looking very hard into her lap. Only Lucinda looked unembarrassed. In fact the elegant young blonde had an exasperated expression on her face.

'It is not germane,' Mrs Frobisher said briskly, 'what your habits have been in the past. What concerns me is your stay here and your season. Throughout that period, I must tell you all, self-abuse will be strictly forbidden. No wandering fingers in the bedroom late at night, girls! I shall expect restraint!'

The big woman chortled with laughter and Angela felt her cheeks flame hotter.

'Well, actually,' Mrs Frobisher continued, walking over to a sideboard, 'I don't expect frisky young fillies to manage without help. If I or the staff catch you at it, you will get a stiff dozen from Norris's cane. However, we cannot be watching you all night now, can we?' She opened a drawer and pulled out a jingling bunch of chain complete with leather collar and cuffs. 'So, starting tonight, girls, when you go to bed tonight, each of you will be fitted with one of these "artificial aids".'

Angela looked at the shackles with a sinking heart. The device was only too familiar from Aunt Anais's house. With something close to despair she wondered when and how she would ever have the relief she now so desperately needed.

'Ooh! What a relief!' Lucinda said as the maid finally got her stays undone and took it away.

She had to admit that the other girls looked very fetching in their corsets. The new girl, Angela was all too obviously unused to displaying her charms, and was blushing amusingly and trying to cover both her breasts and sex as Suzette loosened the laces. Plump little Daphne looked particularly succulent in her cream satin waspie.

The five girls, helped by the maids, continued to undress until even their corsets and stockings were gone. There were only four showers, but Lucinda lingered, letting the other girls go first. There was a reason for this. From where she stood she had an excellent view of the four naked girls as each one waited for Suzette to soap her body in turn. Jane and Angela were clearly the two that had most recently been caned, for distinct, deep pink stripes still barred their bottoms.

Lucinda licked her lips. One day! she thought to herself, imagining the cane in her hand and looking at each naked bottom in turn as the girls showered. One day she would have beauties like these trembling as they awaited her pleasure. The cornucopia of pink and naked flesh before her eyes was almost too much. Her whole body was tingling with arousal now. Did she dare to touch herself surreptitiously? The urge was almost irresistible. However, the memory of Norris's cane was still fresh in her memory. Although the desire to put her hand between her legs was so strong now that her fingers actually trembled, somehow Lucinda controlled the almost overwhelming urge.

When her turn came she allowed the latex-clad maid to soap her body. Not that Lucinda cared if the maid was punished or not, indeed, she would have loved to watch the girl caned again. The fact was that she had noticed how the maid's hand lingered as she soaped the other girls in certain places, and she hoped that Suzette might keep her latex gloved fingers between Lucinda's legs long enough . . .

The door to the bathroom opened suddenly. Instantly a frisson of fear passed through the room. Daphne gave a little alarmed squeak and Angela gasped and coloured. Norris stood as imperturbable as ever, coolly viewing the nubile and naked flesh arranged before him as if critically examining a dinner table setting.

'Lady Lucinda,' he said at last, resting his gaze on her naked body. 'Mrs Frobisher has asked for the pleasure of your company this evening.'

* * *

'This isn't . . . decent!' Angela whispered at last.

'I know,' Daphne whispered back, after a pause, 'but what can we do?'

After showering the girls had been issued with baby doll nighties. These were diaphanous and scandalously short, too short to cover matching, absurdly frilly panties. Each girl's nightie was a different shade of pastel, Angela's being a pretty shade of yellow. Norris had asked them to line up in the corridor while he locked the bathroom door once more. Then he had walked the little line, looking at each trembling girl in turn, as if examining his staff's uniforms for dirt marks.

'Lovely,' he said, stopping in front of Jane. 'Very lovely.'

Squinting sideways, Angela could see him raise his hand to touch gently the tall girl's breast. Jane bit her lip and coloured slightly but said nothing. After fondling her for a moment or two he moved on, stopping again to smile down at little Daphne.

'Settling in all right are we, miss?' he asked blandly.

Angela could see that his hand was travelling up the girl's thigh. Daphne stared straight ahead, blinking furiously, as the butler began to stroke the front of her panties.

'Ah, yes, ooh, Norris, thank you,' the plump blonde girl managed in a hoarse voice.

'Glad to hear it, miss. I'm sure that you will soon get used to being caned. Mrs Frobisher has asked me to give you six tomorrow.'

Daphne had let out a gasp at this, but whether from fear of the cane or in response to his fondling Angela had been unable to distinguish. The butler moved on and stood in front of Angela herself. She could not meet his eyes and dropped her gaze, only to see his hand come up towards her.

Norris had opened his hand and placed his fingers around her breast, which was clearly visible through the transparent yellow nylon of her nightie. He did not squeeze or pinch, he just felt her titty gently, yet this light contact made her head spin and her stomach tighten. It was almost unbearable. She wanted him to squeeze harder, she wanted him to let go. She wanted him to unhand her and to let her go to bed. She wanted him to rip her knickers off and fuck her! Angela's head spun. She had never felt anything like this cyclone of conflicting feelings and emotions.

'You have lovely breasts, miss,' Norris said at last. 'The gentlemen and ladies at the balls will certainly want to whip them.'

The bell rang in the servants' hall, putting an instant end to the conversation.

Jem looked at the two parlour maids and they looked at him and each other.

'One ring,' Jem said in a voice that was slightly strained by anxiety.

'That's you then, Jem,' Chloe said unnecessarily.

He nodded and got up hurriedly.

'She's in her bedroom,' Yvonne said archly, gesturing at the array of bells.

'Yes, I do understand the system, thanks!' Jem said, colouring a little.

'Watch that sweet little bottom, Jemmy!' Chloe called out as he left the room. The laughter of the maids followed him down the corridor as he hurried away.

Valencia Dacourt's Mayfair house was impressively large. Jem had only just begun to find his way around the place. However, he knew that his mistress's room was on the second floor. He made his way down the thickly carpeted corridor with a pounding heart. Pausing at the door, he took a deep breath and then knocked.

'Come,' Valencia's voice said.

She had her back to him. He saw she was wearing a black negligee so long that its hem brushed the floor. It was made of something soft and silky, trimmed with jet-black feathers. Jem let out a sigh of relief. The negligee was not transparent at least. He had been half afraid . . .

Valencia turned and his sense of relief vanished in an instant. In fact for a moment Jem forgot to breathe. Valencia had not tied the front of the gown and it hung open. She stood before him resplendent in a black lace basque. Semi-transparent black French knickers did not help his composure, either but it was Valencia's thighs that he found himself staring at.

From the little he had seen of his new mistress, he had gathered that she was a very fit young woman. All the same, he had not realised quite how powerful looking her exposed legs would be. The sheer black stockings that she wore only seemed to emphasise the sleek muscles of her thighs. He found himself unable to take his gaze away.

'Ah,' she said at last, 'there you are, boy.'

Valencia walked forward until she was standing no more than two feet away. Jem found his downcast eyes now fixed on her magnificent cleavage. The black lace cups of the basque pushed Valencia's opulent breasts up, but failed to veil her nipples entirely. Jem bit his bottom lip and looked up. Not daring to meet her eyes, nor to look down at Valencia's bust, he swallowed hard and fixed his stare on her collar bone. Musky perfume engulfed him; intoxicating, giddying, completely overwhelming.

'How are you settling in?' she asked, huskily.

'Um, er,' he mumbled, completely tongue-tied and befuddled by her presence.

'Uniform OK?' she said very softly, leaning even nearer.

'Yes, ma'am,' he lied hoarsely.

In fact Jem found the pale-blue pageboy outfit slightly humiliating, and the trousers were certainly too tight. From the moment that Valencia had turned around his cock had begun to stiffen. The trousers had been a tight enough fit when it was flaccid. Now he found himself wincing in pain.

'Trousers not too tight, I hope?' Valencia purred archly, reading his mind or, more likely, the expression on his face.

'No, ma'am,' he said through gritted teeth.

'Good,' Valencia said slowly. 'You are a little bit bigger than the last pageboy I had here.'

Footman! Jem thought indignantly. The job that Chloe had told him was going was for a footman, not a pageboy – that was why he had thought the uniform so strange. He should have protested. He should have handed in his notice there and then. There were plenty of jobs about; he did not need to put up with this strange woman and her peculiar, smirking maids. Somehow the words just would not come to his lips. Somehow, his legs refused to turn and take him out of there. Even when the long crimson-varnished nail of her index finger began to move slowly towards the bulge at the front of his too-tight trousers he did no more than take a sort of half step back.

'Stand still!' Miss Dacourt snapped. 'I did not say that you could move, boy!'

Jem flushed at this but somehow found himself rooted to the spot. The nail came slowly closer until it touched the bulge of his cock.

'What's this, boy?' Valencia demanded, giving his erection a sharp prod.

Jem did not know what to say and so kept silent.

'Have you got a stiffy, boy? You dare to come into my bedroom with a stiffy?'

'Please . . . ma'am,' Jem began hoarsely, with absolutely no idea of what he was going to plead for.

'You are going to do yourself an injury in that state in such tight trousers,' Valencia said in a softer, more sympathetic voice. 'I think that you had better take them off, don't you?'

'Lady Lucinda, ma'am,' Norris said simply.

'Ah, there you are, Lucy,' Mrs Frobisher said. 'Very well, Norris, you can go and secure the other little mischief-makers!'

Lucinda heard the door shut behind her but it did not make her feel any less apprehensive. Maude Frobisher's room was surprisingly small; smaller than Lucinda's own large bedroom. It was sombrely furnished, almost masculine in style, with wooden panelling and dark mahogany furniture. There was a large wardrobe and the door of this was open, blocking Lucinda's view of the bedroom's owner.

Then the door closed and Lucinda let out a gasp of sheer astonishment. To date, Mrs Frobisher had always appeared dressed in tweedy suites and had looked every inch the bluff, upper-middle-class countrywoman. The person facing Angela wore leather trousers and on her upper body nothing but a sort of harness made of chains and black leather.

The other revelation was the body this revealed. Mrs Frobisher's frumpy clothes made her look both portly and dumpy. This outfit revealed massive and surprisingly firm breasts and stocky arms that were solid and well muscled.

'Don't you look sweet?' Mrs Frobisher said after a moment of frank admiration of Lucinda's figure. The baby doll that Lucinda wore was a pale blue that suited her blonde hair, she knew, but she also knew just how much it revealed her pert and slender figure!

'Be with you in a minute, petal!' Mrs Frobisher said, turning to a chest of drawers and pulling a drawer open. She pulled out a big handful of black leather straps and gleaming chains, examined them critically for a moment and tossed them onto the bed with a clatter. As Mrs Frobisher carried on looking through the drawer, Lady Lucinda realised with a little frisson of shock that the leather trousers were not trousers at all, but chaps. Cut-away panels revealed her hostess's large and naked bottom.

At last Mrs Frobisher found what she was looking for, a broad leather collar, and sat down on the bed, patting the crimson satin counterpane beside her.

'Come and sit here, dearie, while we get you fitted up!' she said in her usual jovial tones.

Lucinda struggled with herself. There was something strangely comforting about Maude Frobisher's matter-of-fact manner, but the chains and straps, and the woman's peculiar get-up were very far from reassuring. Taking a deep breath, she walked over to the bed and sat down next to the other woman.

'Good girl!' Mrs Frobisher said and gave her a wink. 'Wrists first, I think, give me your left hand please, dear.'

Her heart was hammering hard now, but Lucinda did as she was bid. Mrs Frobisher quickly strapped a broad black leather band about it, repeating the procedure on the right wrist a moment later.

'That's it, now the ankle; bring your foot up, please.'

'Please . . .' Lucy heard herself say in a little voice

very different to her usual confident tones, '. . . what is this . . .'

'Hush a moment, dear, other leg, please!'

Having buckled a strap around one ankle it was a moment's work for Mrs Frobisher's practised fingers to secure the other.

'Would you mind holding your hair out of the way, please, dear?' Mrs Frobisher asked brightly. Lucinda's long and straight blonde hair had been let down after her shower. She gathered it and held it up, out of the way, while the other woman secured the leather collar.

It felt cold around her neck. There was a gleaming steel ring at the front and a chunky padlock on this which hung low enough to brush the skin of Lucinda's chest. It felt cold and deeply strange too. Lucinda felt the desperate arousal she had experienced in the showers come surging back like a tidal wave.

Mrs Frobisher stood up, taking hold of Lucinda's bare upper arm and steering her so that she stood up at the same time.

'Turn around, please.'

Lucinda did and found her arms seized. Some sort of snap hooks on the wrist bands were clicked into place and she found that her arms were now secured behind her.

'Please . . .' she asked again, more urgently this time, '. . . what are you . . .'

Mrs Frobisher had hold of Lady Lucinda's upper arm, and used this to spin her around suddenly. The slap came out of nowhere, cracking hard across Lucinda's cheek, knocking her so that she fell and sprawled back onto the bed. Maude Frobisher lunged forward and grasped a handful of hair. Lucy let out a startled squeal of pain as the stocky woman used this to pull her off the bed and onto her knees.

'Enough of the questions, you hoity-toity little bitch!' Mrs Frobisher said with a snarl.

Lucinda blinked in shock and astonishment. First her hostess had changed her appearance and now her manner was quite different. Maude Frobisher took a length of chain from the tangle on the bed and secured it to the padlock at the front of Lucy's collar, forming a steel leash. Only then did she put her thumb beneath the blonde girl's chin and lift it until Lucy was forced to look into her eyes.

Mrs Frobisher's gaze transfixed her. The jolly-looking countrywoman had quite disappeared and seemed to have been replaced by some sort of perverse and grinning demon. Lucinda could see a world of malice and depravity in those eyes. With her hands secured behind her she felt appallingly vulnerable. For once, Lady Lucinda had no doubts as to what she felt. For the first time since signing that damned contract, she felt pure and simple fear.

Jem stood rooted to the spot. She could not have said that really, could she? Valencia smiled and reached forward and undid the button at the front of his trousers. Jem was simply too stunned to resist. Instead he stood and watched as if mesmerised as she unbuttoned his flies all the way down. As she bent to pull the pale blue trousers down his legs, he found himself looking down her cleavage.

She stood up suddenly and fixed him with a predatory stare.

'What?' she demanded in an outraged voice. 'You filthy boy! Do you dare to stare at my breasts?'

'No, I mean . . .' Jem began, his mind a confused whirl. What on earth was he supposed to look at with her dressed like that, he thought wildly?

Unjust the accusation might have been but he was

hardly in a position to protest, standing with his trousers around his ankles, his erection pushing out the material of his white cotton underpants all too obviously.

Valencia struck with the speed of a cobra. Suddenly, Jem found that his right ear had been grabbed by her talonlike nails. He let out a rather unmanly yelp of pain, as his mistress hauled him over to her bed. Because his trousers were still around his ankles, all Jem's attention was caught up in trying not to trip. Before he knew what was happening, Miss Dacourt had sat on the bed and, with a vicious tug on his agonised ear, propelled him suddenly right across her lap.

'Do you know what happens to dirty boys who come in here with stiffies and ogle my titties? *Do you, boy*?' she roared.

'No, ah, sorry, I mean, please, ma'am . . .' Jem blabbered in a state not far from panic.

His ear had been released, even as he fell across her thighs, but his waist was gripped instead. Now he felt the other hand grab the waistband of his underpants. Jem let out a startled wail.

'Oh, no! Please don't, ma'am!'

Valencia simply chuckled and ignored him, pulling his pants down with so much force that they ripped apart.

'What happens to dirty boys like you is that they get their bottoms smacked!'

He almost sobbed as he felt the last shreds off his Y-fronts hauled down. Now naked, Jem's bottom felt terribly vulnerable. Worse, his erection was rubbing against Valencia's firm thighs. One of the tabs of her suspender belt was just beneath and digging into his cock, squashed down by his own weight. It was an exquisite discomfort; almost painful and yet strangely thrilling too.

A smack on his naked buttock cheek made him yelp aloud in pain.

'Shut up, you dirty little boy!' Valencia growled and smacked him again.

At first the spanks were light. They stung, but it was bearable. That is, the pain was bearable; every new slap added to his level of excitement. Each time he bucked in response to the pain, the tab of the suspender bit deeper into his cock shaft. His naked thighs and belly squirmed against sheer nylon and silk French knickers. After only a dozen or so spanks, Jem let out one almighty groan and came.

'Ach! What are you doing? You filthy, filthy, boy!' Valencia Dacourt roared.

It seemed to be unstoppable. Jem's cock squirted out a great hot stream of jism, some spurting over her thighs, some on her negligee, some on the costly satin bedspread, and more on the floor.

She stood up, sending him sprawling onto the carpet. Jem lay there close to tears, his bare bottom still throbbing, the tattered ruins of underpants around his knees and trousers around his ankles, while his deflating cock still dribbled spunk over the floor.

Valencia strode across to the bell pull and tugged it several times.

'Look at me!' she cried.

Scarlet-faced, Jem turned to face her, only to be blinded by a camera flash. Valencia wound the film on and took another picture, then another.

'What, what are you . . .?' Jem mumbled as the flash bulb pinged again.

There was a soft knock at the door.

'Come in,' Valencia said imperiously.

To Jem's utter horror, Chloe and Yvonne came in. They looked at him wide-eyed and seemed to be trying not to giggle.

'This filthy boy has squirted spunk all over the place. Yvonne, take this and run the film over to Mr Hoskins. Chloe, you can clean up this mess. When Yvonne gets back we can decide what to do with the dirty little boy!'

'Could you just hold your hair up for me, miss?' Norris asked smoothly.

Like Lucy and the other girls, Angela had had her hair let down after the shower. With hands that trembled slightly, she gathered her luxuriant dark hair and lifted it, gasping very slightly at the cold of the collar.

'Thank you, miss, and now the wrists.'

Angela stood by the side of her bed as the butler secured the wrist bands. Without pause he lifted her hands to her throat and padlocked the wrist cuffs to the steel ring at the front of the collar. She fought a surge of panic that came with the realisation that she was now completely helpless. No longer had she any way to stop him if he chose to touch . . .

The idea caused a fresh tremor to pass through her body. Norris stood holding the short chain that held her wrists to her throat. He looked at her inquisitively, staring at her face. Angela looked away.

'Look at me, miss.' It was an order, not a request.

Angela obeyed. The butler's eyes were grey and cold and seemed to see deep inside her. He brought his free hand up and stroked her cheek quite gently. She swallowed slowly. Then he brought his thumb down her cheek to the corner of her mouth and pressed it gently. Angela found her mouth opening, seemingly of its own accord.

'There's a good girl,' he said in a low growl. 'Suck it!'

Angela sucked hard on his thumb. It was not just that he had ordered her to. She seemed almost unable to prevent herself from doing so. His eyes still bored into hers mesmerically.

At last he withdrew his thumb, smiling openly now, and pulled her by the chain until she lay back on the bed. There was a short length of chain attached to the middle of the head of the brass bedstead and he locked this to the collar and cuff arrangement. Now Angela lay helpless, tethered to the bedstead and unable to move her wrists more than a few inches in any direction.

She expected him to go then, both hoping and fearing it at the same time somehow. Norris, however, sat down on the bed and regarded her with open admiration. Wide-eyed, she watched him openly rub the front of his trousers, where there was now a quite discernable bulge.

The butler kept stroking himself with his left hand but reached his right across and let his fingertips touch her knee. In slow, exquisitely, almost maddeningly gentle circles his fingertips travelled up her naked inner thigh.

'Oh, please . . .' she heard herself say before she could do nothing but moan.

It was impossible to bear. Angela found that she could raise her hand enough to bite down hard on her knuckle, but even the pain that this produced did not blot out the impossibly tantalising sensation of his fondling.

'Shall we have these down then, miss?'

'What, oh . . . ah . . . please?' she mumbled incoherently.

After a moment of near delirious confusion, she realised that he was referring to her knickers. He was asking her if he could take them down and . . . the implication was simply too outrageous. Angela let out a little gasp of shock.

'Yes,' she heard her own voice saying, 'Oh God, Norris, please . . .'

'All right, bend over now, Jem,' Chloe said, smiling.

Jem looked at the blonde maid with horror. 'What,' he asked anxiously, 'is that thing?'

Chloe grinned at the naked young man. He stood cowering in the bath, covering his cock with both hands. To his great mortification, it seemed to be getting stiff again.

'You don't know much, do you?' the brown-haired maid said, shaking her head. 'It's an enema, silly. We need to flush you out before we bugger you, don't we?'

'Bugger me?' Jem said, his mouth dropping open. 'But you can't . . . I mean, she wouldn't . . . I mean she couldn't . . . could she?'

'I think you'll find that our dear mistress can do pretty much what she likes, unless you want the world to know what you did all over her!' Chloe said with a throaty chuckle. She put something from a little pot onto the end of the nozzle. 'In fact, I expect that she is buckling a "strap-on" onto Yvonne as we speak, unless she means to have your cherry herself, of course! Now bend over and let me stick this up your bottom. If you keep her waiting she will be very cross. Come on, Jem, bend over, that's it.' The maid's voice was positively creamy with enjoyment as the cold nozzle tip probed his anal ring. 'There now, that's a good boy, in she goes!'

'Has he been flushed?' Valencia demanded.

'Yes, ma'am,' Chloe said.

'Come here, boy!'

His face furiously burning, Jem took a couple of hesitant steps forward. He was still naked but Chloe had produced handcuffs after she had cleaned him, and cuffed his wrists together behind his back. Well, he was almost naked. Perhaps the most humiliating thing of all was that, after she had towelled him dry, the snickering maid had insisted on putting the pale-blue pageboy's pillbox hat back on his head.

Even before the griping in his bowels had begun, even as she had put the nozzle of the enema up him, his cock had responded by becoming hard as rock. Now it stood in front of him, an awful rigid purple-headed proof of his arousal. Nothing that Jem could think of seemed to make it any less embarrassingly prominent.

'What's this?' Valencia demanded, her eyes narrowing and focusing on his erection. She held a long thin riding crop, sheathed with black leather and tipped with a couple of inches of crimson whipcord. She cut the crop through the air so suddenly that he did not have time to step back. The stroke must have been perfectly judged because the end of the crop itself just missed his erection, the whipcord trainer that extended from the tip lashing the middle of Jem's cock, viciously.

'Ow!' he yelped as the pain seethed through him.

'Vile boy!' Valencia said with what seemed more like relish than real anger, 'I hope you do not propose to squirt your filthy spunk all over me again?'

This did cause the maid to giggle behind him. The pain in his cock began to ease but Jem thought it was almost preferable to such utter humiliation. His engorged manhood twitched eagerly, however. It seemed as if the pain and shame he endured only made another mortifying accident more likely to happen.

'Chloe, I think we had better have the rubber sheet out on the floor before this puppy shoots another load over the carpet,' Valencia said.

There was another giggle from the maid. Chloe moved as fast as possible on her six-inch heels. She took a yellow latex sheet from a large chest in the bay of the window and unfolded it on the largest clear area of carpet. In the meantime Valencia used the tip of her crop to raise Jem's chin, until he had to look straight into her piercing eyes.

'I was very tempted to bugger you myself, boy,' she said slowly, and then licked her full crimson-lip-sticked lips hungrily. 'But I want to watch it even more!' She grinned suddenly, her white teeth, though perfect, looked to Jem as sharp as any panther's. 'But, of course, first I have to punish you for soiling my person!'

'Put the chair in the middle of the sheet, Chloe!' Valencia continued. With mounting apprehension Jem watched the maid take an upright chair from the dressing table and place it in the centre of the sheet.

'Right, come along, Jem!' Miss Dacourt said crisply, seizing his ear again and steering him over to the chair.

Jem could feel the cool latex of the sheet beneath his feet as she pulled him across until the polished walnut back of the chair was right against his belly.

'Bend over it, right over. Feet further back. No, wider apart than that.'

There were a couple of short whistles and the smack of crop on skin. Sharp pain in Jem's thighs enforced these instructions.

'Yvonne, get his head down. In fact, straddle him!'

If Jem was confused by this instruction, enlightenment came all too quickly. The maid grabbed him by the back of the neck and forced it downwards. When it was low enough she stood astride him, clamping his head between her thighs. The tickling petticoats and skirts on his naked back, the firm grip of her nylon-clad thighs and naked flesh above the stocking tops and the feeling of frilly knickers on the back of his neck did nothing to ease his state of furious arousal.

Valencia said something but he was not sure what it was. Chloe's thighs were clamped so hard against his ears that he could hear only muffled sounds. However, he felt the chain linking his handcuffs seized and pulled until his hands were halfway up his back, so he could guess what Miss Dacourt's orders had been.

There was a terrible pause. Even the distracting situation of having his head clamped under the maid's skirts could not stop him being aware of how vulnerable was his exposed and naked bottom. Bent over the chair, quite unable to move hands or head, there was nothing that he could do except wait for Valencia's crop to lash his twitching rear.

Jem heard something muffled and vague. But there was nothing at all vague about the pain that seared across his bottom. He let out a startled gasp and could not help his body bucking. Chloe's thighs held his head firm, however, and the awkward position of his arms meant that she was able to hold his handcuff chain in position easily.

All Jem could do was kick his feet back and grind his teeth against the pain. It felt as if hot oil had been splashed in a fine line across his bare bottom. Scared though he had been of the wicked-looking riding whip he had not been ready for such scalding intensity.

Just as the pain had subsided to bearable levels, he heard the muffled whooshing sound again an instant later, and his bare buttocks burst into flame once more. This time he simply could not help himself. Jem just opened up his mouth and bellowed his anguish at the pain.

He felt as if he had been made to sit on a hot griddle. Jem was whipped at least a dozen times by Valencia's wicked crop. Neither mistress nor maid paid the least attention to his yelps and pleas for mercy. Chloe held him firm and Miss Dacourt flogged him hard, and there was not a thing that he could do about it.

Suddenly his handcuff chain was released and Chloe stepped back, freeing his head. Still grimacing from the pain, Jem stood up slowly.

'Ah, look, Chloe,' Valencia said with quite obvious relish. 'The boy is blubbing!'

It was all too true that the tears were trickling down his face. There seemed to be nothing that Jem could do to stop them. It was not so much the pain as the sheer, helpless humiliation of his situation. Valencia and Chloe were looking at him, both girls smirking delightedly at the sight that he presented; naked except for the absurd pageboy's hat, hands cuffed behind him so that he could not even try to hide his rampant erection.

'I am rather concerned that the little toad is about to shoot his load again,' Valencia Dacourt said to Chloe, slowly.

'Yes, ma'am,' the maid replied. 'His thing is twitching quite alarmingly.'

'Get right down and lick the toe of my shoe, bitch!' Mrs Frobisher snapped, tugging the chain with her left hand. The whipcord cat-o'-nine-tails that she wielded in her right was as menacing an implement as Lady Lucinda had ever seen.

The tug pulled Lucinda forwards, and she kept going down, focusing on her captor's feet, as the other woman loosened the leash enough for her to put her mouth close to the polished patent leather of Mrs Frobisher's right stiletto.

Although Lucinda was cowed by Maude Frobisher's manner, revolt bubbled up in her at the last. It was too humiliating! She was Lady Lucinda Beaufort-Grey! To be made to kiss the shoes of this appalling middle-class nobody. She started to raise her head again and opened her mouth to make a protest that never came.

As she moved there was a hissing sound and then the sound of whipcord lashing into naked thigh flesh. Lucinda gave a startled yelp of pain. It was excruciating, stinging the tender surface of her skin. She let out a startled gasp and found that the urge to rebel had suddenly disappeared.

Still grimacing from the stinging in her thighs, Lucinda put her mouth almost on the gleaming black leather, hoping against hope that this would satisfy her tormenter.

'Lick it, you little bitch!' Maude Frobisher said venomously.

Lucy heard the hissing sound again and had to gasp as the whipcord tails lashed into her thighs. For a moment she could not move at all. It felt as if her skin were being blistered.

'Get on with it, slut!' Maude Frobisher said with a sneer.

Still blinking hot tears away, Lucinda did not dare delay for fear of another whip-stroke. Extending her tongue she began to lick. The tears that had begun as tears of pain flowed faster as she felt the true depth of her humiliation.

'That is better. Now you are learning your place! Lick it all over properly unless you want me to skin you!' Mrs Frobisher's voice kept up a constant stream of threats and insults. 'You should see yourself, bitch! Not so fucking high and mighty now, are we? Licking away like a good little slave, terrified that her mistress might give her another one of these!'

Lady Lucinda winced at the hissing sound, even before the cords cracked across her already tender thigh flesh. She opened her lovely lips and let out an agonised squeal.

'Oh no, please, miss . . . it's too big!' Jem wailed as the rubber dildo impaled him even more deeply.

Valencia laughed. 'My God, if I had a guinea for every time I had heard that!' she exclaimed between cackles.

There was a flash and Jem realised that he had been photographed again. He had been photographed while being buggered by a maid. At any other time the idea would have appalled him. However, at that moment he was too concerned by the great rubber dildo inching into him. They had smeared his bottom hole with Vaseline and teased his anus gently to relax it, but the strap-on that Yvonne wore was enormous and he was sure that it was too big to go up him.

'That's it, Yvonne! Get it right up. He can take another three inches at least!'

The maid had entered, quite naked except for the dildo strapped to her body. The whipping had been so intense, the fire in his rear so fierce, that he had blinked at the naked girl for a moment not understanding quite what it portended. Understanding had not been long in coming.

'On all fours, on the sheet!' Valencia had ordered brusquely.

He had hesitated for a moment and she had slashed the riding crop through the air with such startling venom that he had dropped onto the rubber sheet without further delay.

'Now that is a well-whipped arse, ma'am!' Chloe had said between giggles.

'A well-whipped arse waiting to be buggered!' Valencia had agreed.

The latex felt strange under her his hands and knees and the pungent smell was oddly arousing. Even before Yvonne had begun to probe his bottom hole with the tip of her strap-on dildo, his cock was rock hard and twitching ominously. He did not know how he had stopped himself from shooting again as she buggered him.

'Look at his thing!' Chloe said. 'He obviously likes having a rubber cock right up him!'

'Hmmn, it would seem so. Better get it up all the way, Yvonne, the boy likes being buggered!'

'I don't . . .' he tried to protest but a firm thrust made him gasp.

The pressure on Yvonne's clitoral region from the base of the strap-on seemed to be having an effect now, for the maid began to grunt and gasp and her thrusts became more forceful and less controlled.

Jem was unable to resist the temptation a moment longer. As the maid who was reaming him began to shriek in orgasm, he lifted one hand from the rubber sheet and grabbed his own cock.

'What are you doing, boy?' Valencia shrieked in outrage.

He heard the crop whistle from the air and crack against soft flesh, but as his own behind was covered by Yvonne's he guessed the maid must have received the stroke in his stead. Certainly a higher pitch came into her ecstatic shrieks.

One, two, three strokes on his cock were all it needed. It seemed that Valencia had recovered her presence of mind and changed her choice of weapons, for as his semen spurted over the latex sheet, the camera flash blinded him once again.

Angela moaned as Norris slowly pulled down the frilly nylon knickers that matched the yellow of her transparent little nightie. It was not a moan of fear or protest, however. She seemed to be in some sort of delirium. In a strange state that was not quite awake and yet she was certainly not sleeping. Her whole body was so aroused that it trembled at the slightest touch; her mind so fevered with desire that she could think of nothing but the need for him to take her.

Norris did not hurry. The bulge in his trousers was testimony that he was also aroused, but he moved as deliberately and calmly as ever. Even when he had placed the panties beside her on the bed he did not touch her right away. Instead he sat and contemplated the triangle of dark fur below her belly.

'This will all have to go, of course, miss,' he said, lapsing back into the form of address that she was most used to.

Through the fog of her desire Angela wondered vaguely what, 'this' might be. Norris reached out his hand towards her sex and she let out a little whimper of anticipation. But he just pinched a single pubic hair and pulled it out. Angela winced at the sharp pain and failed to suppress a little moan of frustration.

Norris ignored her. 'I will instruct Suzette to shave you in the morning,' he said in his most matter-of-fact tone.

The butler stood and began to unbutton his fly. There was a brief fumble and Angela watched as he pulled his erection from the opening. It was as thickset as the butler was himself and she blinked at the idea of having it inside her.

'Turn around please, miss!' he said simply.

Though the chain that tethered Angela's collar to the bed was short, there was enough play in it to allow her to turn onto her belly. Scarcely had she done so when she felt Norris place his palms on her hips and pull her bottom up. The chain did not allow her to raise her head, so she found herself kneeling prone, with her behind the highest part of her body.

'Legs wider apart for me, miss, if you please!' Norris said calmly.

Angela had little choice but to obey. She moved her knees farther apart, aware that she was exposing her sex to him by doing so. She was so tense now that she barely remembered to breathe.

'Oh!' she said as she felt his finger on her sex lips.

'You are very wet, miss,' Norris said serenely. 'Most satisfactory.'

Then she felt something else, something much bigger than a finger or even thumb, pressing against the opening of her vagina. It was too big, she thought in sudden panic. As he pressed harder she felt a sharp discomfort and nearly let a shriek out, but then his cockhead was in and Angela gave a moan that was as much pleasure as pain.

'That's it, miss, just hold steady for a moment,' Norris said quietly as he pushed the fat shaft of his cock a little deeper.

'Oh, my God!' Angela cried, feeling it push back the walls of her vagina. 'Please, Norris, I think it is too big.'

The butler chuckled at this but continued to inch himself slowly up her.

'You are nice and tight, miss, but it will go, just breathe deeply and stay calm.'

Chained as she was and impaled on his big cock, there was not an awful lot that Angela could do except to obey his instructions and gulp a few deep breaths down.

He pushed again and this time she felt him slide much deeper. She gave a groan that was all pleasure as he withdrew an inch or so and then thrust his cock back in. Angela felt the butler fuck her slowly, deliberately and relentlessly. His cock completely filled her and the sensation, though strange, was also utterly delicious. She wanted him to carry on for ever.

How long the butler reamed her on the bed she could not have told, for the fucking seemed to take her into a world where time did not exist. At last, however, he began to grunt, and fuck her harder and more furiously. Then Angela felt his thick fingers reach around to gently rub her clitoris and almost as soon as she felt that contact she started shrieking incoherently as she came.

Four

'So how did you enjoy Hurtwood House, Lucy, my dear?' Valencia asked with a wicked grin.

Lucinda fought with herself for a moment. Three weeks at Mrs Frobisher's establishment had taught her to curb her tongue, but there were limits.

'If you think I enjoy being whipped, and, and, and, fondled, by servants . . .' she spluttered.

'But it did you good, sweetie, it did you so much good! In fact I think that you should thank me nicely for sending you there.'

'Thank you?' Lady Lucinda went quite stiff with outrage. 'Thank you for that . . . purgatory? You must be barking mad, Valencia!'

Valencia smiled a cold and predatory smile. 'Yes, I really think that you should thank me, even though it clearly was not nearly long enough. Oh, and it is "ma'am," to you from now on, Lucy, my love.'

Valencia tugged at a bell pull. After a brief wait, a young man in a pale-blue pageboy's uniform hurried in. He was about twenty with curly auburn hair, just long enough to add to his anachronistic appearance. His complexion was flawless, but his cheeks a little pink as if from exertion and he seemed to be slightly out of breath.

'There you are, Jem,' Valencia said in an amused

voice. 'What took you so long? I hope you weren't porking one of the parlour maids?'

The slight pink flush on his cheeks flamed scarlet in an instant.

'Oh no, ma'am, I was helping get the ballroom ready as you –'

'All right, all right!' Valencia shut him up with a dismissive gesture. 'The girls can finish getting the room ready. I want you to get me a gag for this little bitch. Then I want you to get ready for your special role this evening.'

'Are you ready for your first ball, Angela?' Aunt Anais asked archly.

They were in the comfortable bedroom that Valencia had assigned them for preparation purposes. Anais was elegant in a pale-blue silk, shoulderless ball gown. Mary, brought by Anais to help prepare the debutante, was putting the finishing touches to Angela's coiffure. The hairstyle was both elegant and simple. Looking in the mirror, Angela could now see why people sometimes compared her to Audrey Hepburn. There was another, more pressing issue however.

'I'm rather nervous,' she admitted. 'Um, Aunt Anais, what about my other things?'

The doe-eyed girl that looked back from the mirror wore nothing but a corset of cream satin, trimmed with white lace. This was longer than the ones she had been laced into at Mrs Frobisher's and it contained her breasts, if only barely – pushing them up until they looked about to burst out of the top.

No other garments had been given her, excluding sheer black stockings, long black lace gloves, and perilously high-heeled court shoes. After three weeks at Mrs Frobisher's establishment, Angela had been trained well enough to keep her hands away from her freshly shaven sex, at least in the presence of her aunt and Mary. However, she remained blithely optimistic that her aunt would produce a ball gown for her.

'Of course, dear. Don't be impatient; we had to get you made up and your hair done first.'

Aunt Anais took a box from one of the bags she had thrown onto the bed. Watching via the mirror, Angela saw her open it and take out something that glittered beautifully. Anais came up behind her, Mary stepped aside.

'There now, this should suit that swanlike neck beautifully!' Anais said fastening the necklace around Angela's throat.

It was a lovely thing; a two-inch-wide choker, completely covered with diamonds. It fastened snugly and made Angela's slender neck look even longer. The only odd thing was that in the bottom of the middle of the choker was a small silver ring. Angela had no time to wonder about this, however, for her aunt had produced two glittering diamond bracelets of the same pattern as the collar. Standing at Anais's request, Angela let Mary fasten one about her right wrist as her aunt did the same to her left. She had just noticed a similar ring and a little silver snap hook on the wristbands and had just realised what they must be for, when she found her wrists pulled back behind her and clipped together.

'There now!' Anais said with satisfaction.

'But please, Aunt Anais . . .' Angela began, feeling her cheeks starting to burn already.

'Be quiet, Angela, you look lovely. Doesn't she look lovely, Mary?'

'Beautiful, ma'am,' the little blonde maid said in a husky voice.

'But, Aunt Anais . . .' Angela said again, finding

that the diamond wristbands were quite strong enough to pinion her hands behind her.

'I said be quiet, Angela. I don't want to smack you before your presentation, in case it leaves a mark, but I will gag you if you cannot hold your tongue. Now, one more item and you will be quite ready.'

Something told Angela that the item in question was not going to be a dress!

'I say, hello, Lucinda, don't you look a treat?' Lord Randolph said grinning at the sight the blonde presented.

'You know Lord Southdean, Lucy?' Valencia said. 'I have to go and do my hostess thing now, but Randolph will look after you for a bit!'

She tossed the little set of keys at Randolph who caught them and put them in the lapel pocket of his tail-coat.

What exactly Lady Lucinda thought of this arrangement could not be determined, for a black rubber ball gag distended her lovely mouth. She made some muffled sounds and her eyes glared back at him. Randolph chuckled and felt his cock get stiff.

'Bye, Lucykins, be good. Take care of her, Randolph,' Valencia said, patting Lucy on the cheek before quitting the apartment.

'I'm so glad that you elected to have a season, my dear Lady Beaufort-Grey,' Randolph said languidly, taking a cigarette from his case and lighting it unhurriedly.

He took a moment to peruse the gagged girl. Lucinda had been laced fearsomely tightly into a corset of the palest blue silk. Broad suspender straps held up black stockings that were so sheer that they only darkened her legs slightly. Full-length, fingerless lace gloves were her only other clothing.

The blonde girl's sex had been carefully shaven, and framed by the lace trim of the corset, suspender drops and stocking tops, seemed exquisitely vulnerable and even more naked than if the girl had worn no clothes at all.

Silver gilt handcuffs held Lady Lucinda's wrists shackled behind her. A pair of similar cuffs circled her ankles, linked by a longer, glittering chain. A gleaming golden collar encircled her lovely neck, above which her elegant face was forced by the gag into a rictuslike grimace.

Randolph took a long draw on his cigarette as he perused the lovely creature. His cock was rigid now, and he was very glad that the dress trousers were roomy. The crossness in Lucy's eyes only made him feel more aroused.

'Damn me, Lucinda, but you are a toothsome little piece.'

He looked at the clock on the mantelpiece. Five minutes before he was supposed to take her down. He walked over to her slowly, enjoying the muffled squeaks that came from the captive's gagged mouth.

'I've wanted to get better acquainted with you for some time.'

He put the cigarette between his lips and with his left hand took hold of her bare arm above the lace glove. Holding her like this he ran the fingers of his right hand down the front of her corset, taking pleasure in the slight 'catch' of the silk.

She made an outraged squeak when his fingers got to the bottom of the corset and continued to circle downwards on warm flesh.

'What a pretty little pussy, Lucy,' he said with a chuckle. 'It seems to be a little swollen, however. Not an insect sting, I hope.'

He slid his finger into her wet, welcoming opening.

'My, my,' he murmured. 'Lucy, I am astonished, you seem to be positively gushing, you wicked little trollop!'

Randolph watched the colour rise to her lovely cheeks and had the satisfaction of hearing her muffled outrage redouble. In fact, he could have sworn that she had said 'bastard'. His erection was getting so stiff that it was almost painful. He would have loved to replace the gag with his cock and have her suck it, but sadly his time had run out.

'You are a bad girl, Lucy, look!' He withdrew his finger and held it up in front of her eyes.

There was no denying that it glistened with her juices. Lucy closed her eyes. Randolph wiped the slick stuff from his finger onto her cheek. Then he released her for the moment as he went to get the leash.

It was a leash, not a ball gown. Anais produced the four-foot length of brightly glittering chain with a leather loop for a handle and a snap hook at the other end, and immediately Angela knew what the little ring at the front of her diamond choker was for.

Hands still cuffed behind her, she was made to walk back and forth across the room on her Aunt Anais's chain, as Mary quickly stripped and put on a different uniform.

'Careful, I know that the heels are high, but you should be used to them by now!' Anais said sharply as Angela teetered. 'Keep your hands up, at the small of your back. The guests will want to see your naked bottom.'

The idea of being displayed this way in front of guests was appalling, though Angela was somewhat distracted from this heart-stopping prospect by what Mary was doing. After stripping to her own white satin corset and familiar frilly knickers, the maid put on a tiny black satin dress. The flouncy skirt of this was buoyed on a raft of white petticoats, and so short that it left her inky stocking tops exposed. Mary's reasonably sensible shoes were replaced with fantastic glace kid creations with six-inch stiletto heels.

'Hold this for a moment, darling,' Anais said.

She lifted the leather handle of the leash to Angela's mouth. After a moment's confused hesitation, Angela took it between her teeth.

There was something peculiarly humiliating, she found, about having to stand there holding the end of her own leash in her mouth, obediently. Still, there was little that she could do about the situation but watch Anais fasten a glossy leather collar about Mary's neck and matching bands about the maid's wrists.

If the maid looked absurd in her tiny French maid's costume, it was not an absurdity that Angela was in a position to appreciate. At least Mary had been allowed to retain her knickers. Angela was only too acutely aware of the nakedness of her own shaven pussy.

'Well, girls, I do believe we are finally ready!' Anais declared after looking critically at both the debutante and the maid. 'Mary, take Angela's leash. You will lead her out for her presentation. Don't go too fast, let the guests look at her and feel her if they wish too. Also take care, because she is not really used to such high heels.'

'Yes, ma'am,' Mary said, bowing her head before taking the leash end from Angela's mouth.

Anais set off, Mary gave the leash a little tug, and Angela had to follow. It was really happening, she realised with a mixture of horror and strange almost suffocating excitement. Corseted and diamond collared and in bondage, she was about to have her shaven, naked pussy put on public display.

* * *

'Seems a pity for your pretty face to be distorted like this. Would you like the gag out, Lucinda?' Randolph asked with an expression of mock concern on his face.

Lady Lucinda nodded vigorously. Randolph's fondling had brought her to such a pitch of desire that she doubted if she could do much more than groan in frustration anyway. But the gag had been in half an hour and her jaw was aching. He unbuckled the retaining straps and pulled away.

'Say thank you, sir!' Randolph said suavely.

Lucinda hesitated. Aroused or not she furiously resented Lord Randolph's treatment of her. To have to thank him was simply too shameful to be endured.

'Thank you . . . sir,' she said at last with ill grace.

Randolph chuckled. 'You have such a long way to go, don't you, Lady Lucinda? I like a bit of spirit in a girl! In fact, I can't wait to get you up to my place. I have excellent facilities for dealing with bad girls like you, did you know?'

Lucinda did know, or at least she had heard rumours. Lord Randolph was supposed to have extensive dungeons, and a matchless collection of equipment, exclusively collected for the tormenting of young ladies. A little thrill of fear shimmied through her belly at the thought.

'Just think about all that, when you try to guard that tongue of yours, Lady Lucinda,' Randolph said as he took up the end of her leash and led her to the door. 'Now then, it is time for your first presentation as a debutante. Chin up, trap shut, hands held above that pert little bottom. It is time for this year's ever-so-slightly reluctant debutantes to come out into our little society!'

'Lady Lucinda Beaufort-Grey!' Valencia Harcourt's voice rang out, loud enough to be heard in the little ante-room where the 'debutantes' were waiting in a fever of embarrassment and anxiety.

Angela watched as the pageboy tugged Lucinda's leash, guiding the blonde girl out of the door. There was a smattering of applause and a few wolf whistles from the room beyond. Angela licked her lips nervously.

Lucinda's departure had left eight girls in the ante-chamber. Each was clad in a variation of the corset and stocking ensemble that was all that Angela wore. Each girl had an attendant holding her leash. Despite herself, despite the churning feeling in her tight-laced belly, Angela could not help but stare at the lovely girls all around her. There were so many pretty naked bottoms and bare pussies; such a cornucopia of shapely stocking-sheathed limbs and satin-corseted waists. The room was thick with a mixture of French perfume and something else, the musky scent of feminine arousal. The scent was so intoxicating that it made Angela feel positively dizzy.

'Lady Sophie Dalbeattie!' Valencia's voice rang out again.

A dark little maid who held the leash of a buxom blonde led the next debutante out. Angela watched Sophie's plump naked bottom disappear out of the door and then heard the round of applause and the catcalls.

Again there was a pause, as the waiting girls listened to the guests shouting out their admiration. Angela caught found herself looking into Anastasia's eyes and seeing her own growing anxiety reflected back at her.

'Miss Anastasia Olgivy!' Valencia's voice called out.

The pretty brunette blinked and licked her lips with a little pink tongue, then her leash was tugged and Angela watched the petite girl teeter out in her turn.

There was a sort of roaring in her ears now. Mary turned and gave her a quizzical look. Angela knew that she was next. The debutantes were being 'presented' according to some arcane rules of precedence. Somewhat to Angela's surprise her parentage apparently meant that she was ranked in the middle of the group. Suddenly she was not aware of the other waiting girls at all, only the waiting audience and her own shameful nakedness.

Angela heard something, but she was so consumed with anxiety now that she was not even really aware that her own name had been called. Mary tugged twice at the leash and so she found herself following, awkward on the six-inch heels, in the blonde maid's wake.

The door of the ante-room led into a large chamber. A dozen or so men and women were sitting in a row of upright chairs which were arranged parallel to a long dining table. Behind the table the three debutantes that had preceded Angela into the hall stood with their handlers.

A set of library steps had been set at the near end of the table and Mary mounted these first, keeping the tension on the leash all the while so that Angela had no choice but to follow. Mounting the steps in six-inch heels was an operation that took all her concentration, and so it was not until she got onto the table top itself that she realised how bright the lights were that illuminated this makeshift catwalk. The round of applause that broke out as she took her first tentative steps onto the table made her only too aware of how well lit her corseted body was, however.

'By God, that is a sweet piece of meat!' a man's voice called out.

'Look at her arse! Did you ever see such a peach?' another called.

'Her arse, *my* arse!' an elegant lady's voice put in. 'That is the prettiest pussy I have seen this year!'

Angela had not known what her first 'presentation' would be like. Of course, as time had passed and she had become aware of how her body, shackled and almost obscenely exposed, was to be displayed she had come to realise that it would be a very different ceremony to those debutantes she had read about in *Tatler*. Still, the crudity of the whistles and calls came as a shock to her. As she was walked the length of the table and back she could not stop herself from blushing furiously and she had to fight to hold back tears of sheer, impotent humiliation.

It could not have taken more than a couple of minutes to teeter down the length of the table, turn and walk back again, but it seemed that she was there, her nakedness exposed by the bright lighting, for an absolute age. Every crude remark about her charms, every whoop and wolf whistle, seemed to burn itself into her brain. The worst was at the end. Just before they reached the stair Mary paused and, taking Angela by the arm, made her turn to face the audience full on.

Angela could not look at her tormenters. She dropped her gaze and stared at the floor. There was another round of applause and a few more coarse comments. Cheeks blazing, Angela stood, appallingly aware that some sort of spotlight had been trained on her naked sex. If she had had to stand that mortifying scrutiny another moment she was sure that she would have fainted.

At last Mary turned, however, and she was being led on legs that trembled now, down the little staircase, and around the back of the table to her place.

* * *

'Angela Carstairs, let me introduce Lord Randolph Southdean!'

After the ordeal of the catwalk, the whole company had repaired to a large and comfortable drawing room where a small chamber orchestra was calmly playing Mozart, apparently quite undistracted by the chained, corseted girls. Here the scene had become more like a strange, informal cocktail party, as the debutantes were introduced to the other guests one by one. As Aunt Anais seemed to have disappeared, Valencia had beckoned Mary and Angela to her side.

He was a handsome man with a dark, aquiline face. Angela had only dared to raise her eyes briefly and had recoiled from his hungry, predatory gaze.

'Delighted,' he murmured. 'Delightful, in fact. Mary, isn't it?' he said turning to the maid. 'Let me relieve you of your charge and then you can trot along and get us both some champagne!'

'Ah, actually, Randolph, I was going to introduce her to . . .' Valencia began in a slightly nettled tone.

'Don't worry, Valencia my dear,' Randolph said smoothly. 'I know the duties of a hostess can be onerous. I shall look after this lovely creature from here.'

His hand gripped the leather handle of the leash firmly. Angela could feel the tension fairly humming in the air, though she could not guess why she was being argued over in this polite manner.

'All right,' Valencia said in a more amused tone. 'Just don't monopolise her, Randolph. Remember that good little boys have to share their toys!'

Randolph chuckled and, pulling on the leash, compelled Angela to follow him over to a plush leather armchair. He sat down in it and she half expected to be made to kneel in front of him. Instead he grabbed her upper arm and pulled her around and onto his lap.

Around the room similar scenes were being enacted. The semi-naked debutantes were being claimed and fondled in various ways. However, Angela was hardly aware of this other than hearing a few startled 'Ohs' as girls were grabbed, for Lord Randolph commanded her full attention.

Dropping the leash and letting it dangle, he gripped the side of her corseted waist with one hand and, to Angela's consternation, used his right to grasp her stockinged knee. Worse, she could feel something hard in his trousers, pressing against her naked flank. The fact that her hands were still locked behind her back made her feel utterly helpless as she tried not to fidget on his lap.

'Well, now,' Lord Randolph said in a low and deeply decadent-sounding drawl, 'you are a pretty little thing, aren't you, my dear?'

Angela did not know what to say to this so she said nothing. Instead she watched wide-eyed as his hand began to travel slowly but deliberately up her stockinged thigh.

'Lovely legs too, sweetheart,' Lord Randolph murmured raptly as he fondled and stroked his way ever higher. 'Just open them up a little for me. I'm sure you have been taught that it is impolite to keep them clamped together like that, my dear!'

Angela *had* been taught, with the aid of Norris's cane. Still, she found it hard to make herself do as he bid and open up her legs. The corset forced her to breathe shallowly and, though she was sitting almost rigidly still, she found herself almost panting as he began to fondle the bare flesh of her inner thighs above her stocking tops.

'Oh, please . . .' she murmured between gasps.

'Shush, sweetheart,' Randolph said in a slightly sterner tone.

Angela had to bite her bottom lip hard as his fingers finally reached her sex. His touch was feather-light and almost impossible for her to bear without moaning aloud.

Randolph chuckled as his strong fingers explored.

'Such a pretty little pussy, Angela, my dear,' he said in a low growl. 'Nicely lubricated too. Good Lord, you are absolutely dripping, you saucy little minx!'

'Lucinda, ha ha, don't you look a treat!' Sir Angus MacLeish said with a chuckle, staring all the while at Lady Lucinda's naked, freshly shaven sex.

Lucinda chewed the bitterest of worms and stared balefully at the floor. Sir Angus was an old acquaintance. Big, red-bearded and kilted, he held a glass of champagne in one meaty fist and in the other a plate piled high with dainty canapés.

'Are you not Valencia's protégé this year, lass?' Sir Angus demanded, glaring at Jem who still held Lucinda's leash.

This seemed to demand an answer. Lucinda took a deep breath.

'Yes, Sir Angus, Valencia is . . . sponsoring me . . . she . . .'

'She's too busy playing hostess to look after you, eh? You poor wee poppet! Never mind, I shall step into the breach, to coin a phrase!'

'No, I'm sure, I mean . . .' Lucinda mumbled in alarm but it was too late.

Sir Angus thrust the plate of canapés into Jem's free hand and, while the pageboy was still looking confused and startled, the big man grabbed the leash. Dismissing the bewildered page with an imperious wave of his hand, Sir Angus hauled Lady Lucinda off to a vacant chaise longue. There was simply nothing that Lucinda could do about the situation but to totter precariously on her steeple heels in his wake.

Alarm had seized her even as he grabbed the leash, however. Lady Lucinda had steeled herself against the indignities – and worse – that she knew the 'ball' would bring. However, she had always imagined that whatever happened she would be Valencia's plaything. After Norris and Mrs Frobisher, that had seemed at least endurable, but Sir Angus was another matter altogether.

He sat down on the chaise longue and set his champagne glass down beneath it.

'Well, my pretty wee lassie,' he said, grinning through his bristling red beard. 'Have you been spanked yet?'

Lady Lucinda blinked at the big man in horror. His thighs, emerging from his kilt, looked as thick and strong as tree trunks. She remembered with a gulp stories she had heard of his prowess as a caber tosser in his more youthful days.

'Yes,' she managed, wishing that he would not stare so at her naked sex that way. 'Um, ah, at Mrs Frobisher's.'

'Ach well,' Sir Angus said and winked at her. He slapped his powerful thigh with a huge hand, producing a startling retort that must have been heard by the rest of the room. Certainly the chit-chat seemed to come to an abrupt halt. 'But, you've no' been spanked by me!'

The sound of the big Scot's hand smacking into his massive thigh made Angela flinch on Lord Randolph's knee. Either that or Randolph's probing finger made her gasp.

'Easy, pet,' he said with a chuckle. 'You are right, though. The done thing is to warm you girls up with a spanking at this point. Of course, you barely need any warming, do you, sweetheart?'

There was nothing that Angela could say to this. She was only too aware of how wet she was between the legs and she simply could not prevent herself from squirming slowly in response to Randolph's practised fondling. All she could do was bite her lip even harder and hang her blushing head.

'Still,' Randolph continued. 'It is tradition and we are sticklers for that, don't you know? Also I am dying to spank that sweet little arse of yours!'

As if cued by the clap of Sir Angus's hand, the little chamber orchestra abandoned the Mozart concerto that they had been playing and struck up a faster and more martial sounding tune.

Unsure of what to do with himself, Jem edged towards the wall. His cock had been rigid since he had first seen the corseted debutantes in the anteroom before their presentation and now it felt almost sore from the continual rubbing against the tight trouser material.

Everywhere he looked was something astonishing and perverse. Here, the girl called Angela was being upturned over a dark young man's knee, her peachy bottom framed invitingly by her corset, suspender straps and inky stocking tops; there the maid called Mary was having her frilly knickers pulled down by a portly gentleman. The band played on apparently obliviously, drowning the gasps and startled yelps that came from the debutantes as they were put across a variety of knees.

There were, however, more guests than corseted girls and several of the maids had been grabbed, and were being pinched and stripped by people who clearly had no intention of being left out of the fun.

'There you are, boy!' Valencia Harcourt's voice stopped him in his tracks.

He turned to face his mistress who looked flushed and very cross. 'Where the hell is Lucinda?'

'Um, ah, a gentleman . . .' he mumbled in confusion, looking around desperately.

At last he spotted them. Sir Angus had put Lady Lucinda over his capacious, kilt-clad lap and was stroking and patting her neat little bottom, grinning from ear to ear. Jem pointed miserably.

'What!' Valencia hissed in a furious whisper. 'I have to go out for a moment and when I come back I find that you have given my girl to that great oaf Angus MacLeish?'

She looked around the room angrily. Some of the guests had begun spanking the girls over their knees, others were still depriving maids of knickers or stroking exposed rears.

'Well, I'm not missing out after all my work!' Valencia said suddenly. 'Neither Angus nor Randolph go for boys, but Anais has had her eye on you all evening and she seems to have collared that little blonde bit, Daphne Willoughby. I expect that she will do a swap if I show her what's on offer. So hurry up and get those trousers off!'

It was true! That was the last coherent thought that ran through Lucinda's brain. She had been spanked, but not by Sir Angus MacLeish. Her bottom was on fire as his great hand smacked across her buttocks time and time again. Almost from the first she started squirming furiously on his lap, but the big man merely chuckled and grabbed her tightly by her corseted waist.

His hand felt like a paddle, it was so hard and big. Lady Lucinda clenched her little fists and gritted her teeth, quite determined not to give him the satisfaction of hearing her cry out. That resolve lasted about six smacks. The spanking was so furious, so scaldingly intense, that she was soon gasping with pain, then yelping like a puppy that had had its tail trodden on. Before long she heard her own voice pleading desperately.

The room was by now full of the sound of bottoms being soundly spanked. Even the chamber orchestra was struggling to be heard over the chorus of shrieks and cries, and the loud, insistent clapping of hard hands impacting on soft rears. Not that Lucinda had any concern for what was going on around her; the stinging in her bottom was far too intense for that. She kicked her legs back helplessly, she struggled and she squirmed, she fought the handcuffs that pinioned her hands behind her back. All quite in vain; Sir Angus simply carried on spanking her like some sort of huge and tireless punishment machine.

'But, but, ma'am . . .' Jem had spluttered, all too aware of his condition and how much taking his trousers down was sure to reveal.

'Take them off, your pants too, boy! Must I fetch my riding crop?' Valencia thundered.

There was something in her eye that he simply dared not disobey, despite the shame of undressing in a room full of people. At least when Valencia had humiliated him the day before there had only been her and her maids to witness his degradation. This time there was a small crowd in the room.

As he reluctantly pulled off his trousers, and even more reluctantly lowered his underpants, he realised with a great deal of relief that few people were taking any notice of him. So many disrobed girls being groped and spanked provided a most welcome distraction from his nakedness and state.

'What's this?' Valencia demanded furiously, slapping is rigid cock hard with her hand. 'Are you insatiable, boy?'

She stepped closer and grabbed his left ear in her evening glove-sheathed hand. 'Just don't shoot your load until I've swapped you, if you value your worthless hide!'

Still gripping his ear and giving it a few entirely gratuitous tweaks along the way, she hauled him over to a sofa close by the orchestra, where an elegant woman had just put the plump little blonde called Daphne across her knee.

For the first time, as he stood blushing helplessly, Jem noticed that the musicians were all women. The cellist and a rather handsome violinist eyed his erection with amusement as they played. Swallowing, Jem looked away.

'Have you seen my new pageboy, Anais?' Valencia asked dryly, retaining a firm grip on his ear.

The elegant lady looked up at his face and then dropped her gaze slowly down his tunic until it came to rest on his erection.

'Well, not *seen* as such, no,' she said smoothly, 'not up until now, anyway.'

Keeping her eyes on his furiously hard cock, she licked her elegant lips daintily.

'He's breaking in quite nicely,' Valencia said conversationally. 'He is very . . . vigorous and fit.'

'Is he indeed,' Anais said in an amused tone. 'Has he a pretty arse on him as well?'

'See for yourself!' With a deft and painful twist of Jem's ear, his mistress compelled him to turn around. 'It is slightly striped because I had to teach him some manners with the crop!'

'Yes, I see. Mmmm . . . that does look tender!' Lady Anais said. 'Well, if I know you Valencia, nothing is for nothing and I spotted that Angus had collared your Lucinda. The perils of hostessing, my dear, awful, I know!' Lady Anais eyed Jem's erection again. 'I suppose that you are proposing some sort of swap . . .?

The little orchestra reached the end of the martial music and switched to a sensuous waltz, not a moment too soon as far as Angela was concerned. Her bottom felt as if it was on fire. Lord Randolph had spanked her pitilessly throughout the march, holding her on his lap by gripping her cuffed hands behind her back. Although he was quite a slender man he proved surprisingly strong. As Angela had bucked and squirmed ever more furiously in a vain attempt to escape the rain of stinging slaps, he had held her down with almost contemptuous ease.

Within a couple of minutes, Angela's voice was added to the chorus of squeals and shrieks that drowned out the musicians' best efforts. The percussion was provided by a dozen or so hands cracking across bare and tender bottoms. Angela had yelped and begged as the pain became ever more intense, but her captor had simply kept spanking pitilessly.

The change in music seemed to be a signal. At last, Lord Randolph's hand stopped spanking her scorched bottom. The pain was still so intense that there was little room for awareness of anything else, but she was vaguely conscious of the fact that the sound of girlish squealing and begging had diminished and the percussive crack of hand on buttock almost ceased.

For a moment, Angela collapsed across Lord Randolph's lap, gasping and sobbing. Her throbbing hindquarters felt as if she had sat on a hotplate and tears were trickling down her flaming cheeks. Yet as the pain subsided she became aware again of the burning need that smouldered in her loins. The music seemed to possess her and she began to writhe on his lap more slowly and sensually.

'Ho, ho, warmed up now all right, aren't you, my pretty one?' Lord Randolph said with a chuckle.

Angela could only moan in reply. His hand on her well-spanked bottom made her wince and bite her lip, though his touch was gentle now.

'In fact, sweetheart, you seem to be positively hot in some parts!' he said with a wicked chuckle.

Still panting from her struggles, and the restriction that the corset imposed on her breathing, Angela might have welcomed a respite, a chance to rest across his lap and get her breath back as her bottom cooled. It was not to be.

'Would you mind standing for me, sweetie?' Lord Randolph asked.

It was clearly not a genuine question for he hooked his free hand in the back of her diamond-encrusted collar and, still holding her pinioned wrists, obliged her to get up. Angela's legs almost buckled and she would have turned over on her heels if he had not held her steady. Fortunately perhaps they did not have far to walk. Randolph simply steered her around to the back of the leather upholstered chair.

'That's it, my dear,' he said suavely, as if she had some choice in her movements. In fact he simply pushed her forward until her legs were against the chair back and then lifted her still-pinioned hands up high, forcing her to bend over it.

The corset resisted this manoeuvre more determinedly than Angela did. Stiffly boned, it creaked in protest as she was forced to bend. In the end he placed a helping hand between her shoulder blades and pushed until she was bent over sufficiently to satisfy him. Angela blinked at the astonishing scenes that were unfolding all around her as she waited to see what Lord Randolph would do next.

She did not have long to wait.

'Now, my darling, just a little wider I think,' he murmured, using his shoe to gently push her feet apart.

Randolph retained his grip on her wrists, but there was a momentary pause. Unable to see what he was doing, Angela looked wildly about the room. To her right she spotted Lady Lucinda on her knees. The blonde girl's pallor and the pale-blue silk of her corset made the scarlet hue of her bottom all the more startling. Lucinda was being made to kneel in front of a big, red-faced and red-bearded man. He began pushing up his great red and blue kilt – Angela looked hurriedly away.

To her left she was astonished to see that her Aunt Anais was holding Jem, the pageboy, by his erect cock. The young man wore only the tunic of his uniform and his pill-box hat. His bottom was also reddened but she guessed that the way he was hopping around had more to do with what Lady Anais was doing with her nails.

At that moment her attention was brought back to her own predicament, for she felt something bulbous and warm nudging into her sex lips.

'Ooh!'

'Easy, girl, just relax and let me get it up you!'

It felt bigger than she imagined it would, and the pressure, though gentle, was inexorable, producing a flutter of near panic in her breast. Lord Randolph held her in position by grasping her wrist in his left hand; she guessed he used his right to guide his straining cock.

'It's too big!' she said in a startled voice as she felt it begin to slide in.

Lord Randolph laughed. 'Don't worry, sweetie, it's true that you are tight but then you are also very nicely lubricated!'

With that, and with a last push, he slid his cock deep inside her. Angela moaned, not knowing if she was crying out with pleasure or with pain. Certainly some pain was still part of the picture. Randolph rammed himself so deeply into her that his starched shirt front bumped into her bottom, which was still smouldering from the spanking. Every time his starched shirt grazed the tender flesh she let out a little mewling sound. Then there was the discomfort of his cock, which simply felt too big to fit inside her. Every time he rammed it home she had to fight the urge to squeal like a stuck pig. But pain was not the dominant sensation. As he slowly reamed her over the back of the armchair, other feelings every bit as intense overwhelmed her fevered brain.

'There now, you little slut, was that not what you wanted?' Lord Randolph demanded.

'Oh, ah! Please, yes! Oh God, don't stop!' a strange voice replied between gasps and sobs and strangulated moans.

The strangest thing about the voice was that it was Angela's own.

'No need to blush, boy, you really have a pretty little cock!'

Jem closed his eyes and prayed. He tried with all his might to think of something unerotic. He tried ice, piles of coal and the ugliest woman he had ever seen, all to no avail. His erection was twitching furiously in the grip of a set of very sharp nails.

Lady Anais was elegant and slender, she had black satin gloves on but she had peeled the right one off in order to spank him. How he had managed not to come over her Dior gown as he had lain over her lap, Jem would never know. The elegant little woman might have been slender but she spanked him with skill and a surprising strength. Jem's bottom was soon smarting furiously; however, that was nothing compared to the terror he felt about coming over her expensive silk gown.

When the music changed, he was allowed to stand up but Anais made him face her and she was now tantalising his throbbing erection by raking it with her long crimson nails. He shoved a knuckle deep into his mouth and bit it hard in a vain attempt to distract from the unbearable sensation. Lady Anais, a smile on her crimson lips, leaned forward with an intent expression and slowly dragged her nails up the shaft of his cock until she reached the glans.

He made a moaning sound, somewhat muffled by his knuckle.

'Oh, is that sensitive, petal?' Lady Anais asked archly, digging the sharp tips of her nails deep into the corona of his glans.

'Please, ma'am . . .' he said between gasps, 'I'm going to, I, I, have to . . .'

'You have to *what*, my sweet?' Lady Anais asked, arching an elegant eyebrow inquiringly.

Blinking away the tears that still flowed from her ferocious spanking, Lady Lucinda stared as Sir Angus pushed aside his sporran and pulled up his kilt. She swallowed hard at the sight of it. Sir Angus's cock, though not particularly long, looked as thick as her wrist, crowned with a bulbous glans in angry purple. Lucinda blinked again.

After the spanking, Sir Angus had maintained his reputation for being a man of few words by simply pushing Lucinda off his capacious lap. She had sprawled on the floor, her bottom still stinging terribly, for a second or two before he used the leash to tug Lucinda up into a kneeling position in between his great, wide-open legs. Thus, as he revealed the monstrous thing beneath his kilt, Lady Lucinda was no more than a couple of feet from it, and the leash, still held taut in his left hand, ensured that, even if she wanted to, she could not rear away!

'Now here's a wee treat for those bonny lips of yours, Lady Lucinda!' Sir Angus said with a wink as he used the leash to pull her to him. 'Lick the shaft now, from the bottom!'

Tentatively, almost afraid to touch the great throbbing thing with her tongue, Lucinda licked it gently.

'No, no! No, like that!' Sir Angus thundered. 'Lick it like a toffee-apple, lassie! Put some enthusiasm into the task unless you want to go back over my knee!'

Lady Lucinda wanted no such thing. Her bottom still felt as if it had been boiled and she did not think that she could bear another round of spanking from that terrible hand. Without more ado she began licking his straining cock, making little upward strokes with her tongue and feeling the hot meat twitch and quiver in response.

Soon, she reached his cockhead and darted her tongue out to tease the rim of his glans. Sir Angus began to grunt out oaths in response.

'All right, you saucy wee bitch! Now take it in your mouth!' he ordered between groans.

Lucinda took a deep breath. The glistening purple glans looked too big to go into her dainty mouth, but she simply dared not risk provoking his punishing hand again. Opening her mouth wide, she took it in, bit by bit, trying desperately not to graze him with her teeth.

'Jesus Christ!' Sir Angus said as her teeth touched the broadest part of his cockhead, 'If you bite me I will flog you so hard, lass . . .'

And then it was in. Lucinda had to breathe through her nose, the great bulbous glans filled her mouth so completely. Sir Angus grabbed her by her carefully arranged hair and hauled her down on him even further. Lucinda let out a muffled little squeak of panic, but found she could still breathe. The hand holding her hair and the other gripping the leash meant that she could not move her head back even an inch. Instead, she tried to move her tongue as much as she could, caressing the swollen cockhead in the hope that that would persuade him not to thrust it further down.

It worked. At least, Sir Angus began shouting a series of blood-curdling oaths. His cock twitched even more violently than before and Lucinda could have sworn that the huge glans grew even bigger the moment before something wet and hot hit the back of her throat.

'Oh, yes!' Angela cried as Lord Randolph thrust himself deep into her.

Everywhere she looked, half-naked girls were being fucked.

'Oh God!' she moaned as he half withdrew his cock, paused, and then thrust it home again.

Lucinda, her bottom still a furious-looking scarlet, was busily sucking the big Scotsman's cock.

'Oh, please . . .' Angela groaned as Randolph fucked her even harder, pinning the fronts of her thighs against the leather back of the armchair.

'Uncle' George was enthusiastically fucking Anastasia over an occasional table. No! Angela's eyes widened as she realised that, in fact, Lord Fakenham was buggering the petite girl.

'Oh, please,' she said again but in a higher voice as her clitoris was crushed against the firm but yielding chair back.

Lady Anais was sitting looking as elegant as ever but with a rather strange expression on her face. Angela looked down and saw the pageboy's naked bottom protruding from beneath Anais's expensive couture skirts.

'Oh, God!' Angela exclaimed as another thrust mashed her clit against the chair back, and that was the last coherent thing she said before she came.

Five

'Good morning, Angela. Slept well I trust?' Lady Anais asked brightly, looking up from her grapefruit.

Lord George glanced up from his *Times* at the far end of the table and grunted a greeting too. Angela blinked hard at the little scene of normality, not quite able to believe her eyes.

'Coffee or tea, ma'am?' Mary asked, standing at the sideboard.

The maid once again wore her sensible and demure uniform. It seemed inconceivable that these were the same people she had last seen engaged in the frenzied orgy that was the climax, in more ways than one, to Valencia's ball. It could have been any upper-class breakfast room. Angela might almost have wondered if last night's wild scenes had been some fevered dream.

She had been given sensible clothes when she had awoken this morning, back at the Fakenham residence. Mary had not even laced her into a corset as usual, instead laying out silk French knickers and a lace suspender belt and bra for her to wear. This lingerie now felt strange and almost tantalisingly light on her body, following the weeks of ferociously tight lacing. Even the spanking had left no trace on her bottom cheeks and Mary had made no reference to the previous night's events, simply helping her to dress demurely and politely.

Angela sat down, took some toast and sipped her coffee. Aunt Anais finished her grapefruit and motioned the maid to take it away.

'So, Angela, did you enjoy your first ball?'

The question flummoxed her completely. Angela felt the colour rising in her cheeks.

'Um . . . ah . . . I . . .' she mumbled in confusion.

'Course she did!' Lord George said from behind his paper. 'Didn't you hear the little minx squealing when Randolph fucked her?' He put down his paper, grinned at Angela and, to her horror, winked. 'Noisiest orgasm I have heard since "Shrieker" Cuthbertson. Quite drowned out the poor musicians when she came!'

'*George*!' Lady Anais reproved him mildly. 'Take no notice of him, Angela my dear, he is an uncouth beast.' She sipped her coffee and continued. 'Now, the next event on the social calendar is the gathering here on Friday. It will be rather different to Valencia's affair. More like an informal dinner really, but you will need the right things. Shall we go shopping after you have finished your breakfast, my dear?'

'Well, boy, I'm waiting for an explanation.' Valencia said, glowering and pointing at the carpet in the drawing room.

'It, it's . . . a stain, ma'am,' Jem mumbled, hanging his head in shame.

'I know it is a stain. I know what kind of stain. It is a spunk stain! What I want is an explanation, you filthy boy!' Valencia Harcourt roared.

When Lady Anais's manipulations had had their inevitable effect the night before, Jem's fears about soiling her silk Dior gown had proved groundless. With deftness that spoke of practice, the elegant

Frenchwoman had simply turned his cock away at the crucial moment, with a not unpainful twist, and so Jem had shot his load over Valencia's expensive deep-pile carpet instead of Anais's expensive dress.

As he had then been obliged to go under Lady Anais's skirts and tongue her to orgasm, he had quite forgotten about the sticky mess. Indeed, he could still taste the Frenchwoman's juices and feel her wiry pubic hair against his face, hours later. So it was hardly surprising that the accident had quite gone from his mind.

It seemed, however, that it had not gone unnoticed by his mistress. Jem swallowed, looked at the barely discernable stain and tried in vain to think of something he could say in his defence.

'She . . .' he began, 'I mean that lady, she touched me . . .'

'You have the effrontery to blame my good friend Lady Fakenham?' Valencia roared.

There was a giggling from behind her. Valencia wheeled around and glared at the two maids who stood there waiting.

'I don't know why you two think it is so funny?' she bellowed at them. 'It is your job to clean up this sort of mess. Why didn't you do so straight away?'

Chloe and Yvonne's expressions changed from smug to alarmed in an instant.

'Please ma'am,' Chloe began, 'I was being . . . being . . .'

'Oh, I would have ma'am,' Yvonne said 'but, but . . .'

'But you were too busy fucking and sucking anyone you could get your hands on. Well, I am going to make you very sorry for being such a pair of sluts!'

'What's all this noise about?' A new voice interrupted the proceedings. Jem and everybody else in the room turned to stare.

Lady Lucinda looked bleary-eyed. Her long blonde hair was down and looking rather tangled. She clearly had not yet dressed as she wore a long silk dressing gown.

'Lucinda!' Valencia said sharply. But then she seemed to rethink. Jem noticed a smile play about his mistress's lips. 'Lucinda, dear, you look simply dreadful!'

'Spot too much champagne, I fear,' Lady Lucinda said and shrugged.

'Not too much of old Angus MacLeish then?' Valencia said with a chuckle.

Taking a sneaky peek sideways, Jem saw pink spots blossom on the blonde girl's cheeks.

'Oh well, at least it's over,' she said, affecting boredom.

'Didn't enjoy it then, sweetheart?' Valencia asked, her voice dripping concern.

'Well, you know.' Lucinda frowned and shrugged.

'That's funny, Lucy,' Valencia said, her face a picture of puzzlement, 'because there is another stain on my carpet just underneath where you were kneeling.'

Jem glanced sideways again and was gratified to see the blonde girl's pink spots go scarlet.

'Oh well, the maids will get the stains out or else, as I am sure they know, they will pay dearly,' Valencia said, shrugging. 'Lucinda dear, once you have breakfasted and dressed, perhaps you would like to help me deal with a small problem. You see –' she turned and gave Jem a smile that made his blood freeze '– there is this young man in my employ who cannot seem to stop squirting his spunk everywhere.'

The Rolls-Royce turned out of Bond Street and up a residential road.

'Just one more stop, my dear,' Lady Anais said at her side.

They had visited the corsetière and ordered some more corsets for Angela. Then they had tried on lingerie at another Bond Street boutique. Angela had been obliged to strip naked once again to try on suspender belts and stockings. She had been painfully aware of her shaven pubis, and noticed the two elegant young shop assistants exchange a knowing glance, but she had managed to suppress most of her blushes. She was growing used to being naked before strangers, she realised with a sort of pang of anxiety. What was happening to her?

Armed as they were with lingerie and stockings, Angela assumed that the next stop would be to purchase gowns. To her surprise the car headed away from the shops she had gone to previously with Lady Anais. Soon it was speeding through an altogether less salubrious area of London. It finally pulled up in an alley with a lot of doors that looked like small factories and workshops. Aunt Anais got out, stepping carefully around the puddles in the alley and rang the bell of a particularly nondescript door.

A rather thin and spotty youth in a stained brown overall opened the door.

'Mr Coping is expecting us, I believe!' Lady Anais said.

The youth looked at Lady Anais in her furs, Angela and the Rolls beyond with ever widening eyes. At last he seemed to shake himself out of his reverie.

'In here,' he said and moved aside to let them in.

It was not a shop really but a workshop. Several men were working on lathes and there was a forge belting out heat in one corner. Various metalwork jobs lay around half finished on benches. Some of the things being put together from steel sheet Angela did not recognise, but several of them seemed to involve steel collars or wristbands and chains.

A small, rather portly, balding man looked up as they entered.

'Ah, Lady Fakenham,' he said, looking at Angela and rubbing his hands. 'This would be the young lady? Quite, quite, well, if you would care to step this way.'

Angela could feel the eyes of the men in the room follow her as she walked behind the man to a door at the far end of the workshop.

'Sorry, but we don't run to a proper fitting room as such,' Mr Coping said as they entered the adjoining room.

It was a sort of office with a desk stuffed full of papers, but there was a battered leather sofa and a rug on the floor.

'If you would care to take a seat, Lady Fakenham,' the little man said.

As Lady Anais sat down Angela made to do the same.

'No, don't sit, Angela. You are here for a fitting. Is there somewhere that she can put her clothes, Mr Coping?'

'Vince will take the young lady's things,' the man said.

'Well, Angela, what are you waiting for? Take your clothes off so that Mr Coping can measure you properly.'

Angela looked at Mr Coping. His bald head was shiny with perspiration. She looked at Vince who had followed them into the office and was staring at her with wide eyes, and then she looked back at her aunt.

'Please . . .' she whispered.

'Now don't be a silly girl, Angela. You only just undressed in the lingerie shop. Think of this as the same sort of thing. Except that here there are men ready to help undress you if you find the prospect too difficult.'

The implication was as clear as it was dreadful. Angela thought of the men in the workshop and their eyes. The idea of being stripped by those rough, oily-handed brutes was just . . . well, it was just impossible! She gave a defeated sigh and took her jacket off.

Of all the times she had had to strip since she came to London, Angela found this to be the hardest. Taking off her clothes in front of Lord George, Mrs Frobisher, even Norris, had been nothing like as mortifying as this was. Every item of clothing had to be handed to Vince, and the spotty youth grinned more broadly every time. After the jacket, Angela slipped off her skirt. Then came the blouse and the youth's smirk became hard to ignore. Next came her slip which the grinning boy took with a hand that was visibly trembling.

Angela hesitated, standing in her bra and panties. She had been so pleased to be released from the corset's iron grip. Now she wished the lingerie was more substantial then the silk and lace confections she had on. Not that it mattered much. The bra was next. Vince could not stop a gasp of admiration from escaping as her breasts swung free. It took a real effort to hand the grinning boy the lacy thing.

Angela stood blushing, covering her breasts with her hands and quite unable to continue for the moment.

'Take them off, Angela or I shall have them taken off for you,' Lady Anais said in a sharp tone.

Angela did not doubt her for a minute. She took a deep breath and let her full breasts swing free, trying to ignore Vince's admiring oath as she bent to peel off the silk French knickers.

'So what's the catch?' Lucinda said slyly before taking another sip of coffee.

'Lucy, you are such a suspicious little bitch! No catch, baby, I just thought that you might benefit from a taste of what you are doing all this for. Things will get pretty challenging for you from here on in. Don't want you shying at the fences, do we?'

Lady Lucinda looked at Valencia coolly across the table. It was plausible, she supposed, but she still did not trust the lovely Miss Dacourt one inch. It felt great to be fully clothed and treated with respect by Valencia's servants, however temporary the sensation. Valencia had insisted she be corseted as usual, but apart from that had let Lucinda choose her own dress; an elegant afternoon frock in royal blue with matching high-heeled shoes.

Most of all, Lucinda wanted to be in on punishing the servants. The last weeks of having to take it had made her desire to give it out all but unbearable.

'Anyway,' Valencia continued, 'after last night's entertainments I could use a hand this morning. All three of them need putting in their place.'

'That pageboy is a peach!' Lucinda put in, finishing her coffee.

'Jem is quite a find! The poor boy is so horny that he shoots his load at the least provocation . . .'

'And then gets punished for it . . .'

'This, of course, gets him aroused again!'

The two young women met each other's eyes and giggled.

'Just be careful, Lucy, dear,' Valencia cautioned. 'I really am getting concerned about my carpet. Damn thing cost me a fortune. If you let him shoot his load over it again I promise that I will have your hide as well!

* * *

'Does she need to take the stockings and suspenders off?' Lady Anais asked in a matter-of-fact tone.

Angela was trying to use one arm to cover her breasts and the other hand to shield her shaven sex from Vince and Mr Coping's gaze. The little man found some glasses on the desk and looked at her remaining underthings with interest.

'No, I don't think so, Lady Fakenham. They are too flimsy to affect the measurements.'

'You said on the telephone that you were developing new lines?' Anais said.

'Yes, yes, nothing revolutionary, just variations on the tried and tested, so to speak. For instance . . .' He picked up something gleaming from the litter of papers on his desk. 'This collar uses a back-plate rather than a chain.'

The thing was a stainless-steel collar of thick hinged metal, at least two inches deep. A further hinge attached a flat piece of steel about the width of a ruler and eight inches or so long to the back of the collar. This plate had two parallel lines of holes punched along its length.

'Oh yes, could we see that on?'

'Of course!'

Angela let out a little gasp as the cold steel touched her neck. The collar was fastened with a clink and secured with a solid padlock at the front. The back plate felt icy, hanging as it did between her shoulder blades.

Although she had been in bondage many times over the previous few weeks, this felt strangely different. There was something about the sheer solidity and weight of the steel collar. It felt massive and immovable, which as far as she was concerned it surely was. It made her feel, somehow, as if she were a slave. This feeling was only strengthened as Mr

Coping fastened equally solid steel bands about her wrists in turn.

Each wrist cuff had a steel ring welded to it, and these had solid steel snap hooks attached. Mr Coping took Angela's left wrist and with a deft twist forced it up behind her back.

'The hooks snap into the perforations in the back plate,' he said demonstrating. 'So it is a simple matter to adjust the length.'

Angela's right wrist was seized and the second hook snapped into place, her arms were now pinioned in a 'backhammer' position, her helpless hands almost between her shoulder blades.

'This is the easiest setting for the subject,' Mr Coping said, using Angela's arm to steer her around so that Lady Anais had a good view of her back.

Angela blinked at the word 'easiest'; her hands were forced up enough to be quite uncomfortable. Pressure from her wrists pulled the steel collar tight against her throat. The collar was wide enough for there to be no danger from this, but it emphasised the feeling of utter helplessness.

'Yes, I see, I rather like that, Mr Coping,' Anais said. 'I'll take it!'

'Well, this is just the demonstration model, of course. I will have to take the young lady's measurements and make one up that will fit her neck and wrists nice and snug.'

'How long will that take?'

'Well a couple of days, it depends. The boys like to work on special jobs and if there are . . . inducements . . .'

'Oh, yes, I'm sure Angela will not mind the usual arrangement, Mr Coping, so long as they are ready before Friday.'

'Oh, no problem at all, Lady Fakenham,' the little man said cheerily.

He took his tape and began to measure Angela's neck. As he had to measure from above the two-inch collar this was a little problematic until Anais ordered her sharply to raise her head. The next part proved easier as the manacles were a little loose on Angela's slender wrists. Mr Coping simply had to measure her wrist where it emerged from the slightly oversized steel bands.

If Angela had hoped that her ordeal would soon be over, that hope withered immediately. Mr Coping took a small wooden packing case, rather under two feet in height, and placed it in the centre of the room.

'Step up, if you please, my dear,' he said, taking her arm and guiding her to the box.

'Oh please,' Angela said in a desperate whisper.

'Stop being silly, Angela,' Aunt Anais said sharply.

Angela bit her lip and stepped onto the box. There was an angle-poise lamp on the desk and Mr Coping switched it on and directed the light full on the naked girl. It was almost unendurable. The manacles forced Angela to thrust her naked breasts out and she could do nothing at all to shield her shaven sex from Vince's grinning leer.

Mr Coping bent to measure her stockinged ankles. He worked deftly and without fuss, but Angela could not ignore the fact that his face was inches from her exposed pussy. Once he had written down the figures in his notebook. The little man turned again to Lady Anais.

'Did you want a waistband too, Lady Fakenham?' he asked.

'Oh yes, I think so,' she replied. 'Mind, she will be corseted.'

'Of course, what is she lacing down to?'

'We might go further. At the moment she is going down to twenty.'

'I see.' Mr Coping looked thoughtful. 'In that case something adjustable, perhaps.' He walked to the door and opened it. 'Bill!' he shouted above the noise of the workshop.

After a few moments 'Bill' came in. He was a tall, rangy man in his fifties with even less hair than Mr Coping, and wearing the same sort of brown coat as Vince. He stared quite openly at Angela and even scratched his crotch.

'Bill,' Mr Coping said as if talking about an order of bearings. 'That adjustable waistband Mr Beazly ordered, has it gone out yet?'

'Nah,' Bill said, eyes still locked on Angela's naked body. 'Still waiting for the extra padlock keys to come back. It was a special Ingersoll, remember?'

'Fetch it, would you, Bill?'

There was a short pause as Bill went out on his errand. To Angela's distress he left the office door wide open. The other two men that had been in the workshop were now standing by a bench and talking, but all too obviously staring through the open door at her. She looked around, avoiding Vince's leer, but even Mr Coping seemed to have dropped his pose of professional indifference and was looking at her with a slight smile on his lips and rubbing his podgy hands together eagerly.

'What do you think?' Valencia asked, stretching her arms wide.

Her corset was black satin trimmed with crimson ribbons. Broad suspender drops, just visible through the translucent black lace of French knickers, supported sheer black stockings that set off her muscular thighs. She turned to the big mirror on her bedroom door, and Lucinda joined her. The blonde girl had stripped to her white corset. White stockings, French knickers and stilettos completed her outfit. The well-built, dark-haired girl all in black and the slender blonde in white presented an extraordinary contrast, rendered all the more dramatic by the slender canes that both young women held in their hands.

'I think,' said Lady Lucinda, still admitting her own reflection and marvelling at how tiny her waist was when laced tight, 'that we will put the fear of God into those sluts!'

The sluts in question were working in the drawing room. All three of Valencia's servants were on their hands and knees. All three were diligently scrubbing at various stains in the thick, cream-coloured carpet. What is more, all three had been made to strip down to little black satin corsets and sheer stockings. Even Jem had been laced into a waspie, red faced and protesting. For once, Chloe and Yvonne had not giggled at him much, however. The two girls were clearly too worried about their own impending fate.

The thickness of the carpet made their entrance almost silent. Valencia cut her cane through the air, producing an ominous whooshing sound. Lucinda took her cue from the other girl and did the same. The effect on the toilers was gratifying. All three froze and then looked around with anxiety inscribed on their faces.

Valencia went first to Jem. She regarded the spot he had been cleaning intently.

'Pretty pathetic, isn't it? Just like you, in fact.'

Jem knelt up and looked at his mistress with an expression of part awe and part terror. Apart from the corset and stockings, he had been made to wear a little apron and Lucinda was amused to see that his erect cock pushed the white cotton outwards like a tent pole.

'Please, ma'am,' he began, 'it isn't dry yet . . . when –'

He was cut off by Valencia giving him a hard slap across the face.

'*I didn't ask for your snivelling opinion!*' she roared.

Lucinda stole a glance at the two maids. They had knelt up too and were watching with wide eyes. They knew all about their mistress's temper, Lady Lucinda guessed, and they had a good idea that they were going to catch it themselves.

'Well, I have had enough of your filthy habits, boy!' Valencia said contemptuously. 'Lady Lucinda can deal with you today!'

Miss Dacourt stalked over to inspect the two maids' efforts.

'Chloe, is that what you call clean?'

'It's red wine, ma'am, I couldn't . . .'

'You should have put salt on it immediately!'

'But, but, I couldn't, I was being . . . you know . . . by . . .'

'Get to my room and wait for me there, you little slut!'

Chloe got up quickly and hurried out after one last anxious glance at Valencia's cane.

Yvonne's work was duly inspected and insulted. This time, however, rather than order the girl out, Valencia simply leaned down, grabbed her by the ear and hauled her to her feet.

'I will probably be some time correcting these two trollops,' Valencia said with a grin. 'Make that filthy creature suffer for me, Lucy. But for God's sake don't let him make any more stains!'

If it was hard to stand naked on her box in the bright light, it got even harder as soon as Bill came back. He handed another gleaming steel contraption to Mr Coping. To Angela's distress, Bill then stood back, leered and even licked his lips. Certainly he made no effort to leave.

'You see how it works, Lady Fakenham,' Mr Coping said.

Angela gasped as the cold steel touched her bare flesh. The little man placed it just above the top of her suspender belt, around her waist. It was much thinner metal than the collar and, though stiff, it was flexible. There was a D-ring welded to one end of the waistband. At the other there was a set of holes for the ring to slot into. A length of chain was welded to the back of the contraption and this dangled, cold against the crease of her bottom as he forced the D-ring through one of the holes.

'Padlock please, Bill.'

Grinning broadly, Bill came forward with a padlock in his hand; he put the hasp through the D-ring, fixing the belt in place. But, to Angela's surprise, neither man clicked the padlock shut. Bill stepped back, but only because Lady Anais had stood to get a closer look at the device.

'Is it solid enough?' she asked doubtfully.

'Perfectly and, though the steel is thin, the edges are chamfered so it won't cut however tight you fix it. The saddle chain is secured to the same lock.'

'Oh really? Would you be kind enough to demonstrate?' Lady Anais asked innocently.

'My pleasure, Lady Fakenham,' Mr Coping replied.

Angela did not doubt it. He reached between her legs to catch the dangling chain and pulled it forward, brushing her sex lips in both directions in a way that she was sure was not necessary. Then he pulled the chain up tight. She let out a startled gasp as the steel chain divided her sex. Mr Coping pulled it even tighter and she gasped again.

'As she seems to be well lubricated already, it won't chafe too much to pull it quite tight,' the little man said in a matter-of-fact voice.

If Angela thought that she had been blushing as much as it was possible to, she found that she was wrong. It was true; she could feel the wetness trickling down the inside of her thighs.

'*Angela!*' Aunt Anais said in a reproving voice. 'I'm afraid she is rather in heat at the moment, gentlemen!'

This caused Vince to almost choke with laughter, Bill to snigger and even Mr Coping to chuckle quietly. If one could die of sheer humiliation, Angela thought, she would be dead by now!

Mr Coping threaded the hasp of the padlock through a link of the chain and clicked it shut. Angela could feel the constriction of the waistband and the pressure of the chain between her legs. Her arms, still wrenched high behind her back, were starting to ache and the collar made her hold her head up, when she wished that she could hang it in utter shame.

'There now!' Mr Coping said with satisfaction. He patted her belly gently and then let his hands travel up until they cupped her breasts, and squeezed.

'She has a lovely pair, Lady Fakenham,' he said appreciatively. 'I'm sure that the boys would love to have a feel.'

'Of course, do call them in. Just so long as the things get to me by Friday. Oh, do stop that silly whimpering, Angela. They aren't going to hurt you, just to take a good look and perhaps fondle you a little, my dear.'

'You look very fetching in that outfit, boy. You are a boy, aren't you, and not a girl?'

Lucinda stood with her feet apart, flexing the cane between her hands, enjoying every moment of the situation.

Jem was beetroot-faced. Clearly he felt the humiliation of being put into corset and stockings very keenly. Clearly, from the way his apron was pushed out in front of him, humiliation was not the only thing he felt.

'Stand up!'

He got up quickly, placing his hands in front of the little apron.

'Put your hands behind your head!'

He hesitated a fraction too long and Lucinda cracked the cane across the back of his left hand.

'*Behind your head, I said!*'

'Aaoow!' he yelped, but did as he was ordered.

Lucinda dropped her gaze to the apron, and the thing that pushed it away from his belly.

'What's this, boy?' she demanded.

'I, ah, um,' he stuttered.

'Say, "It's my stiff cock, ma'am"!'

He looked at her, thunderstruck, for a moment.

'It, it, it's . . . aaow!'

She cracked the cane lightly across the bulge in the apron. Jem doubled up and grabbed his member with a cry of pain.

'*Stand up! Hands behind your head!* Did I give you permission to move? Well, did I?'

'Ah, oh, no ma'am,' Jem managed, his face still creased in pain.

Somehow he managed to straighten up and put his hands behind his head again. Lucinda smiled as she watched the attractive young man tremble and eye her little cane with obvious dread.

'What is it?'

She watched his Adam's apple bob as he swallowed.

'It's my, my cock, ma'am,' he said in a strained voice.

'It's your stiff cock, boy! What is it?'

He licked his lips, eyes still locked onto the cane that she kept waving before him.

'It's . . . my stiff cock, ma'am,' he said.

Oh my God, thought Lucinda, this boy is on the point of blubbing! The idea filled her with a strange joy.

She reached forward with the cane and flipped back the little apron, revealing his erection. It arched up, so stiff that the purple glans almost touched his corseted belly. No wonder the apron looked so odd, Lady Lucinda thought with a smile.

'I know *what* it is,' she said slowly, moving surreptitiously into position. 'What I want to know is what you mean by disrespecting me by being in such a condition in my presence?'

Before he had time to react she slashed the little cane through the air and rapped it across the shaft of his cock again.

'Oh, please . . .' Angela moaned.

'Be quiet, Angela,' Anais said sharply.

Still standing on the little crate, Angela was surrounded by the workmen. Vince had been allowed to put his burden of clothes on the desk. Bill had called the other two men in, and Mr Coping had kept his position fondling her breasts. Rough hands stroked her legs and pinched and smacked her bottom. Hungry eyes devoured her nakedness. She could not step back even when her breasts were pinched and groped by hands a lot less gentle than Mr Coping's, for other fingers pressed their claims from behind and from the side.

'Jesus, she is a fine little tart!'

'Feel these knockers. Lovely and firm.'

'Nice arse too. Fuck me, what I would give to get right up it!'

'She's loving it, too, look at that, she might be posh but what a slut. Look, her juice is running down the insides of her legs!'

Laughter and obscene sucking sounds accompanied these remarks as Angela was groped, fondled and thoroughly pinched. Once or twice she even felt teeth biting into her bottom, and Vince, when finally allowed access to her breasts, began licking them like a friendly dog.

None of these things was the worst part. The worst part was the desperate, almost unbearable arousal. Mr Coping kept a finger in between the chain and her belly. On its own it made the pressure on her clitoris even harder but he kept moving the finger up and down gently. This made the chain move, very slightly, tightening and relaxing against her clit as it did so; gently, rhythmically and irresistibly.

After only a few minutes of this pulsating pressure, Angela let out a lost moan and doubled up. She would have fallen from the box but hands seized her and held her as her body was racked by an orgasm so intense that she just opened her mouth up and screamed.

'You lazy little tarts, why haven't you finished?' Lucinda demanded.

Chloe and Yvonne looked up from polishing the table. 'Sorry, ma'am, but . . .' Chloe began.

Lady Lucinda swished the cane through the air menacingly. She loved the satin costumes that Valencia made her maids wear. Bending as they were over the table to polish it, both maids presented a delicious sight. The little flouncy skirts were so short that their frilly white knickers were exposed. Above the tops of the maids' sheer black stockings, seamed and fully fashioned, pale thigh flesh, naked and vulnerable, was revealed to Lucinda's predatory gaze. She was going to enjoy striping these minxes' thighs and bottoms with her cane.

But first things first, she thought, looking around. Jem, once more allowed his pageboy uniform, was cleaning the dining-room windows. He carried on working, concentrating hard on getting every smear, but Lucinda knew that he was all too aware of her, and of her cane.

'And you, boy, why haven't you finished?' she demanded.

None of them had finished their tasks because she had been careful not to give them enough time to do so. For three days Valencia had allowed her to tyrannise her servants; three days of relentless punishment and humiliation. Lucinda did not know when she had enjoyed three such delightful days.

'Have you been masturbating again, boy, is that it?' she demanded.

'No, ma'am,' he protested, colouring.

This was either true or his stamina was truly astonishing, judging by the bulge in his tight, light-blue trousers.

'I see,' she said icily. 'In that case, knowing your habits and what sluts these are, I can only assume that you have been fucking the maids!'

How much the three servants would have dared to protest against this charge remained uncertain. For at that moment Valencia entered the room.

'Ah, there you are, Lucy,' Miss Dacourt said brightly. In her hand she held an arrangement of leather straps and chains. 'Time to get ready for this evening. Strip, now, if you please.'

'Strip?' Lady Lucinda echoed, looking at the contraption in Valencia's hand, then down at her own cane. 'But I was just –'

'Just going to thrash my poor servants again for no good reason! I know, dear, it's just so unfair, isn't it?' Valencia said with a radiant smile. 'Now, take your frock off, there's a good girl. Now don't pull faces, Lucy. Chloe, Yvonne, Jem, would you mind helping me to strip our little debutante?'

Lucy looked around wildly. Chloe and Yvonne were standing up and grinning at her. Even Jem had put down his scrim and was advancing with a determined look on his face.

'You bitch, Valencia,' Lucinda spat out crossly, flinging the cane onto the floor. 'All right, you lot, get back on with your work. I do know how to undress myself, you know!'

'You are going to look lovely, Angela,' Lady Anais said with a slight smile.

Angela lay back naked on a little white enamel table, as Mary carefully shaved her pubic hair. This was a daily ritual but this time the maid took extra care and Angela had been lying back for what seemed like hours. She had been bathed, her hair shampooed, dried and carefully arranged, her legs waxed and her face cleansed with the juice of cucumbers. The whole afternoon seemed to have passed in these preparations.

'Are we nearly done, Mary?'

'Done, ma'am!' the maid declared, wiping a last fleck of stray shaving foam from Angela's thigh.

'Good, it's time to dress her. Come along, into the bedroom, Angela, I can't wait to see you in your lovely new things.'

The first of the new things was a sort of corset. It was both shorter and more delicate than those she had been used to. Though boned, the panels were held together by flimsy-seeming pieces of black lace. There were little cups of scalloped lace to hold her breasts but these were so small that they left her nipples quite uncovered. At the bottom the thing seemed to leave most of her belly bare. It was laced up at the back firmly but less ferociously tightly than she was used to. Angela guessed that the lace corset was too flimsy a thing to take that sort of strain.

Thin black suspender straps dangled from the lace-frilled bottom of the garment. Stockings of the sheerest silk were rolled up her legs by Mary and fastened to these. Fingerless lace gloves, so long that they came up almost to Angela's armpits, followed. Then there were six-inch stilettos as usual, but again these were covered in black silk. Then Lady Anais took a cotton bag from the bed. Angela knew what was in it immediately by the metallic chink.

'What lovely men,' said Lady Anais. 'Look, Angela, they have done a beautiful job.'

Angela coloured and closed her eyes. She had not been able to get the memory of the workmen and their hungry hands out of her mind for the last three days. After she had recovered from her thunderous orgasm, she had been so mired in perspiration and so covered in oily hand marks that, rather then dress again in her expensive lingerie, Lady Anais had borrowed one of the brown overalls for the return journey.

It had been old, stained, and smelled of oil, metal and perhaps sweat. The odour had stayed in her mind along with the image of the men's leering faces and their groping hands. The most appalling thing was that every time she thought of it something seemed to melt inside her loins.

'We won't fix your hands right now as it will be a long evening,' Lady Anais's voice said, cutting into Angela's reverie.

She let her aunt lock the heavy steel collar around her neck. A length of heavy steel chain, some six feet long, had come with the collar and other manacles, and Lady Anais locked this to the padlock hasp which secured the collar at Angela's throat. This collar, made to her measurements, fitted snugly. The feeling of complete helplessness that had engulfed her in the workshop was if anything even greater. Not only did the solid steel collar fit exactly and immovably around her neck, and the back plate cold between her shoulder blades, the chain and collar together were a seriously substantial weight.

There were ankle bands as well, every bit as massive and solid as the wrist cuffs and collar. Mary knelt to padlock them around Angela's ankles, linking then together with a two-foot length of chain.

'Oof!' Angela grunted as the maid pulled the waistband as tight as she could manage.

'Ooh!' she gasped as her aunt pulled taut the cold steel saddle chain. The padlock hasp secured waist belt and chain as it snapped shut. Angela blinked a few times as the chain worked its way into her folds, and tried not to moan.

'Oh dear,' said Lady Anais, looking at her watch. 'Is that the time? Well, dear, better limber up and run through those shoulder stretches one more time. You are going to have your arms secured for rather a long time!'

'Now then, Lucy dear . . .' Valencia slipped her hand between Lady Lucinda's thighs. 'Let me explain about Anais's evening and what is expected . . .'

Valencia's Daimler sped through a spring downpour, windscreen wipers ticking rhythmically as they purred through empty streets. Lucinda bit her bottom lip to prevent a moan escaping as Valencia's hand stroked the bare flesh above her stocking top, on her inner thighs. The blonde girl wore a fur coat but this had fallen open at the front. Beneath the fur she was not wearing very much at all; the tiniest white satin corset, laced fearsomely tight with Jem's help, white silk stockings and the usual absurdly high stilettos, apart from which she only had her bonds.

A leather collar encircled Lucinda's lovely neck, a slender chain descended from the back of it to haul her hands up behind her back. Another chain, acting as a leash was locked to the front, falling beneath her naked breasts. Though her arms where held high behind her back by this arrangement, these were not the most bothersome chains.

'Ah, Valencia, this thing between my legs, it's too tight, can't you loosen it a bit?'

Valencia chuckled. 'It's supposed to be tight, petal!' She gave the saddle chain that divided Lucinda's sex lips a little tug. 'It needs to be tight to stop anyone going up there that doesn't have a key! Some people have quite elaborate chastity belts on their debutantes and one or two have their girls pierced and the lip rings padlocked, but I find that this arrangement works as well.'

'Ooh, but it's ooh . . . too . . . tight!' Lady Lucinda exclaimed, between moans, as Valencia's manipulations made the pressure on her clitoris even more impossible to bear.

'I know, it does involve a certain level of discomfort, Lucy, sweetheart,' Valencia said, lifting her hand from the chain to tweak her captive's nipple. 'But then, that is not really my problem, is it, sweetie?'

Six

'So, Jem,' Yvonne asked brightly, 'what are you going to do with your evening off?'

For once the girl was not wearing her absurd 'French maid' outfit, but had dressed in a comfortable and rather shapeless housecoat. It did not suit the pretty brunette, Jem thought, but that was fine as far as he was concerned. What he needed more than anything was a respite from almost constant arousal.

Anyway, Jem had put his old clothes on too, which was a huge relief, particularly as the trousers were nicely baggy at the front.

'Don't know,' he said, shrugging. 'Might go for a walk; I have hardly been out of this place since I got here.'

He did not say, but his ambition for the evening was simple. He wanted to give his cock and balls a rest. The constant arousal and frequent ejaculations that had been a feature of the last week had left him with a deep ache in his testicles. Rough handling, sharp nails and even wicked cane strokes had left his dick feeling positively raw.

Jem also wanted to think about his situation. He had been molested and humiliated, beaten and abused, almost from the moment he stepped into this strange woman's house. She had the photos, it was true, but Valencia had promised him that they were only for insurance. If he went to the papers she would use them, she had said, but otherwise he was quite free to leave.

And do what? he wondered as he drank his tea and tried to ignore the pretty girl who was still grinning at him across the table. Go and get another footman's job for rubbish money; to work long hours and be virtually invisible as he had done before? Valencia Dacourt might be crazy, she was certainly a bitch, but he could hardly say his time here had been boring. In fact, if he was honest with himself, he had to admit that the humiliations and pain that he had suffered seemed to have connected with some deep-seated need. At the very least the experience had been so horny and exciting that part of him at least was craving more.

But not tonight, he thought to himself, putting the cup down on the table. Tonight he needed a rest and a bit of cool fresh air. He stood up just as Chloe entered the room. Her shock of blonde curls had been let down to hang free about her shoulders, but it was what she was wearing that made him blink. The maid was laced into a long black leather corset that creaked every time she moved an inch. Black lace French knickers, black velvet evening gloves, black stockings and high-heeled thigh boots, also in black leather, completed the outfit. In her hand she held a small, plaited leather whip.

'Oh, very nice, Chloe,' Yvonne said, with open admiration.

'Do you like it, Jem?' the blonde maid asked with a wicked smile.

'Um, er, isn't that . . . aren't they . . . the mistress's things?' he said weakly.

Yvonne laughed; the brunette stood up and slowly undid the buttons of her shapeless house coat.

Beneath she wore a black satin corset and sheer stockings but, unlike Chloe, the blonde girl wore no knickers and Jem found his gaze stuck to her neatly shaven sex.

'Of course! This corset too,' Yvonne said. 'Haven't you heard the expression, "when the bitch is away the cats will play"?'

Both maids laughed.

'Come along, little mousy,' Chloe said in a husky voice. 'It's play time . . .'

'There's a good girl, you look absolutely lovely, Angela. Now just wait there . . .'

'Please, Aunt . . .' Angela began, only to be silenced by Lady Anais putting a finger to the chained girl's lips.

'Shush, I know it's hard, but that's what makes it fun . . . for us, at least!' Lady Anais winked and swept away.

The dining table had been set for a formal dinner. White linen complemented gleaming polished silverware and elegantly stemmed crystal glasses. It was the grandest and most sophisticated table setting that Angela had ever seen.

However, her aunt had explained, the settings were not for the debutantes but for their sponsors and guests. The debs were due a very different sort of meal.

At one side of the big dining room was a set of French windows. Heavy drape curtains of burgundy velvet covered these, but behind the drapes, steel rings had been set into the doorframes. Angela's long leash chain had been padlocked to one of these. Her wrists, once again, had been affixed to the bottom of the back plate that came down between her shoulder blades from the back of her collar. Thus her arms were wrenched up and back uncomfortably, though not as gallingly as the tight little chain between her legs.

Standing there helpless in this bondage would have been an ordeal at the best of times, but what made it so much worse was the presence of the staff. Mary, Leila and Yvette kept bustling in and out to make last minute adjustments to the table settings and every time the maids came in they gave Angela an amused glance.

This was not so difficult to endure, however. Lady Anais's serving maids wore very little. Leather collars and cuffs, white caps, dainty aprons and suspender belts, black seamed stockings and high-heeled shoes, was the outfit of the night. Only when Leila turned to go out did Angela realise that she also wore a tight saddle chain between her legs. The waistband of the apron hid the waist chain that supported it and, from the front at least, the apron itself concealed the wickedly tight chain.

So, Angela thought, and very nearly smiled to herself as she did so, it isn't just the six-inch heels that are making the little bitches walk so gingerly!

There was no such consolation in the case of Simmonds the butler, however. He stalked in and out of the room, chivvying and reproving the three maids for minor matters in the party preparations. He was so preoccupied and professional that he barely seemed aware of the three maids' lack of clothes. If only, Angela thought as he stopped in front of her, he was as unaware of her own situation.

'Is everything to your satisfaction, ma'am?'

His voice was perfectly and distantly polite, but his eyes told a different story altogether. Simmonds let his gaze trickle down her exposed body, then very, very, slowly, lingering on her naked pussy and again on her bare breasts, he raised his eyes up to meet her own.

'If there is anything I can do for you . . .' he said smoothly.

To her shock, Angela realised that his right hand was in the pocket of his grey striped trousers. The beast was fondling himself as he leered politely at her, she realised suddenly.

'. . . you have only to ask.'

He took one last hungry look at her shaven pussy and then turned to the table.

'Not those, Yvette, you gormless girl! I need the plain crystal decanters for the claret; how many times must I explain it? The cut glass ones are for the port!'

'For heaven's sake, Lucy, have a little more decorum!' Valencia reproved in an amused voice.

'Ooh . . . please . . . ma'am . . .' Lady Lucinda babbled, her eyes unfocused. 'I need . . . I mean I must . . .'

'Yes, dear, I know exactly what it is that you need – but you are going to have to wait for it, you wanton little slut!'

'Nooo . . .'

Lucinda staggered as if drunk and Valencia had to support her with an arm to stop the blonde girl going over on her high heels. The constant pressure of the chain on Lady Lucinda's clitoris, together with Valencia's fondling of her in the car, had brought her to the very brink of orgasm. Just as Lucinda was about to climax, however, Valencia had desisted, leaving the blonde debutante to squirm and moan half-dementedly on the car seat until they arrived at the Fakenham residence.

Getting out of the car and walking up the steps did not help Lucinda's predicament in the least. As she moved the chain rubbed up against her clit the more insistently. The truth was that she was so far gone that she would not have minded at that moment if she had fallen to the pavement and had her orgasm in the street. But Valencia made sure that her charge could get no such release.

'Good evening, Valencia, Lady Lucinda, you look ravishing, my dear!'

Lady Anais beamed as the butler lifted the mink from Lucinda's shoulders, revealing her nakedness and bondage. However, she was so distracted by the burning in her loins that, for once, Lucinda barely cared.

'Here you are, Anais!' Valencia said brightly, passing something that jingled to the other woman.

Even in her distracted state, Lady Lucinda realised with a sudden shock that it was *the* key.

Valencia took the leash and led her charge along the corridor. With enormous effort, Lucinda focused her attention on staying upright on her steeple heels. The fact that her hands were chained behind her helped, as the knowledge that she could not use them if she fell helped to concentrate even her fevered mind.

They were almost the last to arrive and a bizarre sight greeted them in the dining room. One long wall was covered in velvet drapes and, arranged along this in a line were nearly a dozen debutantes. Each girl wore little but a brief corset or basque and stockings, and each had her hands secured behind her and a collar which was attached to a chain that emerged from the drapes. There was something else that Lucinda had in common with the others. Every girl had either a tight saddle chain, secured by a padlock, biting into the soft folds between her legs or else a steel chastity belt securing her pussy.

The faces of the waiting girls, each perfectly made up to complement an elegant hairstyle, displayed a range of expressions. Various degrees of discomfort, apprehension and anxiety could be discerned as well as flushed faces and dilated pupils, distracted eyes and other subtle signs of sexual excitement.

Lady Lucinda's own state of arousal was not diminished by the sight of the chained girls. Indeed, she had to bite her own lip to stop a moan of sheer lust from escaping as Valencia led her to a gap between Angela and Jane, and secured the leash chain to something behind the curtains.

There was not long to wait, which was as well for Lucinda. Unable to use her hands to touch herself she pressed her legs together and performed a sort of strange, upright squirm as she desperately, and ineffectually tried to make her crotch chain move against her clit, that tiny bit that was still necessary . . .

'Well, I must say that Lucinda is looking particularly lovely,' Lord Randolph said, smoothly intercepting Valencia Dacourt as she came back from the dining room to the large drawing room where the guests were assembled.

'There is no doubt that that girl suits bondage!' Valencia said, favouring her friend with a wary smile. 'It's not just her beauty, it is her pride. The humiliation makes her drip like an overripe peach but she does so hate to acknowledge it!'

The maid called Leila came up to them with a tray of champagne dishes. Randolph took one, letting his gaze rest on the girl's small but beautifully shaped naked breasts. She wore a black leather collar and matching wrist cuffs but otherwise was quite naked above the waist. Valencia took a glass too and the maid began to move away, but Randolph detained her by taking her arm. Her light brown skin was warm and smooth. Careful to steer her gently, so as not to upset her champagne glasses, he moved her around so that he could see her from behind.

It was a beautiful and shapely back, the collar seeming to emphasise the grace of her slender neck. The girl's little white apron was tied in a bow at the small of her back and from under this a glinting chain disappeared into the cleft of her pretty bottom. A white lace suspender belt, black seamed stockings, and six-inch heels comprised all the rest of the girl's outfit.

'Rather a good uniform, that!' he said in a drawl. 'Such a sweet peach of an arse should not be hidden under skirts and whatnot! Damn me, but I would like to lay my cane across that pair.'

He felt his cock begin to stiffen as he spoke, for he was speaking the truth and not simply enjoying tormenting the girl. Still he felt her tremble under his touch.

'Let her go, Randolph, she has a job to do!' Valencia said with a shake of the head.

'I suppose I must . . .' he said regretfully and let go of Leila's arm. 'Off you pop, pet, but don't let me run out of champagne!'

He gave the lovely light brown bottom cheeks a pat to set her off on her rounds again.

'Damn,' he said, 'I wouldn't mind if that was mine tonight at all! Where does Anais find them?'

'Algeria in her case, I do believe!' said Valencia. 'So you are not hoping for Lucinda or little Angela again?'

'Ah well, yes, I am growing impatient to improve my acquaintance with Lady Lucinda,' he conceded. 'And Angela is certainly a delicious little morsel.'

He thought about those wide, innocent brown eyes and lovely body and felt his mouth grow dry with desire, a problem that he immediately dealt with by drinking more champagne.

'Well,' Valencia said with a smugness that was slightly worrying. 'Something tells me that you will be out of luck tonight!'

'Oh, yes?' He cocked an eyebrow enquiringly at Valencia.

'Yes,' she said with a confident smile. 'I, however feel particularly lucky!'

'Look,' Jem said, getting up from the parlour table and backing away towards the door, 'sorry, but . . .'

'What's the matter, Jemmy?' Chloe asked, archly advancing on him as he moved. 'Are we not good enough for you, then?'

'Yes!' Yvonne said ominously, moving around the table from the side. 'Seems our little pageboy has got up himself, Yvonne. Only wants to play with Miss Harcourt and her hoity-toity friends.'

Something told Jem that there was no point in arguing with the maids in this mood. He turned and made a run for the outside door. There was a high excited whooping sound behind him. Trusting that their heels would slow them, he charged down the little corridor that led from the servants' hall to the basement door. His hand grabbed the handle and he felt relief surge through him as he turned it, hearing the heels of the pursuing maids clacking behind him on the stone-flagged floor.

The door did not open. It was locked. In confusion Jem turned to face the two young women who had stopped hurrying and were advancing slowly, both grinning gleefully.

'Looking for this, sweetie?' Yvonne said, holding up the outside door key.

The only way out was through them. Jem considered a charge, barging past the two girls in the narrow corridor.

'Come on, Jem,' Chloe said in a husky voice. 'You know you want to really.'

'No, please,' he replied hoarsely. 'I need a break . . . I . . .'

'Tell you what,' Yvonne said with a wicked smile. 'Drop your trousers.'

'Drop my . . .?'

'If you don't have an erection, we will believe you don't want to play and let you go. How's that for an offer?' Chloe put in.

'But if you are all stiff again,' Yvonne said. 'Well, then we will have to conclude that you are just being coy, and want to play with us really, after all!'

Jem looked at Yvonne, and then at Chloe. There was no pity in the pretty maids' eyes at all. He took a deep breath and leapt forward in an attempt to push between them. To his surprise the girls stepped back as if to let him pass. Surprised, he took advantage of his chance to escape, springing forward as fast as he could. Too fast! He felt Yvonne's stuck-out leg too late as he tripped over it to go sprawling on the floor.

With yelps of glee the two girls jumped on him. There was a brief and futile struggle. Soon he was pinned on his back, Yvonne sitting on his chest, her stockinged thighs either side of his face as Chloe, her leather corset creaking lustily, fought to undo his trousers.

'You were right!' Chloe cried in triumph. 'Look, Yvonne! The dirty boy is harder than a ham bone!'

Yvonne did not bother to turn and look; she just grinned down at Jem and pinched his furiously blushing cheek until he gasped in pain.

'See, Chloe,' she said in a hungry, husky, voice. 'I told you the little trollop was just being coy!'

* * *

The pain in her wrenched-back arms was building. So much so that Angela was almost glad to see the elegantly dressed guests enter the dining room. Since the arrival of the other debutantes she had been spared the particular attentions of the butler. But, as each wide-eyed, half-naked girl had been led in and chained up in line, she had seen her own fears reflected back in one pair of wide, half-panicked, eyes after another.

And then there was the odour. All the girls seemed to have been perfumed with costly French scents, which intermingled headily in the dining room. Nor was this all; the musky, unmistakable aroma of feminine arousal mixed with the delicate perfumes and a note of something else, perhaps, she thought, it was the smell of fear.

Combined, these intermingling scents produced an almost overwhelmingly intoxicating odour. As each new girl was led in and chained in line the scent grew in both complexity and intensity, so that by the time a strangely distracted-looking Lucinda was chained in her place the perfume was making Angela feel quite dizzy.

The scent and other things; the enduring pressure of the chain between her legs was even harder to endure than the position of her arms. As the sight of the other girls added to Angela's arousal, she found to her alarm that the pressure on her clitoris became even more intense as her mons began to swell. By the time the guests entered it was all she could do not to moan aloud.

'Oh, my, don't they look lovely!'

'We certainly have a fine crop coming out this year!'

'Little minxes look a bit anxious for some reason, what!'

The ribald comments and laughter of the guests filled the air as men in evening dress and women in the most elegant gowns paraded up and down the row of debutantes, clearly enjoying the plight of the naked and chained young women.

Angela could not bear to meet the hungry and amused gazes of her tormentors and so looked down, trying to ignore the sight of her own proffered, naked breasts, and stare at the floor.

The sound of a gong brought silence to the room. Lady Anais nodded her thanks to the butler who had accompanied her into the dining room with a small dinner gong.

'Ladies and gentlemen,' she said. 'Thank you so much for coming this evening. Most of you were here last year but for those who weren't I will explain the procedure for this event.'

Angela tried to swallow and felt a pounding in her temples.

'All the debutantes are chained, as you will have observed. And all the padlocks securing each girl are keyed alike. Those keys are here!'

Lady Anais gestured to Mary who stood next to her holding a silver champagne cooler. Just as the last time Angela had seen her, the maid wore a demure expression, stockings and her little apron – but very little else.

'Mary will pass among you, and you may each draw out a key. The corresponding girl will be yours for the evening. Dinner will be served immediately. The usual procedure is for the debutantes to serve their evening's master or mistress, under the table during the meal. Afterwards we have various rooms set up for more robust games, and girls may be traded by those who would like a change.'

There was a murmur of approval from the guests

at this and a sort of collective shiver of apprehension ran through the little row of chained debutantes.

'Oh, one more thing!' Anais said as an after thought. 'As we have slightly more sponsors and guests than debutantes tonight, my maids have kindly volunteered to make up for the deficiency. Leila, Yvette, Mary!' The other two maids had been busy at the table but they now joined Lady Anais. In obedience to her gesture each one lifted the little apron that was her principal garment so that the gleaming chains that disappeared between their shaven pussy lips could be seen. Angela felt her own clit throb in sympathy as she saw the colour rise to the three girls' cheeks.

'I assure you that they are by no means second prizes in this draw,' Lady Anais said slyly. 'They make up in experience what they may lack in innocence!'

The tension that had been building in the room was broken by a burst of laughter from the guests. Angela noticed Mary lick her full lips anxiously before setting off with her silver bucket.

A severe-looking woman with grey hair picked out the first set of keys. Each had a number on the key ring, it seemed, and Simmonds had reappeared with a list.

'Jane!' the word went out around the room. The woman came forward and took a good long look at her lovely prey, before reaching behind the curtain to unlock the tall girl's tether chain.

Every time someone reached into the bucket, Angela felt her heart thumping in her chest. Then there would be a pause as Simmonds was consulted and the news would be broadcast through the room in seconds as a name passed from guest to guest.

Angela could not help but hold her breath as she watched Randolph reach in and take out a key. He looked over toward her and smiled wickedly, so wickedly that she thought her heart had stopped for a moment. Then the name Mary was on everyone's lips, an unreadable expression on the maid's face, and Angela felt a strange mixture of disappointment and relief.

The relief was short-lived, however. Distracted by a strange pang of something not unlike jealousy, Angela watched as Lord Randolph whispered something in Mary's ear and saw the blonde girl's eyes widen in response. She quite forgot about who was next up in the lottery, as Valencia Dacourt reached into the silver bucket, until she heard the word 'Angela' ripple about the room.

She looked up to find herself staring into Valencia Dacourt's glittering eyes.

'I shouldn't worry about Randolph, sweetie!' Valencia said with malice. 'Tonight you have me to please, my girl.'

'Argh!' Jem yelled as Yvonne ripped off the wax paper.

'Shut up, you silly girl!' the corseted maid said with a grin.

Chloe stuck the next strip of paper on his legs.

'I'm not a girl!' he muttered sulkily. 'They are supposed to be hairy!'

There was not a lot he could do about his situation. The maids had made him lie back on the big oak table in the servants' parlour and tied his wrists and ankles to each of the table legs. He was helpless and quite naked, spread-eagled on his back as the giggling maids had first shaved the stubble of his pubic hair before waxing his legs.

'Not a girl?' Yvonne slowly dragged a long fingernail up the rigid shaft of his penis. 'Well, I suppose not, exactly with this thing.'

Jem let out a sort of whimper as her sharp nail met his glans and prodded wickedly.

'But we need to wax you because you so look horrid in sheer stockings!' Chloe put in, painting another paper strip with the hot, molten wax.

'But I don't want to wear stockings!' Jem protested, blinking the tears away.

'Don't be silly!' Chloe said sharply. 'Of course you do!'

'But, really . . .' Jem began.

He did not get any further. As casually as if she were pulling a pillowcase from a pillow, Yvonne leaned forward and ripped the next strip of waxed paper from his leg.

It felt as if she had just stripped off a piece of skin. Pain engulfed him but the ropes were well tied and strong enough to hold down his writhing body.

'Argh!' Jem yelled out again.

If Randolph felt a pang of disappointment for a moment it soon passed as he let his gaze rest on Mary's full breasts. He could tell that the blonde maid could sense his eyes on her as she let one guest after another pick their keys from the champagne cooler. He stayed close; indeed, he moved closer and let his hand brush her naked bottom, enjoying the warmth of her skin and the way her pale cheeks went a little pink as he fondled her rear.

At last the maid's task was completed and the guests began to take their places at the table. The butler smoothly relieved Mary of her silver bucket and Randolph felt his cock begin to harden in anticipation of the pleasures to come.

He was seated next to Valencia and opposite Sir Angus and the grey-haired but still handsome dowager Lady Wallingford. Unlike the debutantes, Mary needed no guidance and he did not even feel the need to have her leashed. The blonde maid slipped under the table and he felt her unbutton his flies unbidden. Randolph turned to Valencia beside him. She was busily positioning Angela and pulling up her skirts. It was an awkward and undignified business. He felt the maid's practised hands extract his erection and her hot little tongue begin to lick the shaft and felt well satisfied with the number he had drawn.

Half a dozen oysters had been set out by the staff at each placement during the lottery, and Randolph's waited on a bed of crushed ice. He did not begin, however until the butler, clearly rendered somewhat shorthanded by the raffling of the maids, had served him with wine. Simmonds, who had served Lord Randolph many times before, did not need to be asked to show him the label. It was Chablis, naturally – Anais would scarcely have served anything else with oysters – a 45 Valmur which, Randolph thought with satisfaction, should be just coming round. He allowed himself a smile as he put his nose to the glass and inhaled. Mary's tongue lapped his erect cockshaft as he took a sip and let the steely, perfectly balanced Chablis swirl around his mouth.

'All right, sweetie, on your knees!' Valencia had ordered.

Angela only hesitated for a moment, purely because without the use of her hands to balance it felt awkward, but the pause had been enough for Valencia to grab her nipple in sharp nails and twist.

'Yow!' she yelped as the other woman forced her to get onto her knees. Valencia released the nipple and lifted the tablecloth, still holding the heavy chain secured to Angela's steel collar in her other hand. An astonishing sight had greeted Angela beneath the dining table. Everywhere the guests were taking their seats and their captives were crawling into position. As the debutantes' hands were all secured behind their backs, the guests themselves were pushing back skirts and unbuttoning flies. Angela exchanged alarmed glances with Jane whose mistress for the night was seated almost opposite Valencia. Both girls blinked and gulped.

A tug on the chain brought Angela crawling into position. Valencia Dacourt had pushed her skirt back until her sex was exposed. The elegantly dressed young woman wore no knickers. A neatly trimmed triangle of black fur greeted Angela's wide-eyed gaze. Valencia wore black stockings, and these seemed to enhance the sleek musculature of the young woman's powerful-looking thighs. The chain was tugged again, making Angela crawl forward, between those daunting limbs, nearer and nearer to the triangle of curly pubic hair.

'Lick my thighs, first, both sides and slowly work your way up towards the main course,' Valencia said, reaching under the table with her free hand to grab Angela by the hair and yank her head into position.

Angela had little choice but to comply. Sounds of sucking, licking and clinking chains from elsewhere under the table mixed with the noise of laughter and chink of cutlery and glassware from above. Starting at the very tops of Valencia's stockings, Angela began carefully to caress the muscular thighs with the tip of her tongue.

The pressure on the chain guided her progress. Only after she had thoroughly laved both sides of the thigh above the stocking tops did Valencia tug to bring her head a little higher.

Suddenly a hand appeared in front of her holding an oyster in the half shell.

'Swallow it!' Valencia's voice demanded.

Angela had never had an oyster but she did as she was bid. The cold, delicious juices hit the back of her throat and she gulped it down.

'Lick my fingers,' the disembodied voice demanded.

Angela obeyed, sucking the slightly oyster and lemon flavoured fingers, each in turn until the woman seemed to be satisfied. Then the hand grabbed her head and pushed it down, which Angela took as a signal to begin licking the insides of Valencia's thighs again.

The presence of the other woman's sex was impossible to ignore for a second. There was a musky scent, one element of which was reminiscent of the oyster, and the chain was pulling her ever closer to the dark triangle of fur.

Before too long, Angela had run out of inner thigh to caress. One last tug of the chain was an obvious signal. Angela took a deep breath and began.

'Oof!' Jem grunted as the two maids hauled on the corset laces.

'That's better!' Yvonne said, panting a little from her exertions.

'Starting to get somewhere!' Chloe said brightly.

'Starting!' Jem protested. 'This thing won't go any tighter! I can hardly breathe as it is!'

'Now you know what we feel like, then. And of course it will go tighter. I reckon we can get you down another inch at least!'

There was little Jem could do except complain. After waxing him and washing him, the maids had taken him up to Valencia's bedroom and used the steel rings in the top and bottom of her four-poster bed to bind him in an X-shape. He could only move his neck freely and so there was little he could do when they produced the pretty corset, liberally trimmed with lace and dripping with suspender straps. It was pink satin, a much paler pink than Jem's face once the giggling girls began to lace him into it. The suspenders dangled, tickling his legs and feeling utterly bizarre against his freshly waxed thigh skin.

That sensation had only bothered him to begin with. As the maids began to tighten the corset, the tickling, even the humiliation, ceased to be his main concern. He felt like he was being squeezed by a giant hand around his waist. His protests only drew more giggles from his tormentors, however. The girls kept hauling on the laces until he felt he could barely breathe.

As he got used to the sensation slowly, he faced another problem. He had been stiff for over an hour now and neither the waxing nor the tight lacing had done anything to make his erection subside or even ease. He was on the point of coming, and he knew it.

The problem was that the girls had secured him facing Valencia's bed. If he did shoot his load it was primed to go all over her expensive-looking, pale-blue satin counterpane. The idea was terrifying but the terror only seemed to bring the disaster even closer. He tried his best to think of something else.

The maids hauled again at the corset laces and squeezed his waist down even tighter. It took his mind off the fear for a moment, but his balls twitched in response, to the pressure. Oh God, he thought as he breathed shallowly and deeply. How on earth did I get into this situation again?

Valencia proved to be every bit as juicy as the oyster, and even a little reminiscent in scent and taste. Angela tried to ignore the way the chain rubbed against her own clit, but it was very hard. The scent of cunt simply engulfed her and her own body, chained and shackled as it was, responded on some deep atavistic level. Only too aware that disobedience would have unpleasant consequences, however, Angela tried to concentrate on the task she had been set.

The sounds around her were more muffled now. As soon as her tongue had touched Valencia's pussy lips, those powerful thighs hand clamped around Angela's head. For a moment she had had to fight a wave of panic, brought on by a fear of suffocation. But, though her nose was crushed against the wiry curls of Valencia Dacourt's pubic hair, she found she could, just, breathe through it. She used the tip of her tongue to explore the other woman's pussy lips, dipping it in between them, tentatively at first but then more deeply as the strong thighs squeezed her head in response.

At last she began to lick around Valencia's clitoris itself. From the first flickering touch of her tongue she felt the other woman buck and squeeze those powerful thighs convulsively. Soon the motion became even more violent and Valencia's began bucking and writhing in her seat as she came.

How he got through the first course without coming halfway through, Lord Randolph could not have said. There were five guests on either side of the dining table, Lord George at the head and Lady Anais at the opposite end. Each diner was immaculately dressed and the scene, if sumptuous, was utterly respectable – except perhaps for the demeanour and expressions of the guests.

Every man and woman seated at the table had a pretty girl between their legs, busily sucking and licking with varying degrees of enthusiasm and skill. The way that the diners reacted to this stimulus varied, however. Lady Anais ate her oysters and sipped her Chablis with almost glacial grace, only betraying by the occasional slight tremor or hesitation in her voice that cunnilingus was being performed on her beneath the white damask tablecloth.

In stark contrast, Sir Angus, already even more scarlet in complexion than usual, hardly bothered to try and make conversation with the other guests. He swallowed his oysters quickly and swigged the Chablis like a glass of water, then simply swore and banged the table with his massive fists. Lady Wallingford, by his side, simply sat bolt upright with a rather startled look in her eyes and completely ignored both wine and food in front of her.

Valencia, sitting beside him, made a valiant effort. She had managed her oysters with a measure of decorum, even giving one to Angela, which amused Randolph to see. Then she tried to maintain her dignity as she sipped her wine. The attempt did not last long.

'So, Valencia are you going to go to Paris this year?' he asked archly, ignoring the hot little tongue lapping his cock.

'Yes I, I, I thought I, I might go over in . . . ah . . . sorry, Randolph . . .'

'Fuck! That's the way, aye, suck hard, you saucy bitch!' Sir Angus cried out banging the table so hard that his glass jumped off to shatter on the floor.

'I'm . . . ah . . . rather bored with ah . . . Paris myself . . .' Randolph managed. 'Thought I might go to Florence . . . ah!'

But he had no need to try to continue the conversation, for Valencia let out a lost-sounding moan and grabbed fistfuls of table cloth in each white-knuckled hand.

Cries and groans and grunts were now more common than coherent conversation around the table. The guest's moans mingled with the busy chink of chains from beneath the tablecloth.

Mary had reached Randolph's glans now and it took all his self control to maintain any semblance of conversation as the blonde maid skilfully licked his sensitive cockhead. If anything, he thought, taking a quick swig of cool Chablis as if to compensate, her tongue felt hotter than before. The sensation was almost too delicious to be borne. Randolph picked up the last oyster with a hand that trembled very slightly and waited until he felt the maid take the head of his cock in her hot wet little mouth. At that precise moment he let the oyster slip down his throat, following immediately with the steely tang of the Chablis. If one could die of pure pleasure, he thought, feeling himself begin to spurt into the Mary's mouth, even as the fine wine slipped down his own throat, he, for one, was most certainly doomed!

Seven

'Please . . . I really don't think that this is a good idea!' Jem said hoarsely.

As well as the corset, he now wore sheer black nylons. Crimson lipstick had been applied to his lips and his nails painted the same shade. Somehow, by an almost superhuman effort, he had not come over Valencia's costly bedspread. The maids had let him down only after putting a dog collar around his neck and leather bands about his wrists and ankles, and pinioning his hands in front. Then he had been chivvied downstairs to Valencia's sumptuous drawing room.

'More champu, Yvonne?' Chloe asked, waving the bottle she had brought back from the cellar.

The maids had already consumed one bottle of Valencia's vintage champagne in the bedroom as they had made him up and dressed him. To Jem's alarm they seemed to be becoming more giggly and wilder by the minute.

'I don't mind if I do, old girl!' Yvonne said, in a poor attempt at an upper class accent and proffering her glass.

All Jem's worries about disturbing or soiling Miss Harcourt's bedroom were coming back to haunt him. He looked down. From the frills of lace at the bottom of his corset his cock stuck out at a 45-degree angle. He had been rigid for more time than he had imagined possible. The sight of the two maids and his own humiliation kept him aroused, and yet he had not been given or permitted that final contact that would cause him to come.

'I think Jem should have some too!' Chloe said with a sly smile.

'Jem? I think she is too pretty for a boy's name!' Yvonne said. 'Let's call her Jemima!'

The maids dissolved into a fit of giggles. Jem felt his face redden but there was not much he could do.

'I don't want any champagne, thank you,' he said sullenly.

The maids turned and stared, their giggling suddenly interrupted.

'What makes you think you have any choice in the matter?' Chloe asked coldly.

'Do you want the mistress to come back and find champagne all over her precious carpet?' Yvonne asked, her eyes full of menace.

'No, don't,' Jem said, panic building as he wondered wildly what the two girls intended. 'You know how she is with this carpet, and she will blame you as well.'

'Not if we tell her it was all your doing, Jem. You stole the champagne in the first place, after all!'

'That's right,' Yvonne chimed in, taking another deep swig from her glass. 'All Jemima's doing, wasn't it, Chloe, pet?' Yvonne took the bottle from her companion and walked over to Jem. 'Get on your knees!' she ordered. 'Get on your knees, now, if you do not want to be in more trouble than you ever imagined!'

Jem got to his knees, finding his face only inches from Yvonne's naked and shaven pussy. He licked his lips anxiously. The maid pressed the rim of her champagne glass against her bare belly, just under the bottom of the black satin corset.

'Now,' she said in a high, excited, voice, 'if I was to spill some of this it would run down my belly and spill on the carpet!'

'No, don't!' Jem said, as understanding began to dawn.

'It might be best for you if you were to catch it. Best put your lips against my pussy just in case.'

There seemed to be no choice. Jem leaned forward and let his mouth meet her shaven pussy.

'Ooh!' she said, 'Not there, naughty! A bit lower down would be better!'

She tipped the glass and the champagne began to trickle down her belly. Desperate to stop it spilling on the carpet, Jem had no choice but to suck her pussy lips and swallow as much as he could.

Some of the wine escaped his desperate lapping. Some ran down his chin and neck and, he guessed, onto the pink corset he had been laced into. Some ran down Yvonne's legs to be, he desperately hoped, absorbed by her nylon stockings before reaching the floor. Although the maid let the champagne cascade down her bare belly in a steady trickle, Jem was hopeful that he had managed to prevent any from reaching the carpet.

'Very good!' Yvonne said in a purr as she lifted the empty glass.

Jem's relief was short lived.

'Fill me up, Chloe,' Yvonne said, proffering her glass. 'Oh, and I'd keep sucking, Jemima, if you want me to drink this one instead!'

Jem stuck his tongue between her champagne-flavoured cunt lips and flickered his tongue in an attempt to keep her happy. To his relief it seemed to work. The blonde maid sipped her champagne, letting out the occasional sigh of pleasure as he tongued her.

'That's it, good girl, ooh! Stick it in deeper, that's it, darling!'

'The bitch seems to know how to suck a girl off!' Chloe put in with a giggle.

'Ooh! Yes, she is quite good at it. Fill us up again. Oops, looks like we will have to make another trip to the cellar in a minute. OK, Jemima, look up!'

Jem lifted his eyes to see what he had been dreading. Yvonne had pressed the rim of the glass against her belly once more.

'Now then, sweetie, ready to try again?'

'General, good to see you,' Randolph said smoothly, moving to intercept the portly soldier who was leading Lucinda from the dining room on her leash. 'Didn't get to speak to you earlier.'

'Evening, Southdean,' the general grunted, looking at him coldly. 'What can I do for you?'

'More a case of what I can do for you, old chap. That little maid I won in the old raffle should be just up your street.'

'Quite happy as I am, thanks all the same,' the general said a little huffily.

'Oh, I'm sure you are. Toothsome little piece of arse, isn't she?'

Randolph looked over the other man's shoulders. Lady Lucinda was trembling with barely suppressed fury, her mouth set in a tight line. His cock began to tingle as it engorged once again.

'But maybe I could offer some other inducement. As well as the maid, of course, I mean.'

General Hollis had looked as if he were about to brush past, but he paused and his hostile expression softened just a touch.

'Other inducements?'

'Well . . . I understood that you had a big celebration planned, after the season was over.'

'Retirement do, yes – by God, Southdean, you keep your ear to the ground!'

'Just thought you might like to borrow the old dungeon?'

He had guessed right, he could see the hesitation in the old soldier's eyes.

'Still got that trollop, Belinda, round the place?' General Hollis asked.

'Oh, I think I might have squirrelled her away somewhere,' Randolph lied, thinking that if he could not get Belinda back in time he could always lend the old goat someone else. Still the General was not finished.

'Use of staff?'

Lord Randolph hesitated. He had recently trained two very lovely new maids, and the general and his pals could be very boisterous. It might even cost Randolph a day or two of his own pleasure if he had to give the girls time to recover. He looked at Lady Lucinda, weighing up the bargain.

She was lovely, no question, with her fine blonde hair and glacial Grace Kelly beauty. But it would not have been enough, if it had not been for the expression of pure frustrated fury in her glittering green eyes.

'You drive a hard bargain, general, but yes, use of staff as well.'

'Free run at the port?'

This was really chancing it and Randolph simply laughed.

'Bugger off, old chap!' He held up Mary's key and let it dangle. 'After all, she is only a little tart!'

Randolph kept one eye on Lucinda, delighted to see the pink spots that burned in her porcelain cheeks.

The general chuckled and handed over Lady Lucinda's key. 'A little tart who has already sucked me off this evening, Southdean! You must have lost your mind!'

'Please,' Jem begged, his face contorted with discomfort. I have to go . . . I can't . . .'

'Well,' Chloe said, 'you should have thought about that before you drank all that champagne!'

He had been made to lick Yvonne to climax and then Chloe had taken off her French knickers and played the champagne game. Once he had licked the blonde maid to orgasm things had quietened down for a time. The maids made unlocked the wristbands and resecured them in front of him, making Jem get on his hands and knees between two chairs, so positioned that they could both use his back as a footrest. Then they had started on the third bottle of champagne.

How much Jem had swallowed in his desperate struggle to prevent the streams of wine reaching the carpet, he could not guess. It had been enough to make him a feel little dizzy but not enough to make him truly drunk.

It had, however, been sufficient to fill his bladder to bursting. As he listened to the two maids giggling and chatting away the pressure had slowly built up until now it was almost unbearable.

'That's right, you silly little bitch!' Yvonne said in a slightly slurred voice. 'And you should have gone before.'

'I'm not paying you piss in my time, sweetheart!' Chloe said in what Jem was forced to admit was a not bad impersonation of Valencia's manner and voice.

He bit his bottom lip hard in an attempt to distract himself from the unbearable pressure. While kneeling on the carpet being a footstool, his erection had subsided a little, although his cock was still at least half engorged.

'What do you say, Chloe, shall we let *her* go?' Yvonne said in a gentler voice.

'Or should we let *him* come?' Chloe responded.

The two maids dissolved into fits of giggles so uncontrolled that it was some time before they recovered sufficiently to refill their glasses with champagne.

'Alone at last, my dear!' Valencia said with a sly smile.

Lady Anais had set up her house so that every available room was prepared and Angela had been hauled off to the library. No one else seemed to have had the same idea and the two young women seemed to have the place to themselves.

Valencia took a while to look around, smiling as she saw the array of canes and whips left out on a leather-topped desk, compelling Angela to follow her by tugging the heavy chain. There were several slender marble columns in the library, supporting a sort of upper gallery. Angela was led over to one of these.

'I expect that you would like your arms released now, pet?' Valencia Dacourt asked archly.

'Oh, yes, please,' Angela said, for her wrenched-back arms were aching in earnest now.

To her relief Miss Dacourt unclipped the snap hooks pinioning Angela's manacles to the back plate of her collar. Even better, the imperious young woman allowed her a few moments of stretching until the aching in her shoulders had begun to subside.

'All right, that is enough. Stand with your back to the column and put your hands back,' Valencia said after a minute or two.

Angela did as she was bade. The marble was so cold against her back that she let out a little gasp. She put her hands back and felt Valencia seize her wrists and then, with a snap, her manacles were secured to one another. Now Angela could move hardly an inch, her arms either side of the marble column and locked together behind it. Relief was quickly replaced with alarm.

Valencia Dacourt strolled over to the leather-topped desk and perused the array of implements unhurriedly.

'Now, I wonder if Anais has left the sort of thing I want . . .' she said pensively.

Angela's heart was hammering in her chest now as she watched the other young woman examine the array of implements with increasing alarm. When Valencia picked up a tiny whip with lots of stiff but very slender thongs and turned back with a smile, Angela forgot to breathe for a few seconds.

'Of course she has!' Valencia said smugly. 'Your aunt is always the consummate hostess. I should not have doubted it for a second. Look, a splendid little titty whisk. You see, these tines are made of wire, just dipped in rubber so that they don't lacerate.'

Valencia's predatory eyes bored into Angela's. There was a cruel and delighted look in them that the bound girl did not like at all.

'Tell me, Angela, my sweet. Have you ever had your tits whipped?'

'No . . . no . . .' Angela answered in a hoarse, alarmed voice.

'Well,' Valencia replied with a grin, 'there is a first time for everything, my dear!'

'One!' the maids said in chorus.

'Ah, please!' Jem said with a gasp.

Jem was standing on a mahogany coffee table with his hands behind his head. In front Yvonne stood wielding a flogger – a whip with many tails of thin, flat leather. Behind, Chloe stood waiting with a cane.

'Two!' the girls chorused as the flogger slapped across his cock again.

It was unbearable. The flat thongs stung but it was not that that made him grimace. His balls felt as if they were about to burst and the smacking of the whip against both them and his cockshaft made the moment when he could not stop it ever more imminent.

Yvonne paused to take another swig of champagne. How many bottles had they drunk now? Jem wondered wildly. There were empty bottles on their sides on Valencia's precious cream carpet and he only hoped that they were empty and not leaking wine onto the floor.

'Three!'

This time Yvonne struck harder and the leather tails slapped painfully against his cock and balls.

'Ow!' he sang out and this time he could not stop himself from bringing his hands down to cover his stinging cock and balls.

There was a whistle, and a crack, and pain of much greater intensity flared across his bottom.

'Bad boy! Put your hands behind your head!' Yvonne ordered.

He was not quick enough and Chloe cracked the cane across his bottom again. Jem grimaced and danced a little jig on his coffee table, but somehow managed to put his hands back up behind his head.

'Four!' The two maids said together as Yvonne lashed his erection once more.

'Oh, God, I can't, I mean, I'm going to . . .' Jem babbled.

Wide-eyed, he watched Yvonne pull back her arm ready to lash him once more. He closed his eyes and heard rather then saw the thongs sweep through the air towards him. Then he felt them slap his tender cock and balls again and that was enough.

'Ooh! You bad boy, stop it!' Yvonne cried with delighted outrage.

'Filthy little oik!' Chloe chimed in.

The cane hissed through the air and cracked across his bottom again, but the pain did nothing to stop the come spurting from his cock. Jem watched in horror as it squirted in an arc, clearing the coffee table, to spatter in an irregular line on the precious cream carpet.

'Oh no,' he said as his cock began to deflate and the last dribbles of his spending hit the mahogany table surface.

' "Oh no" indeed, you filthy tyke!' Yvonne said. 'And put your hands back up behind your head, I haven't finished with you yet.'

'But I need to go,' Jem protested weakly, putting his hands behind his head once more.

'You really do have lovely breasts, Angela,' Valencia said with a smile.

Angela licked her lips anxiously as the other girl raised her hand. Miss Dacourt gently brushed Angela's left titty, pushing down the lace cup that veiled the lower half of her breast, then gently caressing the tender skin. She made little circling movements, tantalisingly light. By the time Valencia's fingers met Angela's nipple, it was already standing up as stiff as a little pink soldier.

The finger circled the nipple a few times and Angela could not stop herself from gasping in response. Then Valencia put her head forward and began to kiss the breast. Just as she had done with her fingers, the dark young woman covered Angela's trembling titty with kisses, circling in towards the erect nipple. The pressure on Angela's clit from the saddle chain was driving her wilder by the minute, and the way that Valencia caressed and kissed her titties did not help one bit. At last, Valencia's mouth closed on Angela's nipple.

The tongue circled the tender nub of flesh a few times, the sensation driving Angela to ever-deepening distraction. Then Valencia's teeth closed on the nipple and bit and Angela let out a piercing squeal, though she could not have said if it was from pleasure or from pain.

'Six!' the two maids chorused as the flogger thumped across his lower belly.

'Please . . . I can't . . . I need . . .' Jem pleaded desperately, hopping from foot to foot.

Now he had come there was no doubt which of his needs was the most urgent. The pressure in his bladder was unbearable. Despite two further strokes from Chloe's cane and several blood-curdling threats from Yvonne, he simply could not keep still.

The flogger tails lashed down again, smacking the flesh just above his bladder. The thongs were light, the extra pressure minimal, but it was very nearly enough to set him off.

Yvonne drained her glass and he had a respite from the flogger. It was no respite from his bursting bladder, however, and Jem still had to jiggle and hop and strain to hold it in.

'Bloody hell, it's finished!' Yvonne said, staring stupidly at the champagne bottle which refused to disgorge any more wine into her glass.

'There is another bottle on the chiffonier,' Chloe said from behind him.

'All right, won't be a sec. Stay there and thwack him if he tries to get down, Chlo!'

Yvonne teetered unsteadily on her heels over to the chiffonier. She came back with another bottle of vintage champagne in her hand. Jem grimaced as the pressure got even more insistent, screwing up his eyes against the acute discomfort.

When he opened them again, Yvonne was fiddling with the wire cage of the champagne cork. She pointed the bottle towards his lower belly.

'No, don't!' he said in alarm.

'Er, better not, Vonnie . . .' Chloe said from behind him.

Yvonne shrugged and to his relief directed the bottle elsewhere. Even as she moved it there was a loud pop and a clinking that even in his distracted stated sounded to Jem like a bit of chandelier breaking. Then the champagne was gushing from the mouth of the bottle. It was foaming, pouring out in a frothy torrent, all over the cream carpet.

It was not this that bothered him so much though. The sight of the gushing champagne was the final straw for his overburdened bladder. In apparent sympathy the piss began, first a tiny trickle then a faster one and then a great arcing stream of pee. To Jem's horror it joined the spunk and champagne soaking into Valencia's thick-pile carpet. His face burned with unendurable humiliation as Yvonne and Chloe, after watching open mouthed for a few moments, began to giggle gleefully.

It was pain now – that was certain. The titty whisk was a diabolical invention. The rubber coating on the wire tines might have stopped them from lacerating her flesh but they did not stop them stinging quite atrociously.

Valencia had a dreamy, rapt expression on her face as she lashed first one of Angela's breasts, and then the other in turn. The wire tines hissed through the air like stinging insects and bit into her tender breast flesh wickedly.

At first, Miss Dacourt lashed the skin above each of Angela's nipples. It stung like fury and the bound girl yelped with pain. Then Valencia struck the left of the left breast and the right of the right one. Angela let out a squeal and began to beg.

But there was worse to come. Now Valencia used the wicked little whip to sting the flesh below Angela's nipples. The under breast seemed far more tender and the pain that much more fierce. There was another problem. As the wire tines whipped up into the tender skin, Angela found herself jumping up as if by doing so she could get away from the little whip. Every time she did the saddle chain rubbed up against her clitoris.

Finally, Valencia began to lash her nipples. Already sensitised beyond endurance from the other girl's caresses and bites, Angela felt as though jolts of electricity were passing through her body. She closed her eyes and gritted her teeth against the pain but the jolts were just too violent to be borne. Then she realised that she was no longer being flogged and that the fire was coming from her crotch and not her titties. It was not pain that she was convulsing her body, but white-hot ecstatic pleasure. She had been whipped all the way to orgasm.

'Good morning, miss,' Mary said brightly. 'Lady Fakenham thought you might like your breakfast in bed!'

Angela sat up in bed, rubbing her eyes with surprise as the maid set down the tray of breakfast things on the side table. Then Mary pulled back the curtains to reveal a bright spring day, and gave Angela a quick curtsey before exiting.

There was delicious-smelling coffee, fresh orange juice and a couple of hot croissants – more of Lady Anais's exotic continental ways, thought Angela. It felt strange as it had for the previous few mornings, to awaken uncorseted and unchained, unrestrained in any way in fact. It was as if she had become so used to bondage and restriction that she felt odd and almost insecure to be so free and unfettered. Even the servants seemed to be treating her with a certain respect.

To Angela's surprise, she was not sure that she quite liked the sensation. Certainly it was a great relief at first, not to be humiliated or kept in painful bondage, and her body certainly needed a respite from punishment. But the welts had melted away and she had soon begun to think the strangest thoughts. It was not that she was looking forward to the next 'ball' exactly – the very idea of the upcoming ordeal made her heart pound in her chest and mouth go dry with a sensation not entirely unrelated to terror – but she felt odd and ill at ease having freedom and respectable clothes. It was almost as if her body had begun to crave the stimulation of the whip and the strange security of chains.

Still, the coffee smelled inviting and the croissants were warm and delicious. Freedom had its compensations, she thought, as pastry melted in her mouth.

'Ah, there you are, my dear,' Lady Anais said, walking into the room, as usual, without knocking. 'Have you finished your breakfast? Good, good!'

The elegant woman sat on the edge of Angela's bed and reached over to lift her chin with a slender finger.

'Well, now!' Lady Anais said, with a smile. 'Have you fully recovered from the weekend's exertions, my dear?'

'Yes, I think so.' Angela replied.

The veneer of normality that had descended on the household over the last few days was so profound that Angela found herself colouring a little at the reference to the debauchery of the ball.

'Good,' Lady Anais said, ignoring her discomfiture. 'Tomorrow night we will attend the last event of the season. It is held in a country house some distance from London, so we will be house guests until Sunday. As the drive is considerable, you will get ready after you have bathed. Oh, and it is time you were tight-laced again. Mary will see to your corseting after bathing. All right?'

'Yes . . . Aunt Anais . . .' Angela said uncertainly. 'Ah, might I ask . . . whose ball is it this time?'

The realisation that her little holiday from 'the season' was over had caused Angela's heart to begin pounding in her chest. Lady Anais did not answer at once but smiled at her as the tension in the room seemed to rise higher and higher.

'Of course you may,' Lady Anais said at last. 'Tomorrow's ball will be hosted by Lord Randolph Southdean.'

'Open wide!' Valencia demanded.

'Look,' Lucinda said crossly, 'this really isn't necessary, Valencia!'

It was so unfair, she thought, gritting her teeth so that Valencia could not stick the gag into her mouth.

The last few days had been simply heavenly. The chance to rest after Anais's dinner had been very welcome. Simply not being in bondage had been better yet. But, for Lady Lucinda the real joy had come from being restored to her proper position with regard to Valencia's servants. She had done her damndest to make the days a merry hell for them –

stalking the house day and night with a cane or crop in hand – looking for the least excuse to make the maids drop their knickers or have Jem lower his trousers.

Fortunately, after what she had seen on her return from the ball, Valencia had been happy to let Lucinda make things as hot as she liked for the perfidious servants, only interfering to apply the whip herself on occasion.

Until that morning, it had been quite wonderful. Today, however, Lucinda had awoken, not to an anxious-looking Yvonne or Chloe with the breakfast tray, but to both maids. Yvonne had held one of the detestable corsets in her hands and the eyes of both maids were hungry for revenge.

Lady Lucinda had not fought it. She knew that struggling would only have brought Valencia and Jem into the fray, so she submitted to the wickedly tight lacing and let the girls roll fine black stockings up her legs and fix them to the corset's suspender drops. She had let them put high-heeled shoes with locking ankle bands onto her feet and had not protested when the bands were clipped together with a single padlock. Lucinda had not even struggled when Yvonne had produced the single glove – a great long, fingerless thing of white leather – and proceeded to lace her arms into it behind her back.

When that was done, Lady Lucinda had been pretty well completely immobilised. Chloe had gone off on her business, but Yvonne remained at her side, steadying Lucinda with a none too respectful hand on the other's waist.

'I expect that you will be looking forward to this trip, miss,' the maid had said pertly. 'Have you seen Lord Southdean's dungeons? Ooh!' The maid had licked her full lips, dramatically opening her eyes wide. 'I'm not so sure that I would want to go down there again myself!'

'I'm not scared of Southdean,' Lucinda had contemptuously retorted.

'No, miss, of course not, miss!' Yvonne had said with a contemptuous smile. 'But he did make you squeal quite a lot at Lady Fakenham's, I hear!'

'Listen to me, you pert little trollop!' Lady Lucinda had hissed. 'You had better enjoy it while you can because when I get back . . .'

But she had got no further, for at that moment Valencia had entered the room with a rubber ball gag in her hand.

'Open wide!' Valencia repeated.

Lucinda set her teeth and glared back mutinously. Valencia smiled ominously. Then she reached forward and took hold of Lady Lucinda's nipple with her crimson nails. There was a swift and vicious twist and Lucinda found herself yelping with pain. Instantly the gag was shoved against her mouth, but Lucinda's cry had not opened her mouth wide enough for the rubber ball to go right in.

'Open it, you stubborn little bitch!' Valencia hissed. 'Or I might just twist it off!'

She gave the tender nub of flesh another wicked pinch and Lucinda did as she was told. The gag was rammed home and quickly buckled up. Valencia went to the bell-pull and rang for the servants, before coming back to stand and admire her handiwork.

'Doesn't she look fine, Yvonne?' she asked, looking Lucinda up and down as she spoke.

'Oh yes, ma'am!'

Corseted, gagged and bound as she was, Lady Lucinda could not even argue. She stood, blinking away tears of sheer impotent frustration as Valencia enjoyed her plight all too obviously. Then there was a knock and Jem entered the bedchamber. He was carrying a bulky object made out of black leather. It was as long as a person and wide enough . . . understanding dawned and Lady Lucinda let out a muffled cry of protest. She tried to struggle out of Yvonne's restraining hands as if, hobbled as she was, there could be some way to hop away.

'Now where does she think she is going?' Valencia said with a chuckle. 'Lay it down on the floor, Jem, and then help us zip her in.'

Valencia strode across the room to grab Lucinda by a hank of hair. She wrenched back the blonde girl's head so that she could look straight into her eyes.

'I don't know,' Valencia Dacourt said with a smile on her full lips. 'I don't know what the world is coming to when you cannot even trust the luggage to behave!'

'Hullo, Angela!' Lord George Fakenham bellowed amiably as she stood waiting in the hallway. 'All set for the show?'

After even a few days off the corset seemed impossibly tight. Angela wore a respectable flower-printed frock with wide skirts and a chic hat with matching gloves, but the constriction of the tight lacing made her feel quite different from the last few days.

She stood in the hallway with the luggage, or rather, she had been told to stand there by Simmonds, relaying Lady Anais's instructions. There was a golf bag containing what were obviously canes and whip handles rather than golf clubs, and several suitcases and hatboxes. After half an hour of waiting, her high heels had begun to make her calves ache and she had begun to feel as if she were merely a piece of luggage herself.

'Ah there you are, George!' Lady Anais emerged from the library, putting on her gloves. 'Are you ready?'

'Can't go with you, Anais, my love,' Lord George said, in a regretful tone. 'Something came up. I'll hitch a ride with the general – he's going up tomorrow.'

Lady Anais cocked her elegant head and assumed a sceptical expression.

'Something came up, George? What exactly came up that is so important. Hmmn?'

'Well . . . it's Lancelot. He is in town very briefly. Got some Sudanese girls that he says . . .'

'Lancelot is in England? Then why does he not come to the ball?'

'Can't, apparently,' Lord George replied. 'Got to go to Paris, so he says, on business.'

'And he is going to show you these Sudanese lambs?' Lady Anais asked archly.

'Yes, erm . . .' Lord George hesitated.

'And maybe let you play with them a little?' she insisted.

'Well, I don't know . . . perhaps a bit of slap and tickle . . .'

'George, if you swap one of our maids without my approval I will cut your balls off with a razor. You do understand me, my dear?'

'Oh yes, my love!' Lord George insisted with a sheepish grin.

'I expect you at Randolph's in good time tomorrow!'

'Of course, my sweet!'

'You had better be!'

With that Lady Anais linked arms with Angela and swept out, followed by Simmonds and the maids burdened with luggage. There was a short wait in the Rolls as the equipment was loaded.

'Your uncle is such a goat when it comes to black girls!' Anais said, with an indulgent smile. 'He was in Africa in the army before the last war and, it seems, he never lost the taste!'

This did not seem to require an answer, and Angela certainly did not know what to say.

'It is so provoking that Lancelot cannot come to the ball, too. I have not seen him in ages. Mind you, my dear, it might be better for your poor hide that he cannot.' Lady Anais leaned over and put her mouth close to Angela's ear, and whispered in a confiding tone, 'Between you and me, Lancelot Shaw is *such* an awful beast!'

'No, push the bags right in, Jem!' Valencia Dacourt ordered.

Jem could not see the point really; the boot of the Daimler was capacious and Valencia had only ordered a small suitcase for herself and one for Lady Lucinda packed. Lucinda had been zipped into the sheath-like leather bag which Jem had helped his mistress lay on the back seat of the car. He could not help but imagine what it must be like for the blonde girl. The wild look in her eyes as Valencia had zipped the bag up over the gagged girl's head was still vivid in his mind.

Not that he was given any leisure to think about Lady Lucinda's problems. Wondering what other luggage Valencia had in mind, he pushed the bags to the back of the boot.

'Right, get in!' she said.

'Get in,' he echoed, looking from the small space left by the suitcases in the boot to Valencia, who was glaring at him.

'Did you think that I was going to leave you here to drink my champagne and piss on my new carpet?' she asked menacingly.

There was not a lot that Jem could say to this and so he just hung his head.

'I know Lucy has flogged you for it, but you seem to be incorrigible, young man. As I cannot trust you not to spread your spunk and piss all over my things, I shall have to take you with me. Now, get into the boot. Don't worry, there is plenty of air. I have transported those two little tarts . . .' Jem had been so transfixed by Valencia's diatribe that he had barely noticed that the maids had been giggling in the background until the sound suddenly stopped in response to this remark. '. . . often enough!' Valencia concluded, having paused to glare at the girls.

'You two!' she said, keeping her gimlet gaze fixed on Yvonne and Chloe. 'Behave yourselves this time or when I get back there will be hell to pay. Do you understand?'

'Oh, yes, ma'am,' the maids chorused.

'Lying little bitches,' Valencia muttered. She turned back to Jem. 'All right now, get in the boot with the rest of the luggage!'

Jem swallowed hard, took a deep breath, and then reluctantly climbed into the boot.

'Anais, Angela! So nice to see you!' Lord Randolph drawled, walking down the front steps to meet them.

'Randolph, chérie, you only saw us at the weekend,' Lady Anais chided.

Angela said nothing. The truth was that she was awestruck by Seardon House. Lord Randolph's country house was nothing less than a mansion – a massive yet elegant Georgian extravaganza set in a great park. Although she did not know the full extent of the grounds, Angela realised that they must be very extensive. The car had driven along a country road with a high retaining wall on one side for what seemed to be miles. They had entered through ornate gates and then driven for what seemed to be another eternity along the drive.

Randolph gave an arm to both ladies and led them inside the house. Angela tried, and failed, to fight the urge to gawp. The scale of the place was awesome, the décor magnificent. The steps led up to a great marble entrance hall and double staircase. Lord Randolph led them from this to a hallway and then into a huge and astonishingly opulent drawing room.

'Are we the first?' Lady Anais asked, for there was no one else to be seen.

'Oh no,' Randolph replied. 'But Valencia and Lucy are getting settled. They have been here for some time now. You know how Valencia drives!'

How long had she been encased in this sheath of black leather? Lucinda simply had no way to tell. Corseted, gagged and bound, she had had very little freedom of movement and no way of protesting when Valencia had produced the body bag.

As the solid zip was closed over her head she fought a wave of pure, claustrophobic panic. The gag already effectively prevented her from breathing through her mouth, now she doubted if there would be enough air for her nose.

After a few futile, panicked struggles, however, she began to calm down. She could see no light from air holes but she realised that there must be some sort of ventilation built into the black leather hood part of the bag. The air was thick with the odour of leather, but was perfectly breathable. She could see nothing; all was black. She could hear nothing but the vaguest muffled sounds. The hood of the thing must be padded around her ears, she realised. In fact the leather body bag seemed to hug her all over. As the panic subsided she found herself slipping into a much calmer frame of mind. It was as if the restriction and the darkness had somehow hypnotised her.

A flutter of anxiety had returned as she felt herself being lifted, and again when she felt the vibrations of the car engine. Valencia could be taking her anywhere, she realised. This time it was not claustrophobia that caused her heart to beat faster, but the sensation of utter powerlessness.

However, the motion of the car, the dark, the feeling of being gently squeezed by her sheath of leather, soon combined to relax her again and made Lucinda feel almost sleepy. The journey might have taken a few minutes or it might have been an age, she really could not have said. All she had known was that when she finally felt the car pull up even before she felt herself hauled from the seat by eager hands, she knew that they had arrived at Lord Randolph's house.

There was the sensation of being carried again – this time it seemed to go on for much longer – then she was placed on a floor. Now Lucinda was fully awake again, awaiting release from her leather cocoon, and yet still it did not come. Her arms, still bound behind her back in their single glove, were aching now, and it was hot in the leather bag, so hot that she could feel herself perspiring.

What could Valencia be doing? Lucinda wondered, getting crosser by the moment. She wanted to spit out an oath but the gag meant that only a muffled moan emerged. Trying to kick her legs and wriggle only made her even hotter in her tight leather prison. If only she could get a hand between her legs and ease that awful tingling sensation. But there was simply nothing she could do but wait until she was released.

* * *

'This is your room, Angela!' Lord Randolph said, throwing open the doors.

He had led the way up the great marble staircase, arm in arm with Lady Anais, with Angela trailing in their wake. Behind Angela, three maids toiled, laden with the luggage. The fact that these girls were all attractive did not come as a surprise to Angela, who was growing used to the ways of her Aunt Anais's friends. Less expected was that all three girls looked distinctly oriental. Angela glanced back at the girls several times as they walked the long corridor from the top of the staircase, feeling a pang of guilt about the weight of the luggage as she saw how much they struggled to keep up.

'I've put you next door, in the blue room as usual, Anais. The keys for both rooms and the connecting door are the same.'

Lady Anais walked over to the other door in the room and opened it.

'Very convenient, thank you, Randolph,' she said with a smile.

'Aiko will attend you for the weekend.'

One of the oriental girls gave a little curtsey.

'Her English is not perfect, so tell me if you have any problems, or just thrash her yourself.'

Whether by chance or as an effect of the remark, the girl who had been taking the golf bag from her shoulder dropped it. The bag fell to the floor and some of the riding crops and canes it contained spilled out part way. Angela watched Aiko's eyes widen at the sight.

'I see you have brought the wherewithal,' Randolph remarked, walking over to the wardrobe and opening its door. 'Though, as I told you last year, there really is no need!'

The canes, straps and whips that hung from the inside of the wardrobe door came as no surprise to

Angela; they did, however, make her feel as if her blood had suddenly run cold.

This place was an absolute maze, Jem thought as he followed the back of Miss Fisk, the housekeeper, up back stairs and along twisting passageways. There was no way that he would be able to find his way back to the servants' hall.

Miss Fisk was a handsome woman in her thirties. After he had helped two oriental looking maids haul Lady Lucinda in her leather cocoon up the stairs and to Valencia's rooms, the housekeeper had appeared and told him to follow her. First they went down to the servants' hall and kitchen. In contrast to the rather cool elegance of the upstairs apartments, this was busy and hot and, rather to Jem's surprise, seemed to be entirely feminine.

As well as the housekeeper and the cook, there seemed to be at least a dozen, mostly Asian looking maids, but he saw no men at all. The girls had stopped and looked at him with obvious interest. They were certainly a pretty bunch of girls, but his experiences at the hands of Yvonne and Chloe had made him suspicious of housemaids, for Jem was only too pleased when Miss Fisk told him to follow her again.

He knew that there was going to be another party. The idea made his heart beat fast and his mouth go dry, although Valencia had not told him any details. She had brought him though, and Jem suspected that she had reasons other than wanting to protect her precious carpet while she was away.

They were at the top of the house now and the corridor was narrow with a low ceiling. Finally they reached a door which Miss Fisk opened with her key. To Jem's surprise it was not a single room but a dormitory with a dozen beds.

'That bed at the end is free. Put your bag on it!'

Jem walked along the double row of beds, putting his small bag on the last one. By the other beds there were a few personal items like photos and . . . he blinked . . . lipstick.

'Um, please, Miss Fisk . . .' he began.

'Well, what is it?' she asked impatiently.

'Is this the male staff dormitory?'

'There are no male staff at Seardon House, boy; you will just have to make do,' the woman said briskly.

'But, but . . .'

'Your mistress may keep you in her suite anyway or lend you to another guest, so I should not be too concerned about your accommodation. You are unlikely to see much of it, anyway.'

With these far from reassuring words, the housekeeper gestured for him to follow her out of the dormitory.

'Well now, this *is* cosy!' Lord Randolph said as he passed the port to Lady Anais.

Cosy was not the word that sprang to Angela's mind exactly. True there were only five people at the dinner table; Lord Randolph, Lady Anais, Valencia Dacourt, Lady Lucinda and herself, but the table was massive and set in a dining room that could have seated a hundred guests.

Lord Randolph sat at the head of the table with Lady Anais and Valencia at either side of him. Lucinda sat next to Lady Anais and Angela next to Valencia. Beyond the debutantes the polished teak table stretched away.

'Such lovely girls, Anais and Valencia, you have done yourselves proud this year. I hardly know which I prefer, Audrey . . .'

'. . . or Grace,' Valencia put in with a cynical sneer. 'Yes, Randolph, you said.'

'Well they both suck cock superbly. Lucinda is the more practised, of course, but Angela has *such* an innocent look!'

She could not prevent the blush from rising to her cheeks. Angela raised her eyes to look at Lucinda, expecting to see the blonde girl's face reddening too, but in fact the other had gone pale with what looked like rage.

'Well, Randolph, how do you propose to choose between them?' Lady Anais asked in a husky voice.

'Reckon I'll have to fuck and bugger 'em both! See how much they wriggle with it up 'em!'

'And you think you'll get the opportunity?' Valencia asked archly.

'Don't see why not. This is my ball and my rules. Reckon I can bagsy Angela for tomorrow night. Dance card isn't full already, is it, Anais?'

'Angela, have you the card I gave you?' Lady Anais inquired sharply.

With a trembling hand Angela retrieved the small, gilt-covered booklet from her little satin bag. It was entirely blank inside.

'Yes, Aunt Anais,' she said in a voice that was a little hoarse with tension.

'Well, dear, the gentleman is asking if your dance card is full?'

It was an absurd charade, for Lady Anais had given Angela the card just before they had gone down to dinner. She knew that there was nothing in it as much as Angela.

'May I, my dear?' Lord Randolph stretched his hand out and Angela gave it to him, keeping her eyes lowered as she dared not meet his gaze.

Lord Randolph produced a pen and scribbled something before handing back the card via Valencia.

'Greedy beggar!' was Valencia's only comment before she passed it on.

He had written, 'Randolph S' in a flourish on the top right of the card, and then run two lines right down both leaves, leaving no space for any other names. Angela just looked at it wide-eyed. She had to remind herself to breathe.

'Well, that is the ball worked out, but what about tonight and our other little wriggler?' Randolph said slowly and then took another sip of port.

'If you think you are getting Lucy for tonight . . .' Valencia began.

'Now, now, Valencia, you haven't heard what I am offering yet.'

Angela looked across at Lady Lucinda. The blonde girl's mouth was set in a furious-looking line and she looked as if she were about to explode.

'I am not . . . one of your trollopy maids to be . . . bargained for this way!' she said suddenly, clearly unable to restrain her outrage a moment longer. 'Does what I want have no bearing on the matter?'

There was a sudden, startled silence, all the more profound and oppressive in the massive space of the dining hall. Then Randolph, Lady Anais and Valencia as one burst into a peal of laughter. It was only when this had subsided that Valencia spoke.

'Of course not, you silly little tart!' she said, and began laughing again.

Jem finished his meal and wondered what he should do next. Miss Fisk had taken him back to the servants' hall and he had been served a very decent roast chicken dinner. Despite the anxiety he felt, he had not lost his appetite and made short work of it. He even got a glass of beer to go with it.

He ate alone. The maids kept coming and going,

but he assumed that they must have different meal-times for, though they looked at him and giggled as they passed, exchanging comments in what he guessed was Japanese or Chinese, none of them sat at the big refectory table and ate with him.

Now he was finished he was slightly at a loss as to what to do next. He did not know where Valencia was, however, and supposed that he had better wait where he was.

It was a long wait, and as time went on it became more difficult for him to sit still at the table. When he had arrived the maids had all worn neat and respectable uniforms. Now they seemed to be changing into evening attire that was not respectable at all.

He was first alerted to this by some whispering and giggling. Turning, he found himself staring at a pair of pretty oriental girls who wore nothing but short black satin corsets, sheer stockings and little aprons, as well as high heels on their feet and leather collars around their shapely necks.

The corsets stopped below the girls' breasts and he found his gaze drawn to their firm and shapely titties before flushing slightly and looking away. The girls giggled again and he felt his cock stirring in his uniform trousers.

That particular pair of beauties had only been the start. Half-naked maids hurried back and forth through the servants' hall, their high heels clacking on the stone-flagged floor. Every time a girl passed through his field of vision, Jem felt his cock stiffen. They seemed almost to be slowing deliberately, whether to show themselves off to him or to stare at Jem in turn. One sweet-faced oriental girl hurried through, however, and he only just caught a glimpse of the tears that glistened on her cheeks. As she turned to go into the kitchen she presented him with a full view of her naked bottom, and Jem blinked to see the livid welts that striped her plump behind.

'Bunko was a little slow today!' a voice said in his ear, making him jump.

The noises from the kitchens had masked Miss Fisk's arrival. Jem tried to think of something that would make his erection subside, for the sight of the flogged girl's bottom had made him hard as rock.

'Your mistress will not require you this evening,' Fisk said. 'However, I have a task for you. Follow me!'

To his relief she turned and walked from the room and so the awkward way that his erection compelled him to move was not immediately exposed. Unfortunately, when they were some way down the corridor they met two of the maids coming the other way. The girls giggled and pointed at the bulge in his crotch as they passed.

Miss Fisk said something sharply to them and they hurried on their way, subdued for the moment, but Jem caught a half smile on the housekeeper's face before she swept on again.

After a comparatively short journey, Miss Fisk stopped by a door and opened it with her bunch of keys. Inside was a pleasantly furnished bedroom, very neat and tidy and perfectly respectable in every way.

'This is my personal apartment, boy, so I will thank you to respect my property,' she said.

'Your personal . . .' Jem echoed, astonished.

There was another door in the room and this Fisk unlocked in turn.

'Come along, boy!'

If the bedroom was respectable, this chamber was not. It was almost as large as the other room but was furnished quite differently. One wall was covered with full-length mirrors. There was a small vaulting horse in the centre of the room and an iron cage in one corner, but the thing that transfixed Jem's attention was the wall that faced the mirrors. It fairly dripped with whips, canes and crops and more implements for flogging than Jem had imagined in his wildest nightmares.

'I only have you until midnight as it will be a long day tomorrow!' Fisk said sharply. 'So stop staring like a halfwit and take your clothes off, now!'

Eight

'Have you been buggered often, sweetheart?' Lord Randolph asked suavely.

'No,' Lady Lucinda said tersely. 'Never, actually.'

'A virgin bumhole, how utterly delightful!' he declared. 'And yet you come over as such a woman of the world, you really are still quite the innocent!'

Lucinda said nothing. She stood in Randolph's room biting her lip as he unzipped the back of her dress. It was a large room, half panelled in oak and dominated by a large four-poster bed. At least he had not taken her down to those famous dungeons, she told herself as her dress fell to the floor. Strong fingers closed on the back of her neck and she found herself forced to walk round to the side of the bed. Only when her knees were but inches from the counterpane was she released. There was a piece of cord, a short riding crop, and a jar of Vaseline waiting on the bedspread. Lucinda closed her eyes.

'You do suit a corset, Lucy, but I think we will have it off as well,' Randolph whispered in her ear.

He put his arms around her and, taking hold of the top of the corset forced open the clips that fastened it at the front. Lucy expected him to unclip the suspender straps from her stockings but Lord Randolph did not bother; once it was undone at the front he simply let it fall away behind her still attached. A hand in the small of her back pushed her sprawling over the bed. Lucy let out a little squeak of alarm.

'Put your hands back, darling!' he ordered quietly.

Lady Lucinda's hands had grabbed the crimson satin coverlet and she was gripping this so tight that her knuckles had gone white. It took some effort of will for her to make herself release her grip and put her hands behind her back. The sight of the little black riding crop both made it easier and yet more frightening to obey his order.

It was the work of seconds for her wrists to be secured by the cord.

'Jesus, but your arse looks inviting, girl!' Lord Randolph declared. 'My dick is stiffer than a broom handle. I'm almost tempted to bugger you this instant without first warming your pretty bottom with the crop. I suppose that would be too cruel though.'

'No,' Lucinda said quickly. 'That would be fine, sir, please . . .'

'No, no, girls need warming before buggering, Lucy, sweetie. I would not be so heartless as to ring your arsehole cold!'

Heartfelt as Lady Lucinda's wish to forgo this proposed foreplay might have been, she realised that she was going to be whipped and so she held her tongue. Randolph held her bound wrists with his left hand, picking up the crop with his right. Lucinda took a deep breath and screwed her eyes shut tight as she waited for the flogging to begin.

'So Lancelot is back in England?' Valencia asked.

'According to George. Haven't seen him myself,' Anais replied.

'Why isn't he coming to the ball then?'

'Apparently it is a flying visit. He has to go to Paris tomorrow.'

'Good Lord, that boy does fly around the place!' Valencia declared.

'Perhaps it is a good thing for the debutantes,' Lady Anais said in an amused voice. 'He does tend to be rather hard on the poor girls.'

Not for the first time, Angela wondered what it was that made this man so fearful. She was naked except for gartered stockings and long evening gloves, and the dog collar that Lady Anais had put around her neck. On her hands and knees in between the two older women, her back was being used as a sort of table. An ashtray had been placed on the back of her pelvis, the two women's drinks, feeling horribly precarious, on either side of it.

'Look, poor Angela is trembling!' Lady Anais said. 'Don't worry sweetie. The bad man won't get you . . . this weekend at least!'

Lady Anais and Valencia both laughed at this remark. Angela just blushed and hung her head. She felt Anais's drink lifted from her back and then gloved fingers stroking the inside of her thigh. Biting her lip hard, she tried to think of something else.

'It's amazing really. Not six weeks ago this was a butter-wouldn't-melt little virgin from the suburbs of Birmingham,' Anais said, setting her drink down again on Angela's back. 'Look at this, Valencia.'

There was a pause and, squinting sideways, Angela could see one of her aunt's evening gloves fluttering to the floor. The she felt the fingers, bare now, touch her thigh again. The stroking was unbearably delicate and gentle, and she could not quite prevent a little moan escaping.

'She is absolutely dying for it. Look, she only needs to be ordered to take her knickers of in the right tone and see . . . her juices are running down the insides of her legs!'

'Extraordinary!' Valencia declared. 'May I, Anais?'

'By all means, Valencia, please do help yourself.'

There was another brief pause during which Anais's fingers continued to fondle the inside of Angela's left thigh. Then another set of fingers began to explore the soft flesh on the right.

'Good Lord, you're right!' Valencia said in tones of mock astonishment. 'She is sopping, isn't she?'

Biting her lip was not sufficient to take Angela's mind of the fondling fingers. Both hands were travelling upwards by slow, circuitous pathways. Strange noises were coming from the back of her throat. She needed them to touch her pussy, to rub against her throbbing clitoris. Instead the women tantalised and teased her until her body began trembling uncontrollably.

It was Valencia's glass that fell first. Angela would have sworn that the bitch had put it near too near the edge of its fleshy table on purpose. Certainly a little twitch in response to a firmer pinch of thigh flesh was enough.

'Angela, you bad girl! Now look what you have done!' Lady Anais cried out in outraged tones.

'Will you whip her, Anais?'

'No, she will get enough of that tomorrow, I suspect, and I want to present her unmarked.'

Angela breathed a sigh of relief as she felt the ashtray and other glass lifted from her lower back.

'I shall have to simply spank her with the hairbrush instead!'

'All right, boy, turn around and put your hands on your head!'

Blushing furiously, Jem did as he was ordered, turning to face the housekeeper with a pounding heart.

He was not the only one who had stripped. Fisk was not completely naked as he was, however: she still wore a white girdle and long-line brassiere.

After seeing so many exotic sights, so many beautiful girls in fanciful costumes and erotic lingerie and corsetry over the last few weeks, Jem was surprised to find himself completely transfixed by the sight. Miss Fisk's body was voluptuous and showed signs of bulging from the elasticated underwear in places like the gap between the bottom of the brassiere and the top of the girdle. Meaty, creamy thigh flesh surged from the top of tan stockings that were tethered to the bottom of the girdle.

Miss Fisk had retained her horn-rimmed glasses and regarded him severely through these.

'What the hell do you think that you are looking at, boy?'

Jem could not have said. Perhaps it was the way the girdle evoked the advertisements that had fuelled his first masturbatory fantasises, or the way her mature but still fine body filled the underwear to the point that where was just a hint of strain. What was certain was that the hostile way she glared at him, and the severity of her tone, did nothing to reduce his state of arousal.

Miss Fisk left him standing in the middle of the room as she stalked over to the array of whips and canes. Unlike the bedroom, the floorboards were bare here, and the only sound was the rap of high heels against wood. She moved deliberately and slowly, as though with all the time in the world.

Jem watched with alarm as her hand went up to thoughtfully lift a multi-thonged whip. Then she dropped it and he breathed again, but only for a second. Miss Fisk next lingered over an array of vicious-looking canes. After a short eternity she moved on again. The crops were examined in turn, Miss Fisk touching several before moving onto a selection of tawse and straps.

So it was to be a belt, Jem thought, his bare bottom twitching in anticipation as she fingered her collection one by one. But it was not to be the belt either. Miss Fisk dropped the tawse that she had been fondling, and began to go back down the display again.

'Have you ever had the martinet, boy?' she asked as she reached the multi-thonged whips for the second time.

'No . . . ma'am,' Jem said hoarsely.

At least the little whip that she finally selected looked less vicious than many of those that hung on the wall. It was short, with a turned wooden handle of about a foot long and a dozen or so square-cut leather thongs of similar length.

'Well, then.' She turned and regarded him through her horn-rimmed glasses. 'High time that you were introduced to it! Will you need to be secured?'

'No ma'am!' Jem said, unable to take his eyes from the stiff-looking spray of thongs that swayed in response to her gestures.

'Very well,' Miss Fisk said crisply. 'Put yourself over the horse, with your legs apart!'

'Ow! Oh God! Have mercy, please!' Lady Lucinda heard her own voice begging as the crop cracked across her underbum once more.

She had sworn to herself that she would endure the flogging with icy stoicism. That beast Southdean might flog her body, but her dignity and pride were her own. She was Lady Lucinda Beaufort-Grey, not one of his sluttish servants, and she would show him how a real lady could behave!

This resolution had lasted fully to the second crop stroke. The first had been a vicious lash across the middle of her bottom, and Lucinda had found her breath taken away by the sheer intensity of the pain. The second seemed to set her voice free and she had let out a little squeal. By the third crop stroke her bottom felt as if it were on fire and she had begun to beg between the gasps of pain. It was unendurable; no one could bear such torments. Lucinda was now yelping like a scalded puppy and pleading pitifully.

Lord Randolph simply ignored her and kept whipping her bare bottom and upper thighs quite mercilessly. His only response to her cries, pleas and now frantic squirming as she tried vainly to escape the punishing crop was to chuckle now and then.

He was far too strong for her to escape his grip, seeming to hold her by the bound wrists almost easily, despite the violence of her struggling.

At last he desisted, letting go of her wrists and leaving her to collapse face down on the bed, sobbing pitifully.

'Good God, Lucy! Valencia told me that you were a tender-skinned little trollop, but I didn't realise quite how wet you were!' Randolph declared with a chuckle.

'I, ah, I'm not . . . ah . . . oh . . . wet . . .' Lucinda blubbered, her pride piqued even through the awful pain. 'You . . . hoo . . . must have skinned . . . me!'

Lord Randolph's only response to this pitiable lament was to laugh uproariously. Lucinda heard him walk to the wall and then return.

'Look, my brave beauty!' he ordered with a chuckle.

Still sobbing and gasping, Lucinda looked back over her shoulder. Lord Randolph held a big mirror in exactly the right position for her to see her own bare bottom and thighs.

There was no doubting that she had been whipped. The pale skin of her buttocks was criss-crossed by a score or more lines. These were, however, no more than a livid pink in colour. Blinking her tears away in amazement, Lady Lucinda stared. It could not be possible surely. From the evidence of her own rear, the flogging had been considerably less severe than those she regularly dished out to Jem and the maids. There had obviously been some sort of mistake.

'Well,' she said petulantly, between sniffs, 'it hurt more than it looks like!'

'I suppose that you feel more than the lower orders,' Lord Randolph said pensively. 'Being so well bred and tender fleshed, like the princess and the pea?'

'Yes, well,' Lucinda said, ignoring the last remark, 'of course the working classes do not feel as profoundly as . . . I . . . I mean *we* do.'

'Hmmm,' Lord Randolph said, putting the mirror down. 'So you feel more acutely than the lower classes, Lucy? I'm not sure that I can agree but I certainly hope that it is true.'

Lady Lucinda was still craning around to look over her shoulder. Once he had put the mirror on the floor, Lord Randolph began to unbutton his fly. Lucinda hurriedly looked away, but his last remark puzzled her.

'Why?' she asked in an uncertain voice.

'Because!'

She winced as she felt his hands take hold of her well-whipped flanks.

'I want you to feel it as profoundly as possible,' he continued in an amused voice. 'When I bugger you!'

'Well, then?' Lady Anais demanded.

Angela licked her full lips anxiously, uncertain what she was supposed to do. She wore only her stockings, now held up with elasticated garters, and long lace evening gloves, and she held the little hardwood hairbrush in front of her belly as she stood, trembling a little, in front of Lady Anais and Valencia.

'Sorry, Aunt Anais?' she mumbled when the silence became too oppressive.

'What do you say, girl?' Anais demanded.

'Um, ah, I don't know . . .' Angela said hanging her head, as if by doing so she could hide her glowing cheeks.

'Say, "please, Aunt Anais, would you spank me for being a promiscuous little slut?" '

Angela swallowed hard. She raised her eyes enough to dart a glance at Anais and then Valencia. She saw only amusement and malice, certainly not a grain of pity, in those eyes.

'Um, please . . . Aunt Anais,' she said in what was little more than a whisper. 'Will you . . . would you . . . spank me for being a . . .' At this point she had to pause and take a deep breath, her cheeks flaming. 'For, being a . . . a . . . promiscuous . . . little slut.'

'No dear, I'm sorry,' Lady Anais said crisply, 'but I am saving my strength for tomorrow night's delights. I'm sure that Valencia would oblige you though!'

'Of course,' Valencia said, grinning delightedly. 'Glad to be of assistance.' She slapped one of her meaty thighs so hard that a loud clap echoed around the room.

'Get yourself over my lap, sweetheart,' she said in a husky, eager voice, 'and I will see what I can do!'

'Ow!' Jem yelped as the martinet tails hissed through the air to lash his bare behind again.

'Oh, be quiet, you silly boy!' Miss Fisk snapped. 'You have barely had a dozen so far!'

The thongs cracked across his already scalded buttocks and, despite her orders, Jem let out another cry of pain.

'Please, miss,' he begged hoarsely, 'Oh, it stings so!'

'Well, of course, you stupid boy!' Miss Fisk said dryly. 'It is meant to sting. Wouldn't do you much good if it tickled, would it now?'

With that she lashed him so hard that he could not even cry out for a second. He felt as if his bottom had been seared by a blowtorch. The pain was so intense and sustained that it was a good minute before he realised that the flogging had stopped.

'Stand up and stop snivelling!' she ordered. 'Place your hands behind your head!'

Wincing, Jem did as he was ordered, hoping against hope that she had finished with the martinet. His bottom felt as if he had sat in a patch of nettles. Only slowly did the white fire cool, little by little, to a sort of dull hot throbbing.

They faced each other for a long moment. The girdled woman was looking flushed from her exertions as she eyed him through her horn-rimmed glasses with amusement. She still held the martinet, tapping the end of the handle against her chin thoughtfully.

'So Miss Dacourt prefers you shaven?' Miss Fisk asked with an evil grin, staring at his crotch.

'Yes, ma'am,' Jem managed.

He was not sure if his cheeks could get any redder, but he knew that they must be glowing like beacons by now.

'And what is that, exactly?' she asked slowly, pointing at his erect cock with the martinet.

'That, ah, um, it's my penis . . .' Jem mumbled, unsure what she was asking.

Miss Fisk stepped forward suddenly and gave a sort of flick with the martinet that caused the very tips of the leather thongs to crack across his erection. Jem let out a squeal of pain and doubled up, grabbing his cock in both hands.

'Stand up! I said hands behind your head!' Miss Fisk snapped.

Jem was not able to obey immediately which was something of a pity. The woman took another couple of steps. As he was still doubled up and had his hands over his dick, his already well-whipped bottom was quite unprotected.

She delivered a wicked stroke, right across the sorest part – the middle of his buttocks. Jem stood up again, arching his back away from the stroke, with a gasp of pain.

'I said, put your hands behind your head!'

Blinking back tears of pain, Jem saw her raise the martinet ready to lash his unprotected body once more. With a superhuman effort he made himself get back into position. Raising his hands to leave his cock exposed to her whip was one of the hardest things that he had ever done. The fact was that he simply did not dare to disobey her, and so somehow he stood up straight with his fingers interlocked behind his neck once more.

'Miss Dacourt has not trained you very well, has she?' Miss Fisk said with disdain. 'I must offer our facilities. Lord Southdean does not employ male staff but I am sure that he would allow a temporary exception. How would you like to spend a month here with me?'

Jem had no idea how to answer this question. At that moment in time it was perhaps the most terrifying proposition that he had ever heard. Fortunately, perhaps, she did not seem to expect an answer. Instead she stepped in closer to him.

'You are a very pretty boy, Jem,' she said licking her red lips with obvious relish. 'Do you know that?'

'Thank you ma'am,' Jem managed somehow.

Miss Fisk's face was now inches from his, her eyes bright through the horn-rimmed glasses. Suddenly she leaned forward and licked his cheek.

'Mmmm,' she said. 'Pretty boy's tears, how utterly delicious!'

Suddenly she grabbed him by the left ear, twisting it wickedly and then pulling it so that he had to follow her from the room into the bedchamber.

'That thing of yours looks like it is about to go off, and I say "waste not, want not!" ' Miss Fisk said with a laugh as she hauled him over to the bed. 'Lie on your back and get ready to be fucked, boy!'

She propelled him towards the bed, releasing his ear so that he could carry on towards it and encouraging him by giving his sore bottom a light crack with the martinet.

Jem did not need any more encouragement. He leapt on the bed, only too glad to place his scalded rear out of reach of the little whip's thongs, only concerned that his erect cock was still horribly vulnerable.

'Reach back and grab the bedstead!' Miss Fisk ordered, fingering the martinet as she spoke.

Jem dared not disobey. He uncovered his erection and grabbed hold of the bars of the brass bedstead behind his head.

To his indescribable relief, she did not raise the martinet to whip his cock or belly. Still holding it, Miss Fisk clambered onto the bed and got astride him. The girdle that she wore came down to the level of her pussy, and it was only a glimpse of bottom flesh when she had bent once that had told him that it was open below. The woman grabbed his cock. He winced for it was still very tender from the flick she had inflicted. She looked down at him with an imperious sneer. Her breasts, completely encased in the elasticised material of her long-line bra, seemed huge from this perspective. Her crimson lipstick and horn-rimmed glasses made her look both cruel and terrifying.

His eyes were transfixed by her predatory stare, so that he felt rather than saw her manoeuvre his cock into the hot and wet embrace of her pussy.

'Oh . . . my . . . God . . .!' Jem said as she lowered herself onto his rigid cock.

The sensation was so delicious that he almost fainted.

The back of the hairbrush smacked against Angela's bare bottom with an explosive crack. Angela tried, but failed, to stop a yelp of pain escaping as Valencia punished her bare bottom with pitiless efficiency. The innocent-looking hairbrush stung so much that Angela could not obey Lady Anais's orders to stay still. Instead she wriggled and squirmed on Valencia Dacourt's lap, in a vain effort to escape the rain of spanks.

'Ow! Ooh! Yow!' she yelped, as her bottom felt hotter and hotter.

'Be quiet, you silly girl!' Aunt Anais ordered in a bored voice. 'And do keep still!'

Still the punishing hairbrush cracked against her scorched bottom flesh with pitiless, metronomic regularity. The smacks did not increase in force but as the skin of Angela's rear became ever hotter and more tender, so the intensity of the pain ratcheted up and up until it was quite impossible to bear.

It was not long before she simply could not stand it any more. Pleas for a respite only brought chuckles from Lady Anais and Valencia and a sharp order from the former for Angela to hold her tongue.

Gasping, squealing, blinking away tears, Angela squirmed desperately on Valencia's lap as the back of the hairbrush punished every square inch of bottom flesh.

'Angela, you wicked girl, what do you think that you are you doing?' Lady Anais demanded in a shocked voice.

'Oh! Ah! Please, I can't . . . can't stand it! My . . . oh . . . ah . . . bottom is on fire!'

Angela put her hands back and tried to protect her scalded bottom. The respite was short-lived, however.

'The little minx! Sorry, Valencia, I though she was better trained than this!'

Lady Anais seized her wrists and pulled them forward. Now Angela had no way to protect herself at all.

'You know better than that, Angela!' She heard her aunt's voice through a red mist. 'You will have to pay for such undisciplined behaviour. Really give it to her now, Valencia. Teach her not to put her hands back when she is being punished. Teach that she really must obey!'

'This is going to be a rare treat!' Lord Randolph said with a chuckle. 'For you, my dear!'

Lady Lucinda watched his hand reach over to take the jar of Vaseline from the bed. There was the briefest of pauses as he unscrewed the cap. Then she gasped as his finger applied the cold petroleum jelly to her bottom hole.

'Easy, pet, easy.' Lord Randolph urged in a low growl.

Ignoring the whimpering sounds that she was making, he gently probed her anus with his finger. The touch was practised and assured. Unhurriedly he teased the ring of muscle into relaxation, until at last she felt something larger and rounded pressing up against her bottom hole.

'Just relax, sweetheart!' he said softly.

'Oh, please . . .' she began but then her words became a startled gurgle as he pressed his cockhead home.

'Shush, now!' Lord Randolph said, grabbing her by the flanks and forcing himself deeper.

Lucinda's eyes widened as much as her sphincter muscle as she felt his cock ease deeper into her. It felt so big that it should have hurt but, though she felt her anal ring was stretched beyond its natural limits, the combination of his fingering and the lubrication meant it slid in smoothly. Though her sphincter gripped his cockshaft in a tight embrace she did not feel any real pain.

'By God, girl, you bugger like butter!' Randolph declared between oaths as he forced himself even deeper into her.

Lady Lucinda said nothing. Indeed she could say nothing because she had bitten the bedspread in an attempt to stop herself from shrieking. As he inched in ever deeper it felt like nothing she had ever experienced or imagined. Half delirious with desire, half out of her mind from the strange sensation of impalement, Lucinda writhed slowly on the bed in response to his reaming.

Pain came when he had thrust his cock deep inside her. Randolph's bare belly bumped against Lucinda's freshly welted rear. He buggered her with slow, deliberate but unremitting force, and every time his belly rubbed against her raw-feeling buttocks another surge of heat suffused her rear.

'That's it! Squirm all you like now I am up you, my pretty little wriggler!' Lord Randolph said in a tenser, more excited-sounding voice. 'By God, Lucinda, your arsehole is tight! Jesus! It is gripping me like a bloody milking machine!'

This much was true, she knew, for as his body rubbed against the sore flesh of her bottom, so her anal sphincter contracted in response. The effect on Lord Randolph was obvious but alarming. Lucinda was half delirious with desire now, but her tied hands meant that she could not give herself relief. Though she was being buggered over the bed, her clitoris was in the wrong position to get any solid rubbing from the mattress. She tried to shift but Randolph held her, by his hands and cock, too tightly in position for her to move sufficiently.

'Oh, shit, you little bitch, I am going to come if you don't stop squirming!' Lord Randolph said between gasps.

Lucinda stopped biting the coverlet and let out a lost groan of desire and despair.

But the despair proved to be a trifle premature, for Lord Randolph released his grip on her right flank and reached around her belly until his fingers brushed her throbbing clit gently.

The sound that this provoked from Lucinda could not rightly have been called a moan, a scream or sigh. It was a long exhalation of desire and frustration. Randolph chuckled and rammed into her again, but did not take his hand away.

He only had to ream her bottom hole a few more times before Lucinda felt herself pass the point of no return. Now she screamed in earnest; screams of desperate ecstasy. Her climax seemed to trigger his because Lord Randolph let out a flurry of obscene oaths and rammed himself even harder into her. She felt something wet and hot hose deep into her vitals. Lady Lucinda let out a last abandoned shriek and collapsed on the bed.

* * *

'Ooh! Is it sore, petal?' Valencia asked in tones of mock sympathy.

'Oh, ah, yes . . . ooh!' Angela said in gasps.

She was still over Valencia's knee although Lady Anais had released her hands and she was no longer being spanked. This was a small mercy though because Valencia was examining her brushwork with a far from gentle hand.

'Her flesh is so hot you would think she had been sitting on a stove, Anais!' Valencia declared with a chuckle, as she pinched and squeezed the sore buttocks enthusiastically.

'These girls do tend to, don't they? I suppose she must be a hot-blooded little slut!' Lady Anais replied.

'I wonder if the spanking has taught her any manners?' Valencia said in an amused voice.

Angela's head, which had been raised in response to Valencia's attention to her bottom, hung as she heard this. She knew only too well what the woman would find if she explored between Angela's legs.

'Open your legs, girl! Let us see what is going on down there now!' Valencia ordered.

'Hopefully,' Lady Anais said in a bright, amused, voice, 'the punishment will have taught her to have more respect!'

Only the thought of the hairbrush, still waiting ready on a small side table, enabled Angela to obey and spread her legs wide open.

'Good God, Anais, look at this! The little tart is positively drooling!'

Both women laughed, but Angela could do nothing except hang her head in sheer humiliation. She knew that it was true. Even when she had been being spanked with the hairbrush she had not been able to ignore her own arousal. Not only could she feel the desperate tingle in her vitals, but she could even feel the wetness running down the insides of her legs. She wished that Valencia would stop taunting her above almost all else. However. there was one thing that she wished for even more desperately than that.

'Hot and wet and squirming like a live squid!' Valencia said with a chuckle, 'Are you sure you found this little tart in Birmingham, Anais?'

Angela gasped in delight as Valencia's fingers brushed against her sex lips. She wanted to beg for the fingers to be thrust deep inside her, but she simply did not dare. There was a sort of ache deep inside her vagina, as if it had a need to be filled; fingers, cock, the handle of the hairbrush. At that moment Angela was past caring. She just needed something.

'Please . . .' she heard her own voice desperately begging.

'What is it, sweetheart?' Valencia's voice mocked her. 'What is it that you need?'

'I, I, need . . . oh . . . ah!' Angela babbled as Valencia continued to caress her.

Then, to her unspeakable relief, Valencia slipped three fingers deep inside Angela's pussy. Even as the debutante squirmed with pleasure, the other woman slid her left hand under Angela's belly until fingertips brushed clitoris.

The combination was electric. Angela let out a loud shriek of delight and bucked in response. Valencia's fingers probed deeper into her copiously lubricated cunt. Lady Anais and Valencia both laughed at Angela's reaction, but she was too far gone to care now. Indeed the sound of laughter seemed so distant that she was barely aware of it. The fingers in her pussy and the fingers on her clit were the only things that mattered at that moment in Angela's universe. Then a great shudder wracked her perspiring, naked body and she was aware of nothing at all except her own orgasm.

'Come along, boy! Keep up!' Miss Fisk said briskly, though Jem thought he could detect a certain fondness in her voice now.

As she swept down the corridor imperiously, he hurried along in her wake, head still reeling from his experiences in her apartments. He had lain transfixed on the bed as she straddled him and fucked him steadily. As Miss Fisk had raised herself until only his glans remained inside her pussy, and then dropped herself right down on him again, Jem had merely lain, passive and pinioned by her weight as she rode him expertly.

The way she glared down at him imperiously through her horn-rimmed glasses had made him feel like something small and contemptible. Her full mature body constrained in its white elasticised brassiere and girdle set had mesmerised him as she pumped herself up and down on his rigid cock. Though by no means fat, her body was as substantial as her undergarments, and he had been fairly trapped on the bed by her not inconsiderable weight.

Her pussy had felt extraordinarily hot and slick as she pumped herself up and down on it, so welcoming, in stark contrast to her formidable expression as she sneered down at him from on high. The combination proved potent – before long he felt his balls twitch and he was soon spending his load.

Miss Fisk had come at almost at the same time. Her orgasm had been curiously controlled. The woman had simply spat out a mild oath and a little shudder had rippled through her body. Then she had closed her eyes for a moment and bitten her own knuckle.

He felt tired as he followed her up the back stairway. Too many days of sexual torment by Valencia, Lucinda and the maids, added to the long ride in the car boot, had taken their toll and Miss Fisk's ride had fairly finished him off. Jem longed for bed; his whole body ached for sleep. He might be young and vigorous, he thought as they headed down another corridor, but there were limits, and he had been running on empty for at least a week!

It was with some relief that he saw the dormitory door then. A little longer and he would be able to collapse into bed. Miss Fisk unlocked the door and winked at him.

'Sleep tight, boy! No messing around, you need your rest!'

She stood aside to let him enter the dormitory and Jem blinked at the scene before him. The room was full of girls. Mostly Asiatic-looking, each one was attractive and they all wore skimpy, baby doll nightdresses. Some were standing, brushing hair and chatting, others were already in bed, but every single one had stopped what she was doing and was now staring straight at Jem.

'All right, girls. Be gentle with him!' Miss Fisk said in amused voice.

Jem heard the door close and the key turn in the lock behind him. Some of the girls had begun to move towards him slowly.

'Hi,' he said in a voice that sounded tense and squeaky. 'Wow, I'm tired . . . I guess I'd better go . . . er, straight to bed!'

The passage between the two rows of beds that led to his own bunk was now completely blocked by wide-eyed girls in skimpy nighties. Those that had been in bed were getting out to join the others. A pretty Asian-looking girl stood directly in front of him, her arms folded across her chest.

'This is a girl's dormitory, we only allow men in here for one reason!' she said in an accent that he guessed was Japanese.

'I'm sorry, they put me here. Look, I'm really knackered. If I could just sleep I wouldn't bother you . . .' Jem said hopelessly.

The Japanese girl regarded him with eyes that were amused, but had no pity. Her smile was feline and held not a crumb of comfort.

'Get him girls!' she said.

From all sides the maids leapt towards him, whooping with glee.

Nine

'Do you think it's serious, Doctor Wilmot?' Valencia asked fretfully.

The portly man lifted his stethoscope from Jem's chest and took his wrist, feeling for his pulse.

Jem did not feel quite as weak as he had, but he let the doctor do his work without protest. The fainting fit had alarmed him almost as much as it had Miss Fisk and Valencia, who had sent for the doctor right away.

'He seemed perfectly all right last night,' Miss Fisk said, peering worriedly at him through her horn-rimmed glasses. 'At least when I left him!'

She shot a meaningful glance at Aiko, the maid who had raised the alarm and who awaited further orders in the dormitory, although the other maids had long since vanished about their duties.

Aiko coloured a little. As well she might, thought Jem. At least he thought it had been Aiko who had . . . it was hard to be sure. There had been so many of them and the night had been so long.

'Nothing more serious than nervous exhaustion,' the doctor said at last, releasing Jem's wrist. 'This is a fit young man but he has been overdoing it, I fear! He needs complete rest. I will prescribe a vitamin supplement, but rest is the main thing.' He looked from Miss Fisk, to Valencia, to Aiko with a rather cynical expression.

'Perhaps if a room of his own could be found?'

Only Aiko had the grace to blush.

'Oh yes, I'm sure that could be arranged,' Miss Fisk said smoothly.

'Er how long . . .?' Valencia began.

'I suggest that he has complete rest for a couple of days and abstains from . . . sexual activity for at least a week.'

'A *week*?' Valencia said in an outraged shriek.

Everyone in the room looked at her.

'I mean, he has certain . . . duties . . .' Her voice tailed off and she shrugged defeatedly.

'Thank you, Doctor,' Miss Fisk said, 'We rely on your discretion as always. Would you like to make use of the facilities while you are here?'

Doctor Wilmot licked his plump lips and darted a furtive glance towards the maid.

'Um, well, if it is convenient . . .' he said.

'Of course, Doctor. Aiko will be happy to attend to your needs.'

There was something velvety about the utter blackness that even the pervasive smell of leather could not quite dispel.

When being transported in the car, Lady Lucinda's hands had been secured behind her. This had ensured a certain level of discomfort which had been anti-soporific. This time, however, Lucinda's hands had been pinioned to the front of her leather collar. The great leather sheath she had been zipped into prevented almost any movement, but there was nothing uncomfortable about her situation. Indeed the bag had been placed upon the bed. So this time the darkness and restriction and complete lack of external stimulation made it strangely hard for her to tell if she were asleep or awake.

There was another reason. Her mind was full of the memory of being buggered by Lord Randolph. Or was it that she was dreaming fevered dreams of being violated by him? Whether awake or asleep, the feeling of his cock reaming her bottom hole was so vivid that it seemed almost to be happening again as she lay in her hot black leather cocoon.

Suddenly, without warning, the zip was hauled down and there was an explosion of light. Lady Lucinda blinked blindly for a few moments until her eyes adjusted enough to register the sight of Valencia, glaring down at her.

Valencia wore a lacy black brassiere and a matching suspender belt with sheer black stockings, but not a thing otherwise and her neat triangle of black pussy fur was the nearest part of her body to Lucinda's head.

'Jem is confined to quarters, doctor's orders,' Valencia said disgustedly. 'Those witches Randolph calls maids have sucked the poor little bugger dry. No fucking for a week, apparently. Can you believe it?'

Having seen what Jem had been put through at Valencia's, and knowing what she had put the pageboy through herself, Lady Lucinda could believe it all too easily, but she said nothing, as Valencia did not seem in the mood for an argument.

'Anyway,' Valencia continued, 'I am too horny to wait for this evening so your tongue is going to have to do instead!'

'There now!' Lady Anais said. 'You look lovely, Angela! Good enough to eat!'

The costume for Randolph's ball had proved simplicity itself. Angela had been bathed by one of the oriental maids, and her sex had been deftly shaven again. She had been made up and her hair carefully arranged, then dressed in long, extremely sheer black silk stockings, gartered high on her thighs, and shoulder-length, fingerless black lace gloves. High-heeled court shoes and a simple black leather collar had completed the outfit.

'The dance card!' Lady Anais said after perusing Angela for a moment.

The fine gold chain of the little book was placed around Angela's neck and the cold metallic cover of the little book brushed her skin between her breasts.

'Almost ready!' Lady Anais said walking over to the dresser where a selection of masks had been set out. She perused these thoughtfully.

Lady Anais was resplendent in a full-length ball gown of royal blue silk with matching evening gloves. She chose a mask in the same blue and black for herself, and then paused before taking up a delicate creation of black lacework, that would only half veil the upper part of Angela's face. The maid took this from Lady Anais and put it on Angela with care.

Now that she realised her full costume for the evening was complete, Angela felt terribly naked, but Anais's hairbrush was in sight, on the dressing table, and she managed to keep her hands by her side and not try to cover her newly shaven pussy.

It seemed that she scarcely needed to have bothered. Lady Anais produced a pair of handcuffs and instructed Angela to put her hands behind her back.

'You know the form by now, you must keep your hands high!' Lady Anais said as she clicked the handcuffs around Angela's wrists. 'You must leave all of your bottom uncovered so that the company can see what a peach it is. Do not forget!'

'No, Aunt Anais,' Angela said, a little thickly.

Now she could not hide her shaven sex if she wanted to. It was not the company that she was concerned about however, as Lady Anais clipped a dog's leash to her collar and gave it a tug, compelling Angela to follow her to the door. No, there was one man on Angela's mind as she teetered precariously on her six-inch heels along the corridor. The man whose name was in the little book that hung between her breasts.

'My God, but this year's crop is the finest I have ever seen!' Lord Randolph said quietly.

Valencia took a sip of champagne and inclined her head.

'The fresh meat is certainly rather sweet,' she said with a chuckle.

They were in the Rose Room, a very large drawing room, the centre of which had been cleared of furniture. The debutantes and their sponsors had all come down from their rooms now and a dozen girls, each one naked but for stockings, long gloves and masks were being walked up and down to the accompaniment of music; the same chamber orchestra that Valencia had employed for her ball, having been brought down to play.

'Hard cheese, Sir Angus!' Randolph said in a low voice to Valencia.

The kilted man had stopped to chat with Lady Anais and Angela. Predictably, Sir Angus's fat fingers reached up for Angela's dance card. He frowned on reading that she was already booked and glowered over at Randolph, who raised his champagne glass in an ironic salute.

'You beast, Randolph,' Valencia said with a chuckle. 'Are you ogling the flesh on display, as is quite proper, or simply gloating about having booked that little tart for tonight's fun and games?'

'Why, both, of course!' Lord Randolph a said with a grin.

The general stopped to talk to Lady Anais, and naturally his hand went up to Angela's dance card almost immediately. The old soldier turned and glared at Randolph.

Lord Randolph raised his glass again.

The key turning in the lock woke Jem. It was Miss Fisk, carrying a tray of food.

'There now. You have had a good sleep. Feeling a bit better?'

Jem's dreams had been fevered ones involving being pinned down by a mass of half-naked maids, but at least it had been sleep. He blinked a few times and then cautiously nodded his head.

She was wearing a tweed skirt and matching jacket, with a white blouse that had a ruffled front. With the usual horn-rimmed glasses this gave her even more of a headmistressy look than usual. Jem felt his cock begin to stir.

'Good, well, here is some chicken broth. I can't stay long because it is a busy night, and those maids are a bunch of lazy trollops. Eat it up!'

Jem expected her to go but she did not. He was ravenous, however, so he made short work of the chicken soup and bread, and gratefully drank the fresh orange juice that came with it.

He could feel Miss Fisk staring at him all the time. When he finished she moved the tray and sat on the side of his single bed.

'Give me your hand!'

He obeyed, expecting her to feel his pulse but, instead, she placed his hand between her thighs, pushing back her tweed skirt as she did so.

'Please . . . I need . . .' Jem mumbled in confusion.

'Oh, I know what you need, boy!' Miss Fisk said with an ominous laugh.

She pushed his hand up past the top of her stockings, clamping his fingers between her meaty thighs. Jem felt his cock responding and a sort of tired ache in his balls.

'Your mistress says that she will send you to stay with us when she goes to Paris,' Miss Fisk said, her eyes bright behind the horn-rimmed glasses. 'Six whole weeks! We will work you hard, mind. No slacking, night or day. The maids will be quite excited, I should think. I generally let them spank any new staff, but as you are a boy I think I shall give them leave to cane you until you learn your place . . .'

Whatever the intention of these threats was, the effect was to make Jem's cock stiffen in response to the awful prospect. Suddenly, Miss Fisk released his trapped hand and whisked back the bedclothes. Jem had been given a pyjama top to wear but no sort of bottom, and so his erection was exposed to the housekeeper's glare.

'What's this? You bad boy! You are supposed to be resting!' she said in an outraged voice.

Jem covered his cock with his hands. 'I'm sorry,' he mumbled. 'It was your . . . I mean you . . .'

'Don't blame me, you dirty boy. Well, it was a good thing that I came to check on you, isn't it? No doubt if I had not you would have been masturbating as soon as I was out of the door!'

'No,' Jem said with a groan. 'Honestly, miss . . .'

In truth nothing had been further from his thoughts. His balls ached dreadfully and his cock felt even more raw than before. Jem's sole desire at that moment was rest and a break from the molestation of malevolent women, even if some parts of his body seemed to have their own ideas.

Miss Fisk ignored his protests, however. She went to a chest of drawers in the little room and brought out some straps attached to chains. One of these proved to be a collar, which was soon secured around his neck.

Jem thought of protesting but the memory of being held down by the maids made him realise that it was futile. Wrist cuffs followed and these were fixed by a short chain to a D-ring in the front of the collar. A slightly longer chain secured Jem to the bedstead.

Now that he was helpless, she pulled the bedclothes over him and winked.

'That will stop you wanking away, you wicked boy! I shall send one of the girls in to see to you later. Just try and get some rest!'

She would never get used to this, thought Lucinda as she walked slowly around the room. Naked, other than black stockings supported by a lacy maroon suspender belt and long satin evening gloves in the same colour, her hands cuffed behind her back and trailing the maid who held her leash, she felt a dozen eyes caress her body.

Looking up she saw Lady Wallingford approaching with Anastasia on her chain. The usual form was for the trainers to stop and exchange pleasantries, but as Valencia had relinquished Lucinda's leash to the maid, the dowager simply raised a finger in a gesture.

Bunko stopped and simply waited as Lady Wallingford looked Lucinda up and down.

'Lucinda, dear, how are you? Enjoying your season, dear?'

Lady Lucinda had no idea how to reply to this and so simply stayed silent, hanging her head a little.

'Dear me, gels today have no manners. I asked you a question, dear!'

Lady Wallingford's evening gloves, though full length, were made of fine black leather. She raised a hand to one of Lucinda's nipples and tweaked it thoughtfully.

'Um . . . well, considering that it's not really my kind of thing . . . Ow!' she said as the nipple was twisted suddenly.

'Nonsense, gel,' Lady Wallingford said, releasing the nipple and dropping her hand to Lucinda's pussy.

The blonde girl bit back a startled gasp as the gloved hand probed her cunt lips. The older woman's bright eyes stared into Lucinda's from about six inches distance, and she felt herself colour, for she knew what the probing finger had found.

'Not your kind of thing, eh, sweetie?' Lady Wallingford said with a smirk, withdrawing her finger and raising it until it was just below Lucinda's nose.

The black leather tip of Lady Wallingford's gloved finger glistened with something wet and sticky. Lucinda felt a wave of pure humiliation wash right through her. She looked away.

'I think you are enjoying yourself a lot more than you care to admit, young lady!' the older woman said with palpable relish.

'I'm not, I'm not!' Lady Lucinda insisted, quite unable to stop herself from blushing.

'I think that someone is protesting just a little too much!' Lady Wallingford said smugly. 'Now, I don't want your cunt juice on my gloves, girl, so you had better suck it off!'

Waiting, Angela had found, was always the hardest. She still did not find being paraded naked, in public, easy to endure. Still, if she was honest with herself, there was a sort of hot excitement even keener than the shame she had endured, and intimately bound up with it.

Being leered at and pawed by people like General Hollis and Sir Angus had been hard, but at least she knew that she was protected from their lust by the dance card that dangled like a magic amulet about her neck.

When the parade was over the girls were taken to their partners' separate rooms. Only on the journey up to Randolph's private chambers did the price of that protection really dawn on her. Suddenly Angela felt less sanguine about the coming evening as the maid led her into his room.

Still handcuffed, she had simply been tethered by her leash to the four-poster bed. The maid had given her a contemptuous, perhaps resentful, look and left without a word.

Then there had been nothing to do but stand and wait. At first Angela had looked around the room anxiously. Randolph's bedchamber exuded age, dark wooden panels lining the walls. Although it was warm a log fire blazed away in the grate. The four-poster bed was venerable and there was a massive chest of drawers on one side and a large oaken chest under the casement window.

And that was pretty much that. Though she looked around with anxious eyes, Angela did not espy any whips laid out ready on the bed or bondage equipment waiting on the chest of drawers. The room was strangely plain and free of clutter.

In fact, after the first few minutes, Angela found herself listening more than looking. The door to the room was solid, yet some sounds came through it from the corridor from time to time: the sound of a hand smacking flesh, a girlish cry of pain, guttural laughter, high heels clacking on parquet flooring, the rattling of chains, a heavy man's footfall on the floor.

Angela strained her ears anxiously every time she heard something in the corridor. Her eyes became fixed on the door handle, waiting to see it turn. Little by little the tension built up until anxiety became something akin to terror. Then she heard deliberate heavy footsteps from the corridor.

They were approaching, she was sure of it. He was coming down the corridor to claim his prize. Goose bumps erupted on her flawless skin and the hairs on the back of her neck stood up stiffly as she listened to the footsteps pause beyond the door.

For a moment she stopped breathing completely. Angela's eyes were locked onto the door handle as if mesmerised. She would have swallowed but she did not have enough saliva, so she made a strange dry gulping sort of sound. Then she heard the footsteps move on down the hall, and let out a long sigh of relief.

'Why so tense?' Lord Randolph's voice came from behind her.

The shock was so great that Angela let out a startled shriek and felt her knees go weak. Randolph simply chuckled as he walked over to her.

'Sorry to keep you waiting, sweetheart, that is the worst of playing host. Had to make sure that all the guests had all the toys they needed.'

He produced a blindfold from his pocket and quickly and deftly tied it around her eyes. Angela could now see nothing. There must have been a secret passage, its entrance concealed in the panelling, she realised as she felt him free the leash and tug it. Angela followed him, her high heels quiet on soft carpet and then clacking on something that sounded like stone. There was the slightest sound, which she guessed was the secret entrance closing and then she was following the tugging of the leash down the secret corridor.

* * *

'Phew, it is quite a night, tonight! Things are getting pretty wild out there! I'm Babs, by the way! Old Fisk thought that you might be getting hungry!'

Unusually for Lord Randolph's staff, the maid was European in appearance and English of accent, with a shock of wild blonde curls. She wore a uniform consisting of a tiny satin skirt, buoyed up on frilly petticoats and which was far too short to cover her black stocking tops. Above the waist she wore a maid's cap, a leather collar, wrist bands and nothing else. Her breasts were full and pink and round with delicate little nipples and it seemed that they had been whipped for there were fine red lines criss-crossing them.

Jem eyed this vision with suspicion that bordered on outright hostility.

'Look what that pig, Sir Angus, did to my poor tits!' she exclaimed, putting down the tray of food and drink on the bedside cabinet and cupping her breasts in her hands. She pouted as she proffered them, sitting on the bed and twisting so that her titties were pointed towards Jem. 'Sadistic beast! Would you like to kiss them better?'

'No!' Jem grunted.

'Oh, go on, don't be so rotten. You can lick them too if you would like.'

'I would not like! I am supposed to be resting!'

The familiar deep ache of overworked balls was growing.

'Well, it's not such hard work, is it? Just to kiss a pair of tits?'

She moved so that she was lying on her side, facing him, her breasts just inches from his face. Then she pulled the bedclothes down until his legs were partially uncovered. A nylon-sheathed leg began to draw itself up Jem's thigh as she pushed her titties right into his face. Chained as he was, all he could do was turn his face away, but he found even this impossible. It was as if the girl's plump, freshly whipped breasts held him enthralled.

Then she pushed her titties into his face. A moment later her stocking-sheathed knee rubbed against his cock.

'What's this?' the maid said with a liquid chuckle.

He felt Babs's fingers encircle his cock and groaned.

'Naughty boy!' she said. 'I thought you said that you were supposed to be resting!'

For all Jem's exhaustion, the maid's teasing had been extraordinarily effective. His cock was now quite rigid and, despite the dull ache in his balls, Jem found himself groaning with frustration as she rolled off the bed and went back to the tray.

'Sit up as much as you can, sweetie!' Babs said with a cheeky grin as she returned to his side bearing a plate of ready-opened oysters. 'Babs is going to feed the bad baby!'

'Damn me, but you are a pretty little chit, Lucinda!' General Hollis said thoughtfully. 'Could do with a bit more meat on your bones, but you will do for a starter. What?'

He let out a barking laugh that made Lady Lucinda grind her teeth in fury. There was not much she could do about his exploring hands as she was tethered by her leash to his solid four-poster, and her hands were still securely cuffed behind her back.

'Proud little thing, they say. Don't you like being a debutante, my pretty?'

'Of course not!' she spat out. 'Who would enjoy being pawed by . . .' Lucinda stopped herself at the last moment.

'By . . .?' the general said with a chuckle. 'You would not have been going to say by a fine old soldier, would you, m'dear?'

If Lucinda had been going to reply, his fingers reaching her shaven pussy at that moment would have stopped her. She bit her lip to stop herself from letting out a different sort of moan.

'And yet, you really do seem to be dripping. What is it that gets your juices running like this, little Lucy? Is it the caresses, or the humiliation? Or might it be the pain?'

Lucinda chewed her lip as he explored her with surprisingly deft fingers. One hand delved into her hot and now sopping vagina, the other probed her bottom hole.

'Southdean told me that he buggered you last night, girl!' General Hollis said in a low growl. 'Told me you were as tight as a brand new drummer boy! What! Have to try it, what!' The general barked with laughter once again and tears of sheer humiliation began to trickle down Lady Lucinda Beaufort-Grey's beautiful face.

The air was still and pleasantly cool, yet not so cold as to explain the goose bumps that had bloomed on Angela's flesh. They had gone down a winding staircase, stone to judge from the sound of her heels on the steps, Lord Randolph steadying her by holding her elbow.

Then they had gone on. Twice they had stopped and Angela had heard the rattle of a key in a lock. They seemed to have walked miles.

'They say that the first Marquis was a member of the Hellfire Club!' Randolph whispered in her ear. 'And had this place built to entertain his guests!'

The blindfold was whipped away and Angela found herself blinking, though the light was subdued in the dungeon. What she saw made her belly tighten in fear.

'It was probably just a fancy wine cellar, really. But they must have drunk a lot because there is plenty of space for laying down in the cellar beneath the other wing,' Randolph continued conversationally. 'Whatever it was originally for, I have had it kitted out . . . comfortably.'

They were in a cellar, but like no cellar she had ever seen or imagined. It was huge, stretching away in all directions, its dimensions lost by the gloom. Only directly in front was any wall visible. The ceiling was high and vaulted and there were many brick columns supporting the ceiling. Angela and Randolph were standing in the middle of a space almost like the nave of a church. A row of columns marched on either side of them, over twenty feet apart and the distance to the wall they faced was twice that at least. This hall-like space was well lit, but beyond the columns there was gloom. Ominous shapes, suggesting things like racks and cages could just be discerned in the gloom beyond.

The wall that they faced was bare brick and furnished only with black iron manacles and chains. It had a coarse brutality that made Angela go weak at the knees.

'You expected more opulence, perhaps?' Randolph took hold of her elbow and walked her towards the wall. 'Something with lots of leather, or perhaps guttering torchlight?'

Angela felt his hand placed in the small of her back, gently pushing her towards the wall. She did not know what to say.

'I thought about it long and hard, but in the end I believe that there is a lot to be said for functionality. The brickwork is of marvellous quality, so why hide it?'

She felt him unlock the handcuffs but she was only unshackled for a moment. Lord Randolph locked the hanging manacles around her wrists in turn. Then he knelt and took her left ankle, snapping an iron band around that too.

Panic mounted in her belly as he fastened a second iron manacle around her right ankle. The chains that were secured to the wrist and ankle bands were loose and clanked woefully in the stillness of the cellar, as she moved.

Once he was happy that the manacles were all padlocked securely into place, Lord Randolph walked to one side. His back was to her and she could not see what he was doing, though he seemed to bend a little. Then there was a clanking noise and the chains fixed to her wristbands began to tighten as he worked some sort of winch.

To Angela's alarm, she found her arms pulled out in opposite directions, as well as upwards.

'Oh, please . . .' she begged as the chains really began to tug her arms.

Randolph paused, turned and looked critically at her.

'Another inch or so I reckon should do it,' he said dryly, and worked the winch a little more.

Had Angela not been wearing six-inch heels, then she would most certainly have been forced onto tiptoe by now. Her breasts were forced against the cold brickwork, and she only kept her belly off it by an effort. Then there was another rattle and the chain holding her left ankle began to shorten.

'No, please . . . it's too . . .' She began to babble in a state not far off panic.

'Be silent, you silly trollop!' Randolph said.

Once her ankle had been pulled out some way he stood and walked past her, giving her naked bottom a friendly pat along the way. Then he began winding a third small winch, forcing her right ankle towards him.

Angela let out a helpless wail. Now her body was stretched in a 'Maltese cross', so tight that the tips of her heels no longer touched the floor; only the balls of her feet had any contact with the ground. Her belly pressed the cold bricks too now. She simply could not move an inch in any direction, other than to crane her head around to try and see what her tormentor was doing. Lord Randolph, however, seemed to have disappeared.

'No more . . .' Jem moaned and struggled against the chains that bound him.

He blinked. It was dark and he was on his own. It had been a dream, he realised with relief. The sheets were soaked with his sweat and his cock was almost painfully rigid, but otherwise things were quite different to the dream.

He had been surrounded by half-naked girls, each one trying to force-feed him oysters while several hands fought over his erection. Jem groaned. The aching in his balls was easing but now he was getting terribly frustrated. The wristbands and chains were secure though and there seemed to be no way to give himself relief.

There was a rattle in the lock and the door opened. An oriental-looking girl dressed in a white nurses's uniform came in. She smiled and switched the light on. Cherry-red lipstick emphasised her full lips.

'Hello, my name is Yuki,' she said with a little giggle.

'Are you . . . a nurse?' Jem said.

Her uniform seemed rather tight and her skirt surprisingly short, and so he was not too surprised by her reply.

'Oh yes. Can't you tell by my nurse uniform?' She gave him an idiotic smile and performed a little pirouette. For the first time he realised that she was wearing six-inch stiletto heels. Jem closed his eyes and groaned.

'Have you ever been whipped?' Randolph's voice came out of the gloom.

Angela let out a little startled yelp.

'I mean really whipped, not tickled with a riding crop or flogger?'

He seemed to be awaiting a reply so Angela swallowed.

'No . . . sir . . .' she said in a hoarse little voice.

'Oh, good,' he said in a languid drawl. 'I do like to be able to introduce my guests to new experiences.'

As if for punctuation there was an explosive crack! Angela was so startled that she let out a squeal.

'This is a fine one. Kangaroo hide, Australian of course. It is a signal whip, actually, not a full-sized bullwhip. I don't wish to flay you . . . quite!'

He chuckled, and the sound of his laughter in that chamber was the most alarming thing that Angela had ever heard. There was nothing she could do, however, chained, stretched in an X, naked except for her flimsy lace gloves and sheer silk stockings. Her whole body trembled in anticipation of the lash.

Footsteps, slow and deliberate, were coming towards her. Angela closed her eyes and made a supreme effort not to beg for mercy. She gasped in surprise as she felt his hand stroking her bottom.

'Jesus Christ, you have a lovely arse, Angela!' Lord Randolph said in a low growl. 'It was as if you had been made especially for flogging!'

Then she felt something cold against her face. Squinting sideways she could see the coils of tan, finely plaited leather. To her terrified eyes the whip looked like a particularly malevolent snake.

'A truly beautiful back too. Such a pity that Rodin did not have you as a model!'

She felt him plant a kiss between her shoulder blades.

'It seems almost a crime to mar such sweet perfection,' he said in a thoughtful voice. 'But then, it would be a worse crime not to whip a body that so cries out for it!'

There was the sound of footsteps as he walked back a few paces and then stopped. Angela screwed her eyes shut tight and completely forgot to breathe.

She heard the whistle of the whip cutting through the still air of the dungeon just a split second before it cracked across her back. A line of fire was scored across it from her right shoulder to the left side of her waist. The pain was so intense that Angela found herself fighting the bonds that held her desperately.

The second stroke was not long in coming. This time he lashed her diagonally the other way, from her right shoulder down across her back. Another stripe of white fire burned atrociously across her back. It was too much. It was impossible to bear. Angela opened her mouth this time and shrieked.

The whip whistled through the air and cracked across her back again and again. The sound of leather lash impacting on tender flesh echoed around the vaulted chamber, mingling with the sound of her increasingly shrill screams.

Lord Randolph did not neglect her bottom. His whip lashed her naked body from her shoulders to just above the backs of her knees. Only the small of her back was spared the vicious sting. Angela shrieked and squealed until she was hoarse. She squirmed and writhed like something possessed against her unyielding bonds and ground herself into the unyielding brickwork, as if by doing so she could, somehow, burrow into the wall and escape the merciless whip.

Angela could not have said how many strokes he laid across her tender back and bottom. After the first dozen she was lost in an inferno of pain. She heard a girl's voice pleading for mercy and the punishing crack of leather on soft flesh, but otherwise all she was aware of were the lines of fire, scored across her own tender skin.

Yuki pulled a cream-coloured latex glove onto her hand with a thoughtful expression. Then she repeated the process with the other hand.

'See, Mr Jem!' she said gleefully, holding her gloved hands up at either side of her face and waggling her fingers. 'All very hygienic!'

She picked up a large rectal thermometer from the kidney bowl on the tray she had brought in. Jem eyed it with alarm as she stepped forward. With a free hand she reached forwards and yanked the bedclothes back.

'*Mr Jem*!' she said reproachfully, staring at his erection. 'No naughty thoughts for you, please!' She waggled the thermometer in admonishment. 'Resting! Resting! Now, turn round for me, please!'

Jem looked at the girl. Her plump, voluptuous body was displayed by the crisp white uniform that seemed to him to be at least two sizes too small for her. The skirt was just short enough for him to see the welts at the top of her white stockings. Although he could not see the bare thigh flesh above her stocking tops, the welts put the image in his mind. His cock twitched in response to the image and Jem groaned.

'Turn round, Mr Naughty Patient!' Yuki ordered, frowning.

Jem sighed and did as she had ordered, his tether chain rattling as he turned.

'Very nice bottom!' she said solemnly.

Jem grimaced as he felt the cold thermometer probe his anus. As it slid in he could not quite suppress a little moan. Exhausted or not he needed relief now.

'Please,' he said desperately, 'can't you just give me a hand job?'

'Bad, Mr Jem! Naughty Mr Jem!' Yuki said in tones of outrage so insincere that he was surprised she did not giggle.

The thermometer was pushed a little deeper. Jem sighed and closed his eyes. Then something grabbed the shaft of his cock. He stared down; one of Yuki's latex-gloved hands had taken hold of him and began, gently, to frig him.

'Oh, God, yes, for . . . please, don't stop,' he said between groans.

'Nurses not supposed to give hand jobs,' Yuki whispered into his ear as she frigged him. 'You want, you have to pay!'

'Oh that feels so good . . .' he murmured. 'Sure, anything you want, just don't stop . . . ooh . . . just a little harder, that's it . . .'

The gentle but firm touch of Yuki's latex-encased fingers was strange yet extraordinarily delicious. He was going to come any second, he could feel it.

Then he heard the door of the room suddenly open.

'Yuki! Jem! What the devil is going on here?'

They both froze, Yuki's hand coming to a stop in mid frig in response to Miss Fisk's voice. Then the girl released him and got off the bed.

'I was . . . I thought I better look after the patient . . .' Yuki said weakly.

'By dressing up in that uniform and wanking him off, you little slut?' Miss Fisk bellowed. 'You know as well as I do that that uniform is just for dressing up! If you are a nurse then I am a fucking nun!'

'Easy, sweetheart, easy!' Lord Randolph said softly in Angela's ear.

The lines of fire scoring her back, buttocks and thighs still burned, but it was a warm glow now, only flaring up as his hands travelled over her naked body. Angela sobbed, flinching and trembling from his touch. Her nipples had engorged and, unnoticed during the whipping itself, she had rubbed them almost raw against the brickwork as she had vainly tried to escape the lash. Now she felt them throbbing, as she felt an almost unbearable tingling in her loins.

'There now!'

Lord Randolph's hand stroked her welted bottom. He ignored the gasps of pain this drew from his prisoner. Then he slipped his hand between her legs. Angela moaned as his fingers probed her.

'Well, now,' he said in her ear, his voice a little crisper. 'That whipping seems to have warmed you up, you perverse little slut. You are sopping wet, you know that, my pretty debutante?'

Angela did not answer, she simply bit her lip to stop herself from moaning as his fingers explored her lower lips and slid inside her.

'Would you like me to fuck you, you little tart?' Lord Randolph growled into her ear.

Angela simply sobbed in response. His hand kept probing and she winced as he pressed his body up against her welted bottom. She could feel something stiff and hard under his trousers.

'You are going to have to ask nicely, you know,' he said and chuckled softly.

Lord Randolph brought his other hand around and began squeezing her breast. His erection was now pressed against the furrow of her bottom and his right hand had withdrawn enough for his palm to rub gently against her clitoris. Now she could not help but moan. The lines of fire on her back seemed to have ignited a slow burning in her loins.

'Well?' Lord Randolph pressed his case. 'Do you want me to fuck you, you well-whipped little bitch?'

'Yes!' she said at last, with a desperate sob.

'Well, then, you must beg,' he said with satisfaction.

Lord Randolph withdrew his fingers from her pussy altogether and ran his hand gently up her belly. Then he let his fingertips dance down, stopping just above her clitoris. They were so tantalisingly near and yet not near enough. His teasing fingers were driving her quite out of her mind.

'Oh, please, please . . . fuck me, please . . . ooh, just a little lower . . .'

'Please, *master*!'

'Please, master, sir, oh, anything, please fuck me, master, I can't bear it.' Angela heard her own voice beg in utter desperation.

There was a triumphant chuckle in her ear and the tickling hand was withdrawn, though his left hand continued to play with her throbbing nipple. Then she felt his cock, freed from his flies, pressing against her bottom furrow and she realised that he was going to fuck her, still stretched out for the whipping as she was.

'You don't mind if we do not go to bed, do you, my dear?' he asked smoothly, confirming her suspicion.

'Oh, God, sir, please, just do it . . .' she said with a sob of sheer frustration.

Angela felt his cockhead nuzzling her sex lips. There was a moment of pressure, a sharp pang of pain, and then he was inside her.

'Take it off!' Miss Fisk said simply.

'Please, miss?' Yuki said, blinking at her.

'Get the uniform off, Yuki! I'm going to thrash you!'

The Japanese girl's eyes widened in alarm.

'Oh please, miss! He was poorly. I only wanted to . . .'

'Enough of your nonsense, girl, unless you want your punishment doubled. Take off that silly uniform *this minute* and then go and get me one of the canes from the wardrobe.

Jem did not wonder that Yuki did not argue further for there was something in Miss Fisk's voice, a note of real impatience, that he would not have liked to contradict either. Yuki hurriedly climbed out of the nurse's uniform, revealing a white lace basque and frilly knickers.

Once she had put the uniform over the back of an upright chair she went, with several reluctant, beseeching glances back at Miss Fisk, to the wardrobe. Inside this at the back were half a dozen canes. Yuki prevaricated as if unable to choose between them.

'Oh, for God's sake, girl, just pick one. They are all going to hurt, let me assure you!' Miss Fisk expostulated.

Yuki grabbed a cane and came back with hesitant steps. She did not seem to be looking forward to her fate, Jem thought with a certain satisfaction, whatever game she had been playing.

'Present it properly!' Miss Fisk ordered.

Yuki got down on her knees. She bent her pretty head and stretched out her arms, the cane balanced on her outstretched palms before her.

'Well, girl, what do you say?'

'Please, miss, punish me for my wickedness,' Yuki said in a slightly hoarse, anxious-sounding whisper.

'Very well, since you ask so nicely!' Miss Fisk said, taking the proffered cane. 'Stand up. Bend over the end of the bed, and drop your knickers.'

Jem, whose arousal and frustration had not been helped one iota by witnessing the humiliation of Yuki, felt an odd mixture of relief and disappointment. As Yuki dropped her frilly panties and bent over the iron work at the bottom of the bed, he realised that he would only really see her face during the caning.

Or almost. Yuki's breasts were full and plump and fairly bursting from the lace cups of the basque. Bending towards him as she was they looked as if they were about to fall out of their lace constraints altogether. He could also see her neatly trimmed pubic fur, and her lovely face which was now a poem of anxiety and apprehension.

Miss Fisk took up position behind Yuki. Jem swallowed as he watched the cane go up and back and pause. Then his eyes met Yuki's fear-glazed orbs and the world seemed to stop for a few seconds.

The cane made a low whooshing sound as it cut through the air. Then there was a thwacking sound so loud that Jem's bottom clenched in sympathy. Yuki's face was instantly contorted with pain. Her hands grabbed the blankets and squeezed until her knuckles had gone white, but she did not let a sound escape her lips.

As well as his bottom flinching in response, Jem felt his cock twitch, eager as a setter. He was still desperately frustrated, and now he realised that watching Yuki's face during her caning was going to be every bit as exciting as watching Miss Fisk line the girl's inviting bottom would have been.

The housekeeper raised the cane again. Again the world just stopped for a moment. Then there was a yellow blur, a whoosh and the thwack of rattan on soft skin. Yuki's face creased with pain and Jem's cock twitched in involuntary response.

He groaned and closed his eyes. When the next stroke cut through the air, although he did not see it, he heard its ominous whistle. He simply could not resist the urge to open them again, and did so, just in time to see Yuki open up her plump lips to let out a shrill squeal of pain.

'Oh, please . . . don't stop!' Angela cried as Lord Randolph's cock slid deep inside her.

Both his hands palped her breasts now, so that her nipples were cushioned by his palms, but as he rammed his belly up against her well-whipped bottom, he crushed her stomach hard against the cold brick wall.

It was as if the lines of fire that his whip had inscribed across her back had been a fuse that lit her whole body. Pain and pleasure intermingled as he fucked her until she was no longer sure where pain ended and pure pleasure began. Every thrust bumped her clitoris against the bricks, sending an electric jolt of delight coursing through her hot, perspiring body. Angela began to moan incoherently.

His cock, fucking her from this position, seemed longer and bigger than she remembered. Indeed it seemed to go on for ever, thrusting deeper and deeper into her. She was so wet that, though his erect dick seemed almost too thick to fit in her, the sensation of him thrusting in and out was utterly delicious.

So bound up was she by these overwhelming sensations that Angela was barely aware of what was happening to the man who was fucking her so furiously from behind. Suddenly she heard him shout an oath and then felt his teeth bury themselves in her shoulder.

He rammed himself even harder into her, and her clit hit brick with even more force than before. Once, twice, three times, he pulled back and thrust deep back inside her before she felt him spend inside her. By then her own ecstatic shrieks were echoing around the dungeon vault.

Ten

'OK, sweetie, are you feeling recovered?' Lord Randolph asked gently.

He had released Angela from the chains that held her, catching her as she fell back into his arms, then he had carried her to another region of the dungeon. This had been clearly set up for his comfort for there was a leather sofa, which he had sat in, taking the naked girl in his arms and holding her as she sobbed into his chest.

Naked, thoroughly flogged, exhausted as much from pleasure as from pain, Angela felt a strange security flood through her. She knew that the dungeon held innumerable toys for tormenting girls, but strangely the knowledge no longer frightened her particularly. If she had been pressed to say quite how she felt she would have said content; content to lie enfolded in Lord Randolph's arms, despite the still sore welts that lined her back and buttocks and the menacing devices of the dungeon.

Angela just crooned something incoherent in response to his question. There was a chink of glass against glass and he held a brandy balloon to her lips. Angela swallowed.

The cognac hit her throat and she felt its heat suffuse her. He made her take another sip and then another.

'OK, my sweet, time to go upstairs for the last act. I hope that you are feeling lucky, Angela?'

'Lucky?' she asked as he helped her to her feet.

'Did Anais not explain that this is the last ball of the season?'

'Yes, but . . .'

He took the blindfold from his pocket and put it back around her eyes. Then he clipped her wrist cuffs together behind her.

'Tonight the debutantes will discover who they are to serve until next year's season!'

'Oh!' Angela said, a thrill of fear awakening in her belly. 'I knew, I mean I thought . . . how is . . . how will it be decided?'

'Well, there is a little competition. It involves skill with the whip!'

'The whip . . .' Angela said in an anxious voice as he took her arm and began walking her back through the dungeon.

'Don't worry. It should not involve too much pain. Why do you think I was so concerned to practise on you this evening? Come on now, my little fairground prize!'

'I hope that she was satisfactory, General?' Valencia asked archly.

'Excellent, excellent! The little baggage sucks off wonderfully and buggers like a dream. You have done a good job with her, Valencia!'

Naked, with her hands securely cuffed behind her back, there was little that Lady Lucinda could do but stand and stare at the floor as they discussed her. The general had taken her back to Valencia's room after several hours of energetic games. He was not a young man, but he was still remarkably vigorous, and he had a hard hand. Lucinda's bare bottom was still glowing from its attentions.

'I can't take all the credit. Maude Frobisher did her initial training.'

'Maude! How is the old termagant? Haven't seen her in an age it seems.'

'Well, you can ask her yourself, General. She arrived a little while ago I believe.'

The news that Maude Frobisher was at the house sent a little frisson of fear through Lucinda's belly. She could not have said quite why. After all, she had just been spanked and buggered by the general. What could Mrs Frobisher and Simmonds do to her that was worse than she had already endured? Anyway, she told herself, it was the last night of this debutante farce. Presumably Mrs Frobisher had come to see the final humiliation of the girls that she had trained. The prospect was not one that Lucinda found very pleasing.

Valencia took her leave of the general and steered Lucinda into the bedroom, unlocking the handcuffs.

'How was the general, Lucy, dear?'

'He was a vile old pervert!'

'Well, in that case,' Valencia said with a grin, 'I expect you enjoyed every moment of it, you little tart!'

Lady Lucinda clenched her fists in impotent fury.

'I did not! I did not! I did not!' she said under her breath, trying not to think about the orgasm that had finished the proceedings.

Valencia simply chuckled.

'All right, take off those gloves and stockings and get showered. I need to get you ready for the final act. Quickly now, we need to be downstairs before midnight!'

'He has whipped you very skilfully, my dear. The skin has not been broken anywhere! The welts are fading even as we speak.'

Angela felt a strange disappointment. Why she should want her body marked by Lord Randolph's whip, she could not begin to imagine, yet the idea of the weals fading so quickly seemed sad somehow. She hoped that he would win her later. He would win her, he must!

Anais had made her shower and the maid had fixed her hair and make-up. A deep suspender belt of cream lace, with four drops dangling from it, had been put around her belly. Then Lady Anais had produced a flat cardboard box. In it, between leaves of tissue paper were the sheerest, filmiest silk stockings that Angela had ever seen. Though they were black, and seamed, they were so fine that her legs were barely darker once they were rolled on and fastened to the side straps of the suspender belt.

Angela stood still, waiting for the maid to fasten the front drops, but the maid stood and then, at a word from Lady Anais, left their room.

'Why hasn't she . . .?' Angela began but her aunt stopped her by putting a finger to her lips.

'Shh, dear, never mind about that now. You look quite lovely. You have done me proud, little Angela. I may not see you for some time after tonight. I want you to know that I am very proud of you.'

The elegant woman stepped forward and kissed Angela deeply on the lips, pressing her hot little tongue into the other girl's mouth. To her surprise, Angela found herself responding. She wanted to make love to Anais there and then, but the older woman broke off the embrace.

'Later, my dear, there will be time! But now we must see who wins you!'

'But aren't you going to try?' Angela found herself asking.

'Oh, and I thought you were in love with Randolph! You girls are all so fickle!' Lady Anais said with an arch glint in her eye. 'No, my dear. George and I are going travelling and cannot take such baggage! However, I suspect that the competition will be very hot when your name is called, so never fear!'

It was a room that Lady Lucinda had not yet seen. Used as she was to substantial country houses, she was beginning to realise that Seardon House was of a size and grandeur that was quite beyond her experience.

She hoped that Valencia would secure her for the coming year; after all, it would be worth putting up with the occasional humiliation for the chance to teach Jem and the maids a thing or two.

However, another idea struck her as she looked around the vast hall with its huge portraits of previous Lords of Southdean, and more to the point she noticed quite how toothsome Lord Randolph's Asiatic maids were as they scurried back and forth. How many did he have exactly? she wondered with a little thrill in her belly. Maybe she could fill a similar role here, should Randolph win her. He was very handsome, after all. Whatever his famous dungeons held, it might be worth the sacrifice.

Then she saw Sir Angus grinning at her hungrily and looked away, trying to calm the butterflies that had erupted in her belly. She wished that it was over and that she knew her fate.

The room was filling up now as various guests and debutantes arrived from different parts of the house. After showering, Valencia had made her wear a delicate white lace suspender belt and pure white silk stockings. Strangely, only the side tabs of the stockings had been fastened. The other pair dangled loose, feeling rather odd as they brushed the bare fronts of her thighs. Even odder, Lady Lucinda noticed, was that all the debutantes were dressed similarly.

Jane's suspender belt was black satin with a lace panel, deep and much more substantial than the one that Lucinda wore. Still, the front drops had not been fastened to her sheer black stockings. Daphne had a pink suspender belt, paler than her blushing face or still-glowing bottom but the cream stockings it held, once again, were only fastened by the side.

Lucinda could not guess what it meant, but something fluttering in her belly told her that this strange dress boded the debutantes no good.

'Ladies and Gentlemen!' Lord Randolph said loudly, bringing the hubbub of conversation to an end. 'We have had a marvellous season once again.' He raised his glass of champagne. 'Nineteen fifty-six, a truly great vintage!'

There was a chorus of agreement and a general swigging of wine by the guests. The naked debutantes stole uneasy glances at each other. Angela realised that they were all wondering the same thing; who would win them and what would the mysterious method of choosing be?

'Lady Anais, good to see you. Hello, Angela!' a hearty voice said, breaking her nervous reverie.

Mrs Frobisher had exchanged her tweeds for a rather elegant evening gown; Angela looked at her erstwhile tutor in some surprise.

'Hello, Maude,' Lady Anais replied. 'You did an excellent job on Angie, couldn't be more pleased. Are you competing? You don't usually!'

'No, thought I would make an exception this year, though.'

'Ladies and gentlemen, please!' Lord Randolph said, sounding a little exasperated.

'Huh, Randy Randolph is getting a bit tetchy, isn't he?' Mrs Frobisher said merrily.

'Hush, Maude,' Lady Anais said with a smile. 'Randolph always gets tense. He has his eye on something special, I believe.'

The glance she gave towards Angela was so fluid and subtle that its object might have missed it altogether had Mrs Frobisher not grinned broadly at her.

'Oho!' Maude Frobisher said. 'I *see*!'

'As usual, the order of the debutantes will be drawn by lot,' Lord Randolph said. 'If we can line the girls up, please!'

Lady Anais steered Angela to one side of the room where the debutantes were made to stand in a line. The loose tabs dangling from the front of Angela's suspender belt tickled her bare thighs as she moved and made her notice that all the girls were similarly attired. Once again she wondered what the idea was, but her thoughts were interrupted by Lord Randolph. He walked down the little row of girls, stopping in front of each to let her reach into a black velvet bag.

Reaching inside, Angela felt something flat and cold. She withdrew it. It was an enamel badge, about the size of a playing card, on a silver chain. On the white badge the letter twelve was inscribed in bold black letters.

'Angela, number twelve!' Lord Randolph called out.

Her stomach did a little flip as he took the badge from her and slipped the chain over her neck so that the number nestled in between her naked breasts. Something told her that being last was not going to be a good thing for her nerves.

'All right,' Lord Randolph announced. 'It is time to begin. Will our first debutante step forward, please?'

Plump, blonde Daphne had drawn number one. She stood next to Lucinda who watched the shorter girl step forward with mixed emotions: fear, lust and gladness that she was not the first. Lady Lucinda had drawn number seven and, most of all, she was now afire with curiosity.

General Hollis stepped forward and tied a scarf around the blonde girl's eyes, blindfolding her. Then he took a plump arm and led her to one of the great windows so that she faced the green velvet drapes. A chain ending in a manacle descended from the massive marble columns on either side of the window. Willing hands fastened these to Daphne's wrists and the chains were soon hauled until the blonde girl had to stand on the balls of her stockinged feet.

Another pair of chains fixed to the bottoms of the pillars terminated in larger manacles that were snapped around Daphne's ankles. The length of these was such that her feet were forced three feet apart. Her body was held taut by the pressure of the four separated chains.

'I advise you very strongly to keep absolutely still,' Lord Randolph said to the girl, ignoring the fact that she could barely move an inch.

He patted Daphne's naked bottom fondly and then looked up at the audience.

'Who wishes to compete for this pretty little trollop's services? Remember, friends, that you can only try your skill on three girls in this round.'

'Are we playing one stocking or pairs, Randolph?' called out a rather spotty man that Lucinda had not been sorry to avoid during the season.

'One stocking will suffice. Good God, Jeremy, it has been a long enough night without us playing pairs!' There was a general outbreak of laughter at this. 'Each player has three strokes at his target. The first to drop a stocking wins the girl . . .'

'And if no one drops the stocking, Randolph?'

The voice was new to Lady Lucinda. It was a calm deep male voice, but something about it made the hairs on the back of her neck stand on end. The room seemed to have gone silent and almost held its breath.

'Lancelot,' Lord Randolph said dryly. 'I did not think that you could make it? Welcome anyway. If her stockings are still up after the first round she goes back into the pot, and anyone without a prize can have another crack!'

The laughter that greeted this remark was the last piece of information Lucinda needed. When she saw the maid step into view bearing a tray, it was no surprise that it was laden with whips. Several of the guests stepped forward and chose a weapon. Lucinda looked back at the naked girl chained to the columns. Daphne's naked body was quivering visibly.

Sir Angus stepped up first. He took his stance, raised the whip in his left hand and paused. For a moment it seemed as if time itself had stopped, then the red-haired man threw the whip, cracking it at the very last moment.

The leather cracker missed the stocking tab by inches, exploding empty air to the side of Daphne's left stocking top. The girl in question reacted as if the lash had struck her, shrieking her alarm and struggling in panic against the unrelenting chains.

'Bugger!' Sir Angus bellowed.

He raised the whip and threw it forwards again. This time he was too far to the right. The lash cracked explosively against Daphne's bare right buttock. The blonde girl let out a startled squeal of pain.

'Oh bad luck, Angus!'

'Oh bugger off, Lancelot!'

Sir Angus waited until a thin red vertical line had bloomed on Daphne's bottom; ignoring comments, sympathetic and ironic alike. Once more he cast the long whip forward and cracked it suddenly.

It moved too fast for Lucinda to really see it, but she gained a strong impression that the cracker hit just to the side of the suspender drop. Unfortunately for Daphne, it was the wrong side. The blonde girl let out another shrill squeal of pain.

'Sorry, Angus, bad luck, old boy!' Lord Randolph said suavely.

'Little bitch is wiggling her bottom, she is supposed to be held taut!' Sir Angus muttered with ill grace.

An amused smile flickered over Lord Randolph's handsome face.

'All right,' he said turning to the little crowd of immaculately dressed guests. 'Who's next?'

Jane was unchained and fell into the waiting arms of the general. The tall girl had been particularly popular but her admirers had not been noted for their skill. Angela had watched aghast as competitor had followed competitor, lining Jane's lovely buttocks, even missing by so much at one point that the cracker had struck right between her outstretched legs. That had made the tall beauty howl piteously, and had amused the guests, but the general's skill had finally put an end to the fun.

Angela watched with ever mounting anxiety. Daphne was next. The plump little blonde was stung by five whip-wielding would-be suitors in turn, yet none hit the mark. She squealed and jiggled her fat little bottom as the whiplashes bit into her flesh. Livid vertical welts streaked her pale buttocks by the time Daphne was taken down and put back in the line. Tears streaked the blonde girl's pretty face as she awaited the next round and even more torment.

The next girl, by luck or skill, was won by the first stroke of the whip. Lady Wallingford lashed with cool expertise. A loud crack split the air and, though the tip of the whip moved too fast to be visible, there was no doubt where it struck. The girl's right suspender drop went ping, and her filmy grey silk stocking fluttered slowly down her leg. The audience burst into applause and the dowager Lady Wallingford, smiling for once, curtseyed elegantly in acknowledgment and then stepped up to claim her prize.

So it continued. Four girls were won and three returned, sobbing and wincing, to endure another spell as target. Now it was Lady Lucinda's turn. The blonde debutante was swiftly blindfolded and led up to the pillars where she was chained in place.

The blonde beauty's slender body trembled slightly. To Angela's horror the first to try his skill was Lord Randolph. If he won Lucinda, surely he could not win any other, she thought in panic. It was not just that she felt a warm glow in her lower belly when she thought of Randolph, it was the other man who had arrived so late. Lancelot Shaw did not seem to be able to keep his cold, predatory eyes off her and something about the man made her shiver inside.

Lord Randolph threw his first stroke. Angela's heart almost stopped as she watched it. The whip cracked just a little too far to the left of the right stocking tab. Lady Lucinda's poise vanished in an instant. The blonde girl let out a shriek that might have shattered glass.

Randolph struck again. Too far to the right. The cracker bit into empty air and Lucinda's yelp was of fear rather than pain. He got ready for his third stroke. Angela could not watch, closing her eyes and silently praying.

An explosive crack, a startled squeal of pain. Angela opened her eyes. No white silk stocking was fluttering down Lucinda's shapely leg. It was still securely attached as the naked debutante quivered in her chains.

Next up was Sir Angus once more. Again he tried to whip the left suspender drop off, but his aim seemed to have got worse rather than better. The first stroke laced the middle of Lucinda's plump left buttock. The second was a little nearer but still bit bottom flesh some way from the target tab. The third stroke missed Lucinda altogether. Sir Angus tossed the whip onto the floor disgustedly and stalked away.

Lucinda let out a little shriek of sheer relief as the whip cracked. It was so close that she felt the wind against her left hip. Not only was it relief that she had missed another vicious sting lacing her bottom. She had noticed that only Sir Angus whipped left-handed and she had no desire to be carried off to his remote castle for the rest of the year.

She had scant time for relief, however. Blindfolded though she was, she could sense, perhaps from the way the audience went quiet, that the next competitor was getting ready to lash her. Lady Lucinda set her teeth together and prayed that the person getting ready to try their skill was Valencia.

There was a crack and pain exploded in the very right of her right buttock. Lady Lucinda could not suppress a shriek. It was close, she thought, gasping for breath as the pain coursed through her. How good was Valencia with a whip?

Another wicked crack, and this time the sting was glancing. She felt the elastic fly up and the stocking fluttering down her leg. There was a round of polite applause. Lucinda strained her ears for some clue but there was none. Who had won her services, the use of her tender body for a year? She knew that Randolph was reckoned very decent with the whip but . . .

Her ankles and wrists were released and she fell to be caught by strong arms. It was a woman; a strong woman with full breasts in a velvet dress. Valencia!

Relief flooded though her. This year was not going to be so bad. Lady Lucinda felt the blindfold tugged away and the light blinded her momentarily.

Once, twice, three times she blinked against the light, but the face just refused to resolve into Valencia's.

'Well, Lucy!' Maude Frobisher said, with a grin that froze Lucinda's very soul. 'Won't Norris be pleased!'

Angela was only too popular, it seemed. Though she was the last girl to be chained between the pillars, there were at least half a dozen guests who had not yet won a prize, and every one of them seemed to want to try their skill or luck on her naked body.

The first three strokes missed her stocking tabs but found her tender bottom. The next three were even wilder. One missed altogether and the others laced her buttocks far from the target. The third attempt was nearer, but that was the worst of all. Three blistering lashes snapped into the same strip of skin an inch or so from the suspender strap.

Angela was still shrieking when the fourth competitor stepped up. At least the fire in her flank prevented her from speculating on who had missed, and who was now taking their aim.

The first crack was so close to her sore skin that she felt it as a cool breeze, one that might have been deliciously welcome in any other circumstance. It was Randolph, she felt sure. He had been practising on her and that stroke had been so close.

A sound like a pistol shot split the reverent silence. There was the slightest sting but it was not enough to mask the sensation of silk stocking slipping down her smooth, well-depilated leg. She could not be sure. The certainty that had come deserted her. She trembled as she felt the helpers unlock her wrists and ankles.

The arms of a man in evening dress caught her as she collapsed. The blindfold came off and she was looking up at Randolph. He smiled down at her, a wicked glint in his handsome eyes.

'Lord Randolph . . .' she murmured, more worship than fear in her voice.

'You are such a lovely thing,' he murmured. 'Damned shame!'

'Shame?' she whispered uncomprehendingly.

'Bloody shame! I was close but no cigar. Now that beast Lancelot Shaw has won you, damn his eyes!'

Her shock must have been written in her face because a shadow of regret passed over his handsome countenance.

'All right, Randolph, hand over my property, there is a good chap!' Lancelot Shaw said in a voice that sounded to Angela like a tiger's growl.

Lord Randolph ignored him.

'Look, sweetheart,' he said. 'Don't take it so hard. It's not all bad, you know!'

'Not all . . .' Angela murmured, her mind still reeling, '. . . not all bad?'

'No,' Lord Randolph said, grinning once again. 'I reckon I have a good chance of winning Daphne in the next round. And she is a very pretty little package, after all!'